Hands on the Wheel

by

Karen C. Whalen

*The Tow Truck Murder Mysteries,
Book 2*

This is a work of fiction. Names, characters, places, and incidents are either the product of the author's imagination or are used fictitiously, and any resemblance to actual persons living or dead, business establishments, events, or locales, is entirely coincidental.

Hands on the Wheel

Cover Art by *Diana Carlile*

The Wild Rose Press, Inc.
PO Box 708
Adams Basin, NY 14410-0708
Visit us at www.thewildrosepress.com

Publishing History
First Edition, 2022
Trade Paperback ISBN 978-1-5092-4317-4
Digital ISBN 978-1-5092-4318-1

The Tow Truck Murder Mysteries, Book 2
Published in the United States of America

Dedication

To the hubs, my inspiration and number one fan.

Acknowledgments

There are many people who helped make this book possible: my husband and number one champion, my beta reader Sandra Hilger, my writers' group members Rhonda Blackhurst and Pam Wells, and tow-truck experts Amanda Sawyers and Rina Moore. My editor at The Wild Rose Press, Ally Robertson, and cover artist, Diana Carlile, deserve mention for their extraordinary contributions. Also, a special thank you to my readers.

I let the coffee shop door shut behind me and started toward the stairs…when all of a sudden Haxxed appeared out of nowhere!

The deadly gangster right here in front of me. Me by myself. No one else around. *Yikes.*

I sprinted for the bottom step, but he caught the back of my shirt and my feet only cycled in place like tires spinning on ice.

Haxxed flung back his head and laughed.

I stammered, "Not f-f-funny!"

"I'm here for Clem's stuff." The man speaks! His voice was commanding like a tyrannical character right out of a scary video game.

Cold sweat ran down my spine and my pulse raced like I was on a caffeine rush. "She-she took everything over to Demented's pl-place when she moved out."

"Everything?"

"I swear." I placed my palm over my heart.

"On your mama?"

"Sure."

He stared hard at me before releasing my shirt. I ran up the steps, feeling his eyes searing my back, and I dived inside the door.

I threw the deadbolt and stepped away, out of breath. Boss sniffed around my ankles while I pressed in Ephraim's number with shaky fingers. I shrieked into the phone, "One of the gang members was just here. He cornered me in the parking lot when I was by myself."

Ephraim's voice came back loud, too, "Is he still there?"

I checked the peephole, then scoped the lot from the window. "I don't see him. But I'm sc-scared."

"I'm on my way."

Other Wild Rose Press Titles by Karen C. Whalen:

Everything Bundt the Truth
Not According to Flan
No Grater Evil
A Stewed Observation
Just What I Kneaded
Peaches-N-Creamed
Wasted Thyme
Toes on the Dash
Hands on the Wheel

Chapter 1

Could I ask for a better day? Windows down, hair blowing in the breeze. Wearing my high heels. Driving my tow truck.

You heard me right. Me, Delaney Morran, known as the high-heeled tow truck driver, owner of Del's Towing. I'd landed a contract in my hometown of Spruce Ridge, Colorado to remove abandoned vehicles from the side of the road. Me, and another towing company on a rotating basis.

Last night I'd spotted a Honda Impreza, all-wheel drive, deserted on County Road 6, not yet orange-tagged. Since I wanted to get a jump on the competition, I returned this morning to check for the haul-away sticker and pulled my truck up behind the black Impreza with darkly tinted windows. The city had not ticketed the car for removal, but I might as well scout it out since I was here.

Gathering my long, curly red hair into three bunches, I quickly braided over and under, then secured the end with a stretchy tie. I climbed down from the truck cab and stepped onto the pine needles that covered the wide gravel shoulder. I stretched my arms up to the clear May sky and gazed through the tops of the waving pines. The tall trees cast long, cool shadows over the road. I loved being my own boss, helping people, working in the great outdoors. There's nothing like it. There was no way I'd ever want a desk job.

I hoofed it over to the Impreza's door and stumbled to a halt.

Yowzah! The driver still sat inside. I could see the outline of his body through the tinted window, his head lolling to the right. Had he slept in the car overnight? Did he need assistance?

I rapped my knuckles on the door, but he didn't move. I plastered my face against the glass, cupped my hands around my eyes, and peered through for a better look. *Oh, no.*

Dried blood masked his features. Pale hands hung from the steering wheel. A nasty odor hit my nose and I gagged.

You can guess what that means.

Was it the crimson stains or the white fingers that got to me? *Whatever…* I went down and that was the last thing I remembered.

When my eyelids fluttered open, my shoes with the pink bows were propped up on the Impreza's back bumper. What was that rust color on my heels? And why were my feet on the bumper?

Hands held my arms while I tried to elbow my way to a sitting position. A police officer knelt by my side. "Keep your feet up."

"What happened?"

"You fainted, and the blood needs to get back to your head."

"Blood?" My vision fogged with floating black dots and my brain felt fuzzy. For some reason I wished he hadn't mentioned that word. "What am I doing here?"

"That's what we need to ask you. A passing

motorist called in someone lying on the road next to a black Impreza and a red tow truck. A female in pink high heels."

"Me?"

"Yes, you. Do you know the occupant of this vehicle?"

My head spun as I inspected the stain on my shoe and the scene came back to me. My chest constricted like I'd been thrown against the seatbelt after stomping on the brakes. "The dead guy?"

"Who else would I mean?"

"What happened to him?" Closed my eyes. Squelched the urge to vomit.

"Answer the question."

"I don't know him. At least I don't think I know him. I didn't get a good look at his face, you know, because of…" I squeezed my eyes tighter to stop the whirling sensation and rubbed a place over my heart to keep it from pounding like a speeding engine.

"Tell me what happened."

"I spotted the Impreza last night, so I came back to check for the impound sticker. That's my tow truck." I gestured behind us, thinking a desk job wouldn't be so bad after all, then opened my eyes and peered up at the police officer's balloon-like face. Round cheeks, double chin, no neck. Not an officer I recognized. Spruce Ridge was a small enough town you'd think I'd have seen him before. He considered me with a serious expression. My freckled face was certain to have turned red to match my hair. I hated my red-headed tendency to blush. "I'm better now. Can I get up?" My heart still thumped, but the dizzy sensation was receding.

He planted his feet wide apart and helped me to a

stand. I held onto his arm while I steadied myself. His middle carried a few extra pounds, but he was strong and solid compared to me, short and shaky. He said, "You should be examined by the paramedics. You might've hit your head when you fainted."

Yup, the back of my head throbbed. He directed me to an ambulance on the other side of my truck. Several police cars with lights flashing blocked the westbound lane, and a traffic cop in a safety vest waved passing motorists to move along. An EMT in a black jacket with *MEDIC* printed across the shoulders felt all over my skull for bumps, shined a light in my eyes, took my blood pressure, and told me I was free to leave. But before I could, the chubby officer handed me a witness statement to fill out.

When I finished with that, I acted brave and all, climbing into my tow truck, but it took several deep breaths before I turned the key in the ignition. I sat there while the engine idled, imagining my dad in this same seat, hands on this same wheel, telling me *chin up*. At least that's what I thought he might say. I had to be tough. I'm a vehicle recovery specialist now. It was a known fact that people committed suicide in their vehicles. Horrible, yes, but you never knew what to expect when approaching an abandoned car. Surprising things happened in the towing business, blindsiding you.

How I made it to my best friend's coffee shop, Roasters on the Ridge, I don't know, but the crowded café known for fresh roasted beans appeared in my windshield. I parked my truck in the rear lot, although I normally didn't keep it there, and hauled myself up the staircase that hugged the dark wooden clapboards to my apartment above the shop. The keys dropped from my grip twice before I got to my door, then it took several attempts to unlock it before I managed to get inside.

After I collapsed on the sofa, I let my head rest on the cushion with my arm covering my eyes. The news would soon be all over social media, but I decided to not go there. Instead, I called my new boyfriend and colleague in the towing business, Tanner Utley.

"Hey Tanner, everything's fine, but I had a brush with the police and I'm a bit off balance. If it's okay with you can we cancel tonight?" I didn't want my boyfriend to see me in this hot mess. I needed time to even out.

"What happened?"

"I found a dead guy."

"No! Another one? That sucks."

"Damn straight." What were the odds!

"What happened? Anyone you know?"

"Not this time." I gave him the details in a few brief words.

He made sympathetic noises, then said, "You sure you don't want me to come by?"

"I'll be fine. But, can you cover my calls this weekend?"

"Sure, Laney. Take a break and relax. Let me know if you change your mind about tonight and I'll come over if you need me to. Miss you."

"Miss you, too." We disconnected before I had second thoughts.

I watched mindless television the rest of the day. Outside the windows, darkness had fallen, so I closed the curtains and stepped into a hot shower. I touched my forehead against the ceramic tiles with each word, *why-didn't-you-leave-that-car-alone?*

Note to self: never walk up to an abandoned vehicle that hasn't first been given the all-clear by the city.

I tried to sleep but tossed and turned with gut-wrenching, body-jolting nightmares. Dreams involving a black Impreza on the side of the road with lightning bolts coursing across the sky, illuminating a dead man with bony, skeletal hands. Creepy, grasping hands, mummy hands, with straps of linen falling off the bones, grotesque fingers freakishly stuck to the steering wheel.

Pretty scary stuff.

The kind of dreams that made it impossible to sleep.

After that first *gawd-awful* night, I spent most of the weekend bleary-eyed and zoned-out on the phone with Tanner or at Kristen's apartment across the hall drinking gallons of hot tea. I fell asleep on the couch on Sunday, not even making it to my bedroom. When the sun shone through the blinds on Monday morning, I told myself, *one more day*. Just one more day, then I'd face the world.

Grimacing at the crick in my neck, I staggered around to dress in jeans, a tee-shirt, and a pair of black flats, then crept down the staircase to the employee entrance in the back of the coffee shop.

"Morning, Kristen," I greeted the owner, my best friend and neighbor, as I made a beeline for the espresso machine.

"You back with the living?"

My hands stilled over my steaming cup of joe.

Kristen gave me a weak smile. "I guess I could've

6

worded that better."

The heavenly scent of coffee filled my senses when I took my first swallow. No other fragrance calmed me like Kristen's latest batch. The familiar sights and smells and sounds covered me like an old, familiar sweater. Epic, inspirational music played at a low volume, punctuated with the occasional popping sound of roasting beans. Distressed-wooden shelves showcased soft bags of beans, mugs, and bottles of flavored syrups. Antique skis and poles, snowshoes, and ski boots adorned the walls, in character with Spruce Ridge, an upscale town surrounded by rugged beauty, known as the gateway to the mountains and a desirable location between Denver and Vail.

I set my hot mug on the counter with a sigh and contemplated Kris, now busy at the sink.

There's a lot I could tell you about her, but if I only had one word to describe Kristen Guttenberg, it would be *good*. And if I could add another couple of words, I would add *through and through*. She's my age, taller than me by four inches, and today she wore high-rise jeans, sensible plastic clogs, and the café's black apron embroidered with a swirl of steam above a coffee mug. Her gray eyes, dark brows, and shiny, shoulder-length brown hair made me secretly envious. What I wouldn't do for shampoo-commercial smooth hair like Kristen's. And, she owned her own successful coffee shop. My towing business was in early stages, yet.

"Can you handle the cash register while Delaney and I take a break?" Kristen asked the barista by the name of Guy behind the pick-up counter. He was an eight-months-sober, English Lit major.

"Will do." Guy finished capping drinks and called

out customers' names, "Pierce, Dominick, Roscoe."

Three teenagers in tee-shirts and baggy jeans sauntered over to collect their orders. The teen who picked up the cup marked for Pierce did a complicated hand-bump with Guy, then the three baggy-pantsers reclaimed their seats in front of wide-screened laptops. Book clubs, church groups, and video gamers frequented Roasters on the Ridge. These three had *gamers* written all over them, computer nerds who played here instead of at home so their parents wouldn't know how much time they spent in the gaming world.

Kristen and I crossed over to the square table near the window and relaxed onto the hard, metal chairs. I twiddled my tiny espresso cup around on its saucer. "I'm still having bad dreams."

"Dear Lord." Kristen gave me an exaggerated frown face. "Did you at least get some rest with Tanner covering your calls?"

"Some."

Tanner Utley owned several trucks, a front loader and two flatbeds, and had taught me how to operate my truck, a Fulcan Xtruder self-loader, the best in the industry. I'll tell you more about my boyfriend later. And my truck, too. Right now, I couldn't do either one justice.

"I promised myself today's the last day I'm taking off work." I dipped my head down. "But what if I don't feel like towing anymore? What if I come across something nasty, like, you know, *that*, again?"

"Surely not."

"Tanner tows from accidents all the time, some of them pretty bad. I'm sure he's seen worse things, or at least stuff that's just as gross." My lips trembled and my voice quavered. I was still a little freaked.

"You can do it. You'll be fine." She patted my hand.

"Do you think so?" I didn't feel fine, although we'd been having this same conversation repeatedly over the last couple of days.

"You've had to deal with a dead body before," she reminded me.

"But other than that?"

She gave me a shake of her head. "You are *so* strong, girl!"

"I wish." I shuddered at the memory. "But it's not the same this time. Last time someone else found the body. I never opened the trunk of that car, so I escaped that little discovery."

"True." Kristen sipped on her iced vanilla coconut milk latte while I fiddled with my double espresso.

Tears threatened hot behind my eyelids. "Kristen, I don't know if I can deal with this kind of thing." I was sort of a wuss; a cream puff when it came to this.

She patted my hand again. "Remember what I told you. You'll be okay." My fierce friend was the master of pep talks.

But, would I be okay? I wondered if my dad, Del Morran, found any dead people in deserted vehicles or if he towed away cars from fatal accident scenes. It was his tow truck I was driving. He'd been an auto mechanic and tow operator, both. It'd be ironic if he'd found bodies, since he was the victim of a deadly car crash himself. When he died, I felt abandoned, which made no sense because I didn't even know him. I'm twenty-eight now and my parents divorced when I was seven. My only contact with Dad had been impersonal birthday cards and Christmas gifts. Del Morran hadn't left me many memories, but he did leave me his name and his Irish red hair…and his tow truck. The letter I'd received from the estate attorney with news of my inheritance was a bit of a shock. His death robbed me of the chance to know him, and I felt sad for what might have been. Somehow driving his self-loader gave me a *déjà vu* kind of feeling, a connection to him I never had when he was alive.

When the café door eased open, the three gamers glanced up from their table, and a handsome police officer with short-cropped, salt and pepper hair, and a handlebar mustache over a prominent chin, strode inside. He wore the crisp, tan uniform of the City of Spruce Ridge Police Department.

The teens snapped their laptops shut, and scooted past the policeman and out the door. What was their hurry?

Kristen gave the new arrival a welcoming smile as he claimed the empty chair with his back to the wall. She said, "Good morning, Zach." Officer Zachariah Bowers had a crush on my best friend, and she returned the interest, but neither had made a move…at least, not that I knew about.

I echoed her words, "Good morning," then asked him right off, "You heard about the dead guy I found?"

Kristen got up from her chair. "I'll be right back with your coffee."

"Thanks, Kris." Zach's gaze followed her until she disappeared behind the counter. He turned to me. "Yes, we've identified the victim, if you want to know." Having Zach hanging around Kristen was like having a policeman in the family, and I could get insider information.

"I want to know."

He rubbed his big chin. "The victim's name is Quincy Davidsen."

"Quincy Davidsen. Doesn't ring a bell."

"He lived in Denver."

"What was he doing in Spruce Ridge?"

"That's the question."

Kristen thrust a steaming coffee cup at Zach and resumed the seat across from him.

"It's terrible that he died here." I tagged on as an afterthought, "He shot himself in the head, Zach."

The officer sipped his coffee, then dabbed the foam off his mustache with a napkin. "That's not what happened. It's a homicide."

"Are you for real? You're kidding, right?" I don't know why I said that. Why do people say that when they hear bad news? But I had to ask, "How do you know for sure?"

"He was shot with the door open. When you found him it was shut. That and other clues."

I thought about the closed door, the victim's hands, the way he sat behind the steering wheel. So, okay, not a suicide. That meant a murderer was at large and I felt my heart clench. "Do the police think he knew his killer?"

The officer propped his elbows on the table and hung his head down. "Ephraim is taking over the investigation. You can ask him, but I doubt he'll tell you much."

Kristen flipped a lock of her straight brown hair over her shoulder. "Why does the sheriff get all the homicides?"

Zach answered, "The city only has a small department. The county is better equipped and trained. A city officer has been staying on site, but the crime scene is about to be released and the vehicle needs to be towed to a secure lot. Delaney, do you still want the work?"

I asked, with a little hitch in my voice, "Has the car been cleaned up?"

"The police don't do that. They want it kept preserved, as is."

My coffee didn't taste so good anymore. Did I want the job? *No.* Could I forget the scene? *No, again.*

Kristen nudged me with her elbow. "Towing the vehicle will help you get your confidence back."

"I don't know, Kris."

She rubbed my arm. "Well, do what feels right for you."

"What's this?" Zach asked.

Kristen told him, "Delaney's been having nightmares."

Zach studied me while I crossed my arms and tucked my fists under my elbows. He asked, "You got a good look inside that Impreza, didn't you?"

"Uh, yeah. I keep seeing that man's hands on the wheel." The memory came flooding back so I shut my eyes. "He'd slumped over, but his hands…they were still holding onto the steering wheel." I opened my eyes. "How is that possible? It was weird, spooky."

"Nightmares and flashbacks are classic symptoms from encounters with death. It's a form of post-traumatic stress disorder." Zach's eyebrows puckered. "First responders get support from trauma counselors. Everyone in law enforcement…the officers, firefighters, paramedics, dispatchers…there's a place where they can go to get help. Sounds like you could benefit from a visit to a counselor, too."

I knew what PTSD was. I'd learned about it in one of my college psychology classes. I asked Zach, "How do people get over the nightmares?"

"It helps to keep positive, like doing something good for the community. A lot of police officers mentor, even adopt, at-risk kids, stuff like that. Also solving the crime achieves closure for the detectives working homicide cases."

I nodded. "Solving the crime. Closure. I see how that would help."

Zach drubbed a fist to his forehead. "Oh, no," he groaned.

I assured him, "Don't worry, I'm not getting involved this time, not if my mental health is the price."

He let out a snort of disbelief.

"If you find out anything more, you'll let us know, won't you, Zach?" Kristen put a hand on his arm.

He had a moment of tight-lipped silence, then he placed his hand over hers. "I'll let you know what I can, but there are things I can't discuss."

I asked him, "When will the police want the Impreza towed?"

"As soon as they release the scene." Zach gave me a concerned appraisal. "You don't have to take the assignment."

"Are you going to?" Kristen's eyebrows arched upwards.

I scrunched my nose in a *pee-yew* face, but if I planned to make the towing business work, I needed to toughen up. I said, "Maybe." That was the best I could do.

"You know I'll be praying for you." Kristen smiled in her soothing way.

"Thanks, Kris." I drained my last drop of espresso.

Note to self: Get closure. Get courage back. You can do this. Don't quit when the job turns *sucky*.

Kristen asked Zach about his efforts to collect baseball equipment for underprivileged kids, so I took that as my cue to leave and rose from the table. "See you later." After tossing my empty cup in the trash can, I took my usual shortcut out the back door. On my way upstairs, my phone rang.

It was the police. "Delaney, can you move a vehicle for us?"

"The Impreza?"

"That's the one."

Leaning hard against the stair railing, I drew in a deep breath and thought about it for a moment, glad Zach had given me the heads-up that I might get the call. I'd just given myself the *I can do this; I can do this* speech, so I answered, "Okay, I'll be there shortly."

I repeated the mantra all the way to County Road 6. This will get me back in the game. A quick and easy tow.

But my heart ticked up in speed the closer I got to the spot. My truck windows were closed this time. No carefree breeze blowing in. No cute stilettos on my feet either, not today.

When I pulled in behind the police cruiser, I barely noticed the snowcapped mountains or the blue sky. What did catch my attention were the "Police Hold" warnings spread across the Impreza's windshield and the red splotches that dotted the pavement. Marvelous.

A bead of sweat trickled down my forehead. I mouthed the words to myself, "Hang in there, just hang in there. Everything's fine."

Which I didn't believe for a minute.

Chapter 2

An officer in a yellow vest with silver reflective tape marched up to my truck. "You're here to remove the vehicle?" He spoke in a deep, gravelly voice.

Taking a moment to breathe, I swung down from the cab and faked a ton of bravado. "Yes." *Good.* I sounded okay.

"You need to sign a chain of custody form." He held out a clipboard and I scribbled my name on the page, my signature all wobbly. He pointed further down. "And fill in the location where you're taking the Impreza."

"Where do you want me to take it?"

"Spruce Ridge doesn't have a city impound lot, so you have to use a secure area of your own. You can charge the owner storage fees, you know."

With a tight grip on the pen, I filled in the address for Tanner's yard. I'd hauled other vehicles to my boyfriend's impound lot since I didn't have one, but this was the first time I'd had to deal with a police hold or sign a custody form. I handed back the clipboard. "If the owner's dead, how do I collect?"

"There's usually a next of kin, and if not, then you can apply for the title, determine who the lienholder is, and sell the Impreza. That's a long process, though, and that's well after it's been released from police-hold."

I stretched out my hand. "Can I have the keys?"

"The evidence lab retains the keys. You can't open the vehicle. It has to remain locked." He tapped a finger on the chain-of-custody form. "Says so right here."

I hadn't read the fine print, of course. "That's okay. I can tow without the keys." I stepped back and lobbed a quick glance at the all-wheel drive vehicle I was about to take responsibility for. All-wheel is common and requires a particular procedure.

Here's the deal when towing: if the car is front-wheel drive, the front wheels need to be lifted off the ground, if rear-wheel drive, the back wheels need to be lifted, and if all-wheel, all four wheels have to be raised. My self-loader elevated only one set of tires, either the front or the back. The Impreza was all-wheel drive, which meant I had to use tow dollies on the wheels not lifted by the truck. Got that? It took me a while to understand it, too. Luckily, I had a vehicle encyclopedia to tell me which makes and models were front, rear, or all-wheel drive, and I had a set of tow dollies.

The officer watched me crouch down to release the heavy dollies from under the truck bed. Once I released the clips, the dollies rolled out. I pushed them over to the Impreza and positioned the first set around the front driver's side tire to jack the wheel up with the foot pedal. Catching sight of the interior, I gagged a little, hoping the officer was not paying attention. He wasn't. He was watching traffic. I leveraged the other dolly in place, then pulled myself up into my truck and tried not to think about what was inside the vehicle.

I took a deep, fortifying breath. This was the part I liked best. This was when the magic happened.

Now's the time to tell you about my Fulcan

Xtruder, a self-loading tow truck, red with a logo on the door of a black stiletto. Besides being a good-looking vehicle, it had a nifty integrated lift. That's a wheel-lift system controlled hydraulically from inside the cab. The button on the wireless remote operated the T-bar that lowered to the ground. The scoops, which those of us in the industry called "claws," hadn't lined up with the wheels, so I backed up another foot, then pressed a second button. The claws went under and around the rear tires, and the back of the Impreza swung into the air. My tow dollies had lifted the front; the boom had lifted the back. All the wheels were off the ground. I was ready to roll.

Cool, huh? Told 'ya.

My stomach muscles relaxed. Going through the familiar motions put me at ease. Especially when everything came together like this. The feeling of doing a good job, being helpful, did relieve stress just as Zach had said it would. I waved goodbye to the officer and took off, the Impreza rumbling behind, a sense of accomplishment boosting my spirits.

The officer signaled for me to stop and yelled, "Where's your tow lights?"

Oops. So much for everything going well.

After I attached the beacons to the Impreza, I switched on the roof's LED light bar and steered onto County Road 6. I gave myself a stern talking-to. *No biggie. So what, you forgot the lights? Keep it together, keep it together.*

I drove up to a ten-foot-high chain-link fence topped with circles of razor wire and keyed in the access code. Tanner's place resembled a mini, high-security prison yard without the guard turrets. I navigated through and the gate shut behind me automatically. Reversing into an empty spot, I jackknifed the Impreza and had to make a couple more attempts. After lowering the rear wheels, I removed the dollies and replaced them under my self-loader, then climbed back into my truck to leave.

Did I need to do something to secure the vehicle? Did I need to check it out better than this quick once-over from inside the truck? *Yes.* I was responsible for the Impreza. The police document I'd signed said so.

I eased open the door and spilled out until my heels hit the pavement. I did a walk-around the sedan to make sure the yellow police warnings remained in place. The burning Colorado sun had oxidized the black paint to gray in spots, and time had rusted the rear bumper. No one would want to steal this car, but all the same I crept over to the driver's door to make sure it was locked.

Big mistake!

Ewwww. A little dizzy here. No need to check the other doors. The car *was* going to be fine. *Just fine. No problem-o.* I tapped in a text message for Tanner to let him know I'd stored the Impreza in his lot. Then I jumped inside my truck and steered back onto the road.

Alrighty, then. I'd towed the Impreza. I'd gotten that behind me. Yes, sir, I could move on now. If only I didn't feel like an imposter, lil' ole me driving this big truck, competing with the brawny, all-male towers in town who showed up at bad accident scenes left and right. They didn't get queasy. They held it together. I could do that, too. Not a big deal.

I had turned into such a good con artist, I was even conning myself. I'd just have to do what I always did— bluff my way through it.

I locked up my tow truck at Oberly Motors down the street from Tanner's place and strolled over to the mechanic's bay. I loved visiting with Byron Oberly, the man who'd bought my dad's autobody shop. I inherited the towing business. Byron Oberly bought the mechanic business. This is where I normally parked my truck when I wasn't out on a job.

Byron was in his fifties, gap-toothed and stocky, with dirt under his fingernails, stains on his hands, and smarts in that worldly-wise brain of his. Sometimes I wished he was my dad, even though he was an ex-convict. It's true, he'd spent some time in jail. But he was one of the good guys and would've made a great father. In fact, his niece called him *Old Man* and so did I. He said he liked being the *Old Man*.

He caught sight of me and made his way over, embracing me in a bear hug. He smelled of engine fumes and spent motor oil. "How ya' doing, Delaney?" His deep, rich voice sounded like a trained actor's.

"You heard?"

"Sure did. Come on inside."

I followed him through the door. The lobby presented a clean, welcoming space, with a comfy brown sofa and matching club chairs around a black coffee table covered with old car magazines. A coffee-maker with single-serve pods sat on a corner shelf. Crisp, green plants hung in baskets in front of the window. The mocha color on the walls suited a living room more than an autobody shop.

I admired the breeze stirring through the pines outside the glass frontage, while Byron plopped his big frame down onto the sofa, considerably lowering that end. He said, "I spoke ta' the police."

My head snapped in his direction and a nervous laugh came out of my throat. "Why did you do that?" Not only did I wish Byron was my dad, he often acted like it, in a protective, parental way. Was that why he'd talked to the police?

"I called 'em when I heard 'bout the body bein' found. I drove past that Impreza on Friday night. I was behind the guy and saw him pull over, then I kept goin'."

I tripped over my feet as I took the chair opposite Byron.

"You okay?" he asked.

"Yeah. I drove by the Impreza, too, at a quarter after eight or so. It appeared abandoned then."

"I saw him around seven."

"You know it's a homicide?"

"Yeah, it was on the news."

I chewed my lower lip and we stared at each other in an understanding, sharing moment. We'd both seen the Impreza. We'd seen the driver. Maybe we'd just missed laying eyes on the killer, too. I asked, "Did you spot anybody around the car?"

"Nah. I didn't notice any other cars in that turnout." Byron brought a red cloth out of his overalls and wiped his forehead before returning the rag to his pocket. "The Impreza was driving real slow in front of me, like the guy was on his cell phone or somethin'. I was glad he pulled over to let me get by. That's how I remember him."

I braced my feet on the floor and sat forward. "Too bad you can't place anyone else there."

"Well, that new tow man with the green truck was behind me. I told the police 'bout him, too. I didn't make out where he went; only the next time I looked in my rearview mirror, the tow truck wasn't there anymore."

"That green truck is my competition." I asked, "What were you doing on County Road 6?"

"I live out that a' way."

I always pictured Byron at the autobody shop, never at home. I hadn't given any thought to where he lived.

He fidgeted on the end of the couch and asked, as if this was the real thing he wanted to talk about, "Tanner taking good care a' you? Treatin' you all right?" Byron had introduced us and felt responsible for how Tanner behaved around me.

Old fashioned, much?

At the thought of Tanner, a blush migrated from my neck up to my cheeks. Now's the time to give you the lowdown on my *totally crushworthy* boyfriend. He's tall—somewhere over six feet. Long legs and slender. Dark blond hair and heavily tattooed arms with a geometric pattern, a bald eagle, and another ink job of his favorite song lyrics. Muscles, too, from spending a lot of time at the gym. He was serious about his business while raising two younger siblings after his parents died. He was certainly good-looking, ambitious, and reliable, but what I liked most was his down-to-earth expertise with his tow trucks, and how he handled customers. Tanner was the best tow man in town.

I flopped back in my chair. "I've talked to him on the phone but haven't seen him for the last couple of days. He's busy handling my calls along with his own." I needed to do something about that situation.

A teenager ambled in from the work bay wearing a

knit cap and a grease-stained shirt with a picture of a crossover Indie band on the front. He had an earbud in one ear, and another earbud hanging by a cord around his neck. Axle Guttenberg, Kristen's cousin, an immature teen and the brother I never had, since I was an only child. Axle had recently come to work for Byron.

"Hey, cuz'." That's what I called him, my lil' cuz'.

"Hey, Delaney. Can I catch a ride home with you?" He turned to Byron. "That is, if it's okay for me to leave. I finished the Tesla." Axle acted all cool and important with his earbuds and his cell phone permanently attached, but his eyes shone with excitement, and the corners of his mouth hinted at a smile. Byron had allowed him to handle an expensive paint job.

The Old Man glanced at the wall clock. "You've been here since five this mornin'. I think you can leave now. Let's hope you always get this enthused 'bout a job."

"When are you going to get your driver's license back?" I made a *tskking* noise. "Oh, never mind. You can be trusted under the hood of a car, but not behind the wheel."

Axle flicked my braid up and the heavy plait hit me in the face. "Har. Har. You're such a moron."

"Stop calling me moron." My last name was pronounced *More-ann*—close enough—so Axle often called me *moron*.

"I'd think you'd be used to it by now."

"Just stop." I gave him a death glare.

"Who's going to make me? You and who else?"

"I haven't heard that one since second grade." I

23

swiped the earbud out of his ear and smacked him upside the head, gently of course, because he was my next best friend after Kristen.

"Yeah, deal with it." Axle flapped his hand.

We walked out the door side by side. He gave me a shove, and I lurched a few steps before knocking into him with a hip-bump. I scrambled into the driver's seat of my silver Fiat I'd left parked at Byron's when I'd last taken out my truck, and Axle folded himself into the passenger compartment. My Fiat 500 was a tiny two-door, something like a Smart Car.

As I turned out of the lot, Axle asked, "You doing okay? It's been a few days now."

"Who told you?" I knew he didn't listen to the news and we hadn't talked since I'd found the dead guy.

"Kristen. Pretty gruesome, she said."

"Yeah." I felt like downplaying it. "Are you free to go out with me on some tows?"

"'Course. Just say when."

"I'll call you." Having Axle along would give me some needed courage.

I turned in to the mobile home park in the bad part of town and pulled up to a white, rusted trailer with a sagging awning over the front door. A car backfired from somewhere. I jumped in my seat and rubbed my hand over my heart. So much for being brave.

"You don't look okay," Axle pointed out.

I shook my head. "You need to move out of here, Axle. This place isn't safe."

He laced his fingers through mine and gave my hand a shake. "I'm more worried about you."

I stuck out my tongue. "I'm worried about you."

"No, *you* the one."

"No, *you.*"

We both smiled. He dropped my hand and clambered out of the passenger seat. "Thanks for the ride. Just so you know, I'm working on getting my license back."

I feigned shock. "Get the heck out."

"For real." He gave me a wave as he opened the door and went inside, shutting behind him the loud *RRR-ruff-ruff-RRRR* snarling of his Rottweiler mix named Boss.

On the way out of the trailer park, I drove past rough men wearing black, short-sleeved tee-shirts showing off dark tattoos. Their dull eyes followed my Fiat as I steered in the other direction. These sketchy guys always seemed to hang out around here, sitting on top of picnic tables, doing nothing besides making me scared and jumpy.

Once back on the main road, I placed a call to Tanner. It was time for a chat with my boyfriend. Too many days had gone by. "What's up?" I asked him. "You missing me or did you dump me for another girl?"

"What are you talking about?" He sounded worried.

"I'm teasing you!" *Jeez*, he must really be overworked. "Where are you?"

"Corner of Sims and Main."

"Be right there. Don't go anywhere." I spun my little Fiat in that direction and found Tanner in his black self-loader behind the furniture store. I climbed out of my car and into the passenger seat of his truck. "Hey, everything okay? You seem in a weird mood." I flashed him my best smile.

"Sorry. I thought you were serious." Tanner slid his arm along my seatback and settled a hand on my shoulder. Smooth.

"*Moi*, serious?" I grinned. We were still in the flirty, getting-to-know-each-other stage, but I thought he at least knew by now when I was teasing. "Did you get my text that I towed that Impreza over to your lot?"

"I got it. Are you working again?"

"Yep. I can take my calls back now." If I said it out loud, maybe that would make it come true. I punched the button on my cell to stop my tow calls from forwarding to Tanner. "I appreciate you covering for me." I was grateful for this sweet guy who had my back.

"I'm glad you're doing better." He brushed a strand of hair from my face. "I've missed you." He drew me closer. His fingers stabbed into my hair, and he gave me a deep kiss that made my toes curl and my stomach do a cartwheel.

"I've missed you, too." My hair tumbled out of the braid. Tanner always managed to break it loose.

His cell rang. *Ugh! Interrupted!* He went to hit the button, but I grabbed his hand first. "Come over for dinner tonight?"

"Okay." He nodded, then answered his phone. A call for a tow, so I leveraged open the door and got out. He was more experienced in the business and received a lot more calls than I did.

Once home I started a pot of coffee to give me a jolt of caffeine, then went straight for the pink stilettos I was wearing when I stopped at the Impreza. Holding them high over the trash can, I said a quick eulogy and paused for a moment of silence, remembering the good times. For four-inch heels, they were comfortable, and I'd received a lot of compliments on this pair, but that blood wasn't coming off. I dropped them and they whooshed into the can.

After changing into jeans and a different pair of pink heels—yes, I had more than one pair—I strutted around in front of the mirror. *What would these heels look like with my denim pencil skirt?* I tried on the skirt with the shoes and posed in front of the mirror again. This is what I'd wear tonight for dinner with my man.

The doorbell rang, so I trotted over, but paused with my hand on the knob. The killer didn't know about me. He couldn't possibly know where I lived. Still, I stopped to stare out the peephole. When I saw a familiar dark blue uniform, I threw open the bolt.

Sheriff Ephraim Lopez's frame filled the doorway.

Chapter 3

The county sheriff was taller than me by ten inches, older than me by ten years, and had the bronze complexion of his Mexican heritage, with chocolate brown eyes, long, black eyelashes, and thick black hair. He smelled like citrus, jasmine, and musk—clean and fresh and appealing.

Sheriff Hotty eyeballed me in my pink stretchy top, pencil skirt, and pink stilettos. "You doing okay?"

Ephraim had given me signals in the past that he was interested in me, but we were both involved in a murder investigation then, and by the time the crime was solved, I was dating Tanner. There was no doubt Ephraim was an attractive man, but Tanner and I were still in early days and I needed to give our new relationship a fair chance. Besides, the rumor around town was that this hot-blooded Latino was a player, and I didn't need that.

I folded my arms across my chest. "Yes. Come on in." I turned to escape to the kitchen with Ephraim on my heels, saying over my shoulder, "I heard you've taken over the homicide investigation."

"Yeah. The city isn't too happy, but the county has more resources. I'm so sorry you were the one to find the body. I know the scene had to have been upsetting."

I stopped at the kitchen counter and turned to wrinkle my nose at him. "You need to ask me about it, right?"

"That's why I'm here." He inched closer and electricity passed between us. I looked into his eyes for a moment too long before glancing away. He said, "But that's not the only reason. I wanted to make sure you're all right."

"Would you like some coffee? It's fresh." When he nodded, I stretched up on my toes to grab two mugs, forcing him to take step back. I filled the cups and handed one over. "I'm not exactly okay. I've been having nightmares."

His head bobbed up and down. "I know what you mean. Like flashbacks, right?"

"You've had them, too?"

"It's common."

"Zach says I need closure."

Ephraim held his mug squarely in front of him. "What do you mean?"

"You need to solve the crime, Ephraim, so I can have resolution." I didn't add, *or else I need to solve it*, but you guessed it…it did cross my mind.

"I will, and you can help me out." He laid a handwritten paper on the counter. "Here's the statement you filled out at the scene. Can you read it over?"

I swallowed a gulp of coffee and picked up the report, my wrists shaky. I lowered myself to a counter stool, and Ephraim slid in next to me while I scanned through it. The words brought back the image of the man in the driver's seat with his fingers curled around the steering wheel.

My head felt light and woozy, like I'd just stepped off a cliff. My heart accelerated as if I was plummeting in a free fall. Tears pressed at my eyes and I could hear the blood pulsing in my ears. I snapped the paper and set it back down and waited a moment to catch my breath.

Ephraim asked, "What's the matter?"

I held up a hand. "Give me a second." Was my mind playing tricks? Had the nightmares taken charge of my memories? Because there was more, a lot more that hadn't registered until now. What exactly had I seen? I asked Ephraim, "Were the guy's hands tied to the steering wheel, like with strips of plastic, maybe?" I rubbed my wrists as if I felt the pain.

"The victim's hands were secured with zip-ties."

I kept myself upright by leaning my elbows on the counter. "That's so weird, but that's why his hands didn't fall away from the steering wheel when he was shot. And, there's something else." I fiddled with my earlobes. "He had on earrings, silver, dangly, in the shape of lightning bolts. And he had tattoos on his knuckles. Letters, spelling out B-O-L-T." I splayed out my fingers.

"You're very observant. Do you remember anything more?"

"Someone threw papers all over the passenger seat and the floor. I'll bet they were searching the vehicle for something." My hand flew to my nose. "He'd been there overnight, hadn't he?"

"He was likely killed between seven and eight the night before."

"Byron Oberly told me he saw the Impreza around seven. And you know I drove by around eight. So, you think he was shot some time in between?"

Ephraim's head went up and down. "I'd like you to keep these details to yourself. We aren't going to let the public know about the zip-ties, for one thing." He stood and folded my statement into his pocket. I hopped off my stool and walked the mostly untouched coffee cups over to the sink. I turned around and caught him watching me.

"I'm sorry I had to ask you these questions," he said with a frown.

My hands still shook. "Yeah, talking about it brought it all back." And then some.

"Witnesses often recall more the next day after the shock wears off."

I grunted, stopping short of a laugh. "The image of the guy is stuck in my head now."

"Give it time. How about this for a distraction?" His grin took up his whole face. "You look nice tonight. I think your shoes are fine."

I glanced down at my pink heels. "Thanks."

"Remember that time I came by and you offered me a beer instead of coffee?"

"I do." I knew he would decline, but I asked, "You want a beer? I have some pale ale."

"Can't, on duty." He seemed disappointed. "Take care and call me if you think of anything else. Or if you just need to talk."

"There *is* something I want to ask."

He moved closer. "What's that?"

My mouth had dried up, tasting like dusty brown pine needles, and I cleared my throat. "Once the Impreza is released, who's responsible to clean it? Not me?"

His lips formed a thin line. "No, the owner. There are restoration companies that decontaminate crime scenes. I recommend they use one of those."

"Okay. Thanks, Ephraim."

"Don't forget you can call me if you need someone to talk to. I understand what you're going through."

"Okay." I followed him to the door, then turned the lock behind him after he left.

My cell rang and I dashed back to get it. Was it someone in need of a tow? I should get back to work and put the dreaded crime scene behind me.

I answered with a quivery voice, but it was only Mom calling. "I heard on the news the police found a man shot to death in his car. That didn't happen anywhere near you, did it?"

Might as well get this over with, even though I didn't want to talk about it anymore. "I had to haul that vehicle off the side of the road."

"What!"

My dry throat sucked in air, and I went to the fridge for a bottle of water. "It's part of the job, Mom. And, yes, it was pretty gross, so I took a couple of days off."

"You want to come stay with us for a while? We could go shopping. Out to lunch. You should get away from that town, it'll do you good."

My mom moved to Denver after my parents divorced, taking me with her, while my dad had stayed in Spruce Ridge. After a time Mom remarried, and her second husband, Will, seemed to make her happy with her new life. But when Kristen scouted for locations to open her coffee shop, I suggested this small town and the two of us moved here. That Dad still lived in Spruce Ridge was a draw, but he'd died before we'd had a chance to reunite. I told myself it was because I was too busy helping Kris get her new business off the ground.

That's what I told myself. But I should've made some kind of effort. Once I quit Roasters, Mom encouraged me to move back to Denver, but I had a business to run here in Spruce Ridge, thanks to Dad's gift of the truck. Spruce Ridge was home to me now.

I answered, "Thanks, but I can't take any more time off. I need to get back to work. Tanner's been covering for me." I was nervous and not entirely sure I was ready to tow again, but I was going to try and it was a great excuse to give Mom.

"I'd like to meet that young man of yours." Mom hadn't liked my last boyfriend, and she wasn't sure about this one, either.

"You met him at the coffee shop a few weeks ago."

"I didn't get a chance to talk to him. I'd like you to invite him over for dinner."

"Sure, Mom." Arguing was no use. "I'll let you know when Tanner and I can make it." I didn't mention we were getting together for dinner tonight. An evening alone with Tanner beats out a meal with the parents.

Mom extracted my solemn promise I'd call her back soon and we disconnected.

It was time to get ready for our dinner date. I was dressed, now I needed to prepare the meal.

I stuffed the dirty coffee cups in the dishwasher and went to the freezer for Italian sausage and mozzarella cheese. While the sausage defrosted in the microwave, I stirred up some pizza dough in my big yellow mixing bowl. Once the batter was left to rise, I chopped a garlic clove and half an onion and rifled through the fridge for anything else I could add. Leftover broccoli florets, baby spinach, and tomatoes. I diced all those up fine, too, then browned the sweet sausage, and added tomato paste and spices, and set the flame on low to simmer.

When Tanner walked through the door, he had on a sexy grin that made a warm spot in my stomach. He snuggled me up against him for a kiss. Yep, I was glad we weren't on our way over to Mom and Will's. After he let go of me, we assembled the pizza, and I slipped the pan in the oven. We cracked open a couple of those pale ales I'd told Ephraim about.

I hoped my face didn't turn red thinking of Ephraim, glad I'd placed the coffee mugs in the dishwasher and out of sight. I asked Tanner, "So, you didn't tell me before, but how many tows did you cover for me? A lot?"

"A few, and people were disappointed I didn't wear high heels." He laughed.

At five-foot-two, I barely reached the gas pedal without the help of three-inch pumps. The heels were my brand and set me apart from the all-male tow drivers in town. It gave me no end of satisfaction when customers asked for the high-heeled driver. "Were there any calls from the police for me?"

He shook his head. "Nope, just regular customers. No city jobs."

"Hunh. You know that new towing operation, the guy who drives the bright green truck? Have you seen him around?" His green truck was as distinctive as my red one with the logo.

"Yeah."

"He's on the rotation with me for the roadside tows."

"I know."

"Do you think he's getting all the city calls?"

"Maybe there haven't been any stalled cars to tow. Sometimes there are long stretches without breakdowns." He chugged a few gulps of his cold brew, then said, "I heard Ephraim's handling the Quincy Davidsen murder investigation."

Wait for it...yes, there it was...the flush heating my cheeks. "He came over to ask me some more questions."

Tanner's eyebrows shot up. "Did he stay long?" Tanner was a hunky guy, made all the other girls' heads turn, and I was amazed he wanted me, so I was surprised every time his *rival-radar* appeared.

"No. Not at all." I almost shared the details from the murder scene, but Ephraim had warned me not to, and besides, I was afraid I'd get all barfy or burst into tears like an idiot. "He just went over my statement, then he left."

"Man, the pizza smells good." Tanner opened the door to peek in the oven. The smell of sautéed onion and browned sausage wafted out.

Oven mitts on my hands, I extracted the steaming pan and set it on the stovetop. Tanner ran the pizza wheel over the pie. We each snagged a piece, and Tanner quickly went back for a second, then a third.

I asked, "Would you like to invite your brother and sister over for pizza sometime?"

Tanner didn't like them to be alone too much, and I knew his aunt often watched the kids in the evenings and after school, even though the oldest, the girl, was a teenager.

"Sure." Tanner drained the last of his beer and turned on the tube.

I was curious to meet his family. *Ugh.* I sounded

like my mom, but I asked, "When?"

"I'll let you know."

He turned the station to the Rockies. Baseball was one game I could follow. He settled himself on the white loveseat and I snuggled up next to him.

The word-art above my sofa spelled out, "Family," and the mismatched floral pillows on the two facing loveseats shouted out "shabby chic," the style I loved. Tanner was a masculine contrast in this femininity. We inched closer and closer to each other. Even though the game was tied in the ninth inning, we were in a clinch when his cell phone went off. Someone stranded on the road needed a tow. This was the life of a tow man. Or tow woman. Everything comes to a halt when you need to go out on a job.

"Will you be okay tonight? Should I come back after I'm done with the tow? If it's not too late?"

"No, I'm fine. Go ahead. I don't want your aunt to have to stay up late with the kids."

He ran down the stairs with a quick wave goodbye.

Dang it. Why did I say that? I was all right while he was here, but now I wasn't sure I wanted to be alone.

I feared the nightmares that awaited me during the midnight hours.

Chapter 4

Skeletal hands reached out to me, a circle of red pooled at my feet, and a sickly metallic scent filled my nose. Lightning pierced the darkness exposing the edge of a cliff, a steep drop-off, just inches away. I couldn't take a breath. I couldn't move a finger. I couldn't feel a thing.

I tried to twitch. Really hard. Concentrating, concentrating…a strangled noise from my throat woke me up. Midnight. Blankets clammy with cold sweat. Phone ringing.

Should I let this call go? No one would blame me for pushing this one out; I just woke up from a freakin' nightmare after all! But before my mind knew what I was doing, my hand reached out for my cell. "Hello, this is Del's Towing." I swung my legs over the side of the bed to sit up.

"I'm sorry to call so late, but I'm broken down off Main Street in the alley behind the brewery. My car won't start and I need a tow."

Welp, I couldn't sleep anymore tonight, might as well do this. I wrote the man's name on the notepad I kept by the bed, plus his make and model, and told him I'd be there no later than twenty minutes. I snapped open the curtain. Pitch black outside, no stars.

My skin prickled with goosebumps.

I was always afraid of the dark yet chose a career

that often took me out in the night. Laughable, right? Like a vertiginous mountain climber or an allergic beekeeper or a deaf composer. There was one, you know, Beethoven. I'm not unique in this. Add the Impreza on top of being a natural scaredy cat, and well…I dialed up Axle. I needed my lil' cuz' along to give me some backbone.

"You awake?" I asked him.

"Am now. You got a tow?"

"Yes. On my way over." I went to my closet for clothes and boots with heels. My hair went into a ponytail and I went out the door.

The nighttime temperature had dropped and the parking lot sparkled with frost. Spring in the Rockies meant you could sunburn during the day but freeze at night. I ran my window defroster for a few minutes until the windshield became clear. Monochromic buildings, washed black and white in the dark, hunkered down beside the coffee shop, asleep like everyone else. The only illumination was from the occasional lamp bleeding out from behind a curtained window. The scent of moisture in the breeze made the night smell clean and crisp, and the clouds on the horizon reflected light from the moon, forcing me fully awake.

After I picked up my tow truck at Byron's shop, I pulled into Axle's trailer court. When he slipped into the cab, I handed him my auto encyclopedia. "Find Mitsubishi Lancer. Is it front or rear-wheel drive?"

"I don't need to look it up. Front-wheel is standard, but it's available in all-wheel, too." Axle was better than an encyclopedia.

"Thanks. I don't like to ask the customer unless I

have to. I don't want them to think I don't know what I'm doing."

"The high heels might give them a clue."

I'd left myself wide open for that one. That was the downside of my trademark shoes.

Columbine Court was empty, but Main Street had a few cars. When I pulled into the alley behind the brewery, I hit the brakes hard. A man next to a bronze-colored Lancer had a baseball bat held loosely in his hand.

I sank my teeth into my lower lip and breathed out, "Uh-oh." I might as well be back in my nightmare.

Axle whirred down his window and stuck his head out, his ball cap on backward. "You the one who called for a tow?"

"Yes. You Del?"

"Del's Towing. Can't you see the name on the truck?"

"Okay, good." The man sounded relieved. He sent a glance over his shoulder where shadowy dumpsters overflowed with garbage. Rats likely scrounged around the debris. The man's eyes skimmed the alley one more time, then he placed the bat into his trunk, casual-like.

"Come on, Delaney, it'll be okay." Axle shoved his door open.

I tumbled down from the cab, my boots making a sharp sound on the pavement. I'd chosen heeled boots in green, the color of money since I was back on the job.

The man laughed. "Ha. You *do* wear high-heels."

"That's right." I threw my shoulders back and approached the vehicle like I belonged there. When in doubt, look like you know what you're doing. He couldn't guess I was just as scared of the dark, rat-infested alley as he was.

After I checked with him (the Lancer was front-wheel drive) my customer said, "I need the car towed to my buddy's house a couple of miles away. He's coming to get me. I'll give you the address and we can meet there."

I calculated the charge and he passed me his credit card, which I swiped through the card reader on my smartphone. Just as I handed his plastic back, his buddy pulled up in a Mustang, rear-wheel drive. My customer hopped inside and they took off.

Axle listened to tunes, earbuds in, as I maneuvered my hulking tow truck into the tight space in front of the Lancer. A dog howled from somewhere in the night and the wind swirled a tumbleweed into a dust devil, but I shook off the scary-movie vibe. Axle tapped his knees in time to his music and a low buzz came from his earphones. I squared my shoulders. I was ready.

I hit the controls, then put the truck in first gear. Halfway down the block, I noticed the Lancer still parked in the alley behind us, unmoved. I reversed back into place while Axle threw me a *what-the-heck* expression. This time I concentrated, making sure the claws captured the front tires and lifted them high in the air.

Cutting the corner short while turning out of the back street, I heard the groan of twisted metal and jammed on the brakes. Axle and I blinked at each other. I put the truck in park and we both got out. The Lancer was hung up on a telephone pole, and an ugly metallic-gray scrape cut through the beautiful bronze paint on the driver's door.

"Do you think he'll notice that, Axle?"

My cuz' just gawked at me, dumbfounded.

"I guess this means an insurance claim."

We climbed back in the truck. I hit the gas, the Lancer skimmed the pole with another metal shriek, we both cringed, and I completed the turn onto Main.

So, it should've been easy sailing after that, right? But backing into the driveway at our destination, I jackknifed the vehicle twice. It's just too painful to tell the whole story. Okay, my eyes threatened to tear up, so Axle dug out my insurance information and dealt with the customer, and then I blew through the stop sign at the corner when we left.

I said it was painful.

At least the customer didn't get his baseball bat back out.

Still, Axle white-knuckled the door all the way to the mobile home park. No earbuds in, no music blaring. He didn't tease me like he usually did, but kept tossing worried glances my way.

Enough said. Not going to talk about it.

My breath remained caught in my chest even after I pulled up in front of Axle's dilapidated trailer. The dark night did nothing to improve its appearance. "I guess I might not be ready to get back to work, Axle."

"You're a bit emotional, Delaney."

"I know." I hated my quick-to-water eyes.

"The customer didn't notice, no worries." He popped open the door. "Call me when you have another tow."

"Yeah, okay." No way was I ready to go out on late-night jobs on my own, that's for sure. "Why don't you move into my apartment, Axle? I have an extra bedroom. It's small, but you'd have the use of the kitchen and living room, too, so you'd have plenty of space."

He gave me a wide-eyed once over. "Where's this coming from?"

"You could help me with expenses, and I wouldn't have to come over here and get you for late night tows." The more I thought about it, the better it sounded, especially after my performance this evening. For added incentive, I said, "I'll take you to work in the morning. You could ride with me over to Byron's when I pick up my truck. And go out with me on tows at night. My apartment's real nice, Ax. It's just across the landing from Kristen's."

We both glanced at his rickety trailer. Axle gave me a slanted flick of the eye, which made me think he was about to turn me down, when blue and red strobe lights and the *whoop-whoop* of a police siren came from a street to the west of us.

I asked, "What do you think's happening over there?"

Axle took off his ballcap and rubbed the top of his head before plopping the cap back in place. He shrugged in a *who-cares* attitude.

"That's it. You're moving in with me, buster." I asked, "Do you need to give your landlord notice?"

"Nah. I don't have a lease. I pay weekly."

"You're probably paying too much."

"Probably am."

"Come on, cuz'. Do it."

Axle clicked off his seatbelt. "Ask Kris if I can bring my dog. I've been hiding Boss from the landlord."

"A Rotty is pretty hard to hide. Another reason to move in with me. I'll speak to Kristen and let you know." It'd be nice to have a guard dog around my apartment, too. That'd be a bonus. I liked Boss, who looked and sounded mean but was really a softy. No one knew that besides Axle and me.

Axle pushed himself out of the car and raised his hand in farewell.

Another siren started up a couple of blocks away and I wanted to run after him and drag him home with me, but instead I stepped on the accelerator, clutched the steering wheel tighter, and sped out of the trailer park.

Once I hit Pine Street I felt in safer territory. I loosened my grip and a vehicle pulled up alongside me, a green tow truck hauling a Ford Taurus, front-wheel drive, with an orange impound tag on it. The driver had a long beard and I did a double-take. I recognized him. My competition. And I never got a call from the city about that Taurus! Was the city assigning all the tows to the green tow truck driver now? *Groan.*

That reminded me of my responsibilities to the Spruce Ridge PD, so on the way to Byron's to drop off my self-loader, I pulled into Tanner's lot. The Impreza was hunkered down in the dark shadows between Tanner's flatbed and a Toyota Corolla, front-wheel drive. Fear grabbed my stomach hard, like sharp, hot espresso beans jumping around in my belly, burning my insides. I sat with the doors locked, wishing Axle was still with me, and gave myself a mental slap, *be brave, be brave.* I was in a secure, locked yard, and perfectly safe. But I had the *heebie-jeebies.*

I got out, clutched my hoodie around me, slightly

sick, and inched my way over. The yellow, police-hold warnings remained in place, the edges of the stickers ruffling a little on a breeze I couldn't feel. Perhaps a ghost passed by. I strained my ears and couldn't hear a thing, not even traffic from Pine Street only a few blocks away. I circled the vehicle and avoided facing the windows. There was no need to peek inside, I told myself.

Nothing appeared disturbed. Nothing except me. *I was disturbed.*

****

My bedroom door rattled in the early morning hours. Skeletal hands grasped and turned the doorknob to get inside. Why did I feel the need to open the door? *Don't do it*, I told my sleepwalking self, but I unlocked the door anyway, and there stood Kristen. She mouthed the request, *your rent, your rent*. Then I woke up.

Eek. That was a twist to my nightmares. Why did they have to return to haunt me some more?

But my dream reminded me the rent was due. I knew I was low on funds, but just how low? I threw off the covers and opened my laptop to log in to my bank's website. Yup, lower than a dry creek bed in a box canyon. In other words, scraping bottom. And, car and truck insurance payments were coming up in addition to the rent. Not taking care of my tows over the weekend had made a dent in my finances. Can you tell my mind's been in a fog?

That my landlord was my friend didn't matter. I needed to be absolutely, completely certain I had the cash because I couldn't let Kirsten down. The money was crucial for her to pay the lease on the building. In the morning I'd get busy and try to drum up business, but right now I needed to clear my head, so I watched the shopping channel until the sun rose.

Once morning arrived, I got ready for the day, then strode through the employee entrance to the coffee shop. Now that I was working in my own business, I no longer had to exchange my heels for sneakers or don the Roasters on the Ridge apron. Kris had a full staff and didn't need me to work here anymore.

Guy, the English Lit major, who was also a recovering alcoholic, swept the shadowy front entryway under standings of aspen trees. The pink-haired teenage girl at the espresso machine, who had been homeless before coming to work here, was doing better and had found a place to live. I could tell Sierra would be a solid employee, but Guy...I wasn't sure about Guy. He didn't like me. It was obvious he wanted to be Kristen's favorite employee and resented my presence.

He stopped sweeping when he clapped his eyes on me, then hustled back through the front door and rushed behind the counter, crowding me out of the way. "You can't just waltz in here and help yourself to coffee."

My cheeks warmed. I said, "Kristen doesn't mind. Why? Has she said anything to you?" His eyes narrowed to slits, so I handed him a fiver. I didn't want to take advantage of my friend.

Kris had a few minutes to spare before opening, and my arrival was always an excuse for a timeout, so I went into the backroom to ask her, "Take a break?"

"Of course."

I wagged my double shot at her as we grabbed a table among all the empties. "I paid for my drink this time."

"Delaney, I never want you to pay. You always

show up at closing to lend a hand. Please, let me provide you with coffee."

I gave Guy a death stare and he ducked behind the tall espresso machine. Was he trying to be a jerk? Or was he trying to be an honest employee? Kristen gave people the benefit of the doubt and maybe I should, too, and just ignore Guy. She was a good example, helping people, giving back to the community, and I had a chance to do the same, starting with Axle.

"Kris, here's my rent." I handed her a check. Less than fifty bucks was left in my account now. "I want to ask you a question and I need you to answer honestly, as if I wasn't your friend, but just a regular tenant."

She went rigid. "What's the matter? Something wrong with your apartment?"

"No." I took a deep breath and crossed my fingers. "Could I sublet my extra bedroom to Axle? He needs to get out of that trailer park and it would help me out, too."

She broke into a smile. "Why, that's a nice thing to do. Of course, Axle can live here."

I knew it! I knew it!

"And his dog, Boss?" The Rottweiler mix weighed sixty-or-so pounds and had black with brown paws, a brown muzzle, and big, sharp teeth. He'd chewed on Axle's furniture so I'd have to watch him. Kris might not want the destructive animal living in my apartment.

Her eyes flickered, but she said, "Yeah, okay."

I popped out of my chair and hugged Kristen. "You're the best!"

I texted Axle to give him the glad tidings and we exchanged a few texts making plans. When Kristen got up to return to the counter, I bade her goodbye, latte in my hand. I got into my truck, set my drink in the cupholder, and cruised down busy Pine Street toward Main, then hooked a left on Industrial Lane.

I hurtled up the canyon, past the business park, and overtook what looked to be an abandoned Lincoln Navigator, rear-wheel drive. Out-of-towners' vehicles often broke down on the side of the road because they were not equipped for altitude. But instead of stopping, I continued to the turnoff for the ski resort, pulled to the side, and rolled down my window to the delicious aroma of woodsmoke and the dry scent of pine needles. The sun shone brightly, heating up the morning, giving me a boost of confidence. After a few more moments, I reversed direction and overtook the Lincoln once again. That's when I noticed the orange tow-tag on the back window. I really should've stopped and snagged the Lincoln, but I didn't. I kept going. Where had that confidence boost gone?

Chicken, much?

Once back in town I headed for the entrance to I-70, the busy highway that led to several more ski resorts. A couple miles from Spruce Ridge, a Honda Accord, front-wheel drive, sat at an angle on the shoulder. This was my second chance at a tow job and I wasn't going to lose my nerve this time. I was almost sure of it. I pulled over in front of the Accord and reversed so that the back of my front-loader was inches from the front of the Accord. *Get out*, I told myself. *Get out and check the car, take note of the VIN. Go look. Do it. Do it now.*

First I failed to haul away the Lincoln, now I was scared to approach the Honda. My stomach churned like milk in a frother and a bitter taste crept up my throat.

Just then a call came in from Nancy Abington from the Abington Auto Store. "Delaney, I have a job for you. Do you have time?"

I was saved by a call for a repo!

Nancy had newly acquired the car dealership from her husband, Rob, as part of their divorce. She was a quick learner, ambitious, and a smart businesswoman, and she used me for repos, not my favorite job but a respectable job, nevertheless. It could be dangerous because folks who didn't make their payments were often angry about their cars being repossessed, and towers had to be pretty sneaky to capture the vehicles, but I had a few repos under my belt now. And even though risky, it felt safer than towing abandoned cars.

I said, "Sure, I have time." I took down the make, model, VIN, and owner's contact information, and Nancy told me to work with her company's repo agent, Patrick Crump. This vehicle was a black BMW 5 Series, rear-wheel drive, owned by Bianca White, a local realtor.

I flew down I-70 and returned to Spruce Ridge to cruise by White's home address and wasn't surprised to find her BMW was not out in the open. Next, I drove past the realty office in a corner shopping plaza. No BMW there, either. I texted Patrick Crump to let him know, and he replied that he would check nearby grocery stores and the mall. If he spotted the BMW, he would contact me and I could try for a mall grab.

In the meantime, I returned to the BMW's home address to wait. After an hour, the target vehicle appeared from two blocks away. As it neared, the garage door automatically rolled up and the BMW disappeared inside. The door unfolded back down and a few moments later a light went on in the kitchen.

Arguing with myself about what to do next, I sat there contemplating the job. Repossessing cars seemed mean, but even though owners were given every chance to voluntarily return the car, they kept the vehicle without paying for it, and that was stealing. As a repo agent, I recovered what amounted to a stolen vehicle. I'm sure Abington Auto Store had talked to Bianca White already, but maybe all she needed was a few words from me and this matter could be resolved.

I rang the bell. When White pulled open the door, I said, "I'm with Del's Towing. Abington Auto sent me over to take possession of the BMW. I'm sorry about this, but could you please open your garage?"

She turned pale and clung to the edge of the door. "I just can't make my payment. I'm only starting out as a realtor, and it's been rough. I have a closing in two weeks. I can make the payment then."

Oh man, I knew the feeling, all too well. "I understand. I can't negotiate for Abington, but I can ask someone there to get in touch with you."

"That'd be great." She beamed as if it was a done deal.

"I can't guarantee what they'll say, but I wish you luck in your job. Hopefully your business will pick up even more after your first closing." I gave her a nod and a smile. I felt a little better, like I was helping someone, but I had a feeling in my gut Abington Auto Store would've wanted me to recover the vehicle.

On my way out of the neighborhood, I hit speed dial for Tanner, put the speaker on, and propped my phone on the dash. Hearing his voice would brighten my outlook. After we exchanged hellos, he asked, "You want to get together later tonight?"

Another date. *Yeah-ez.*

"Yes, I do. No, no I don't. Axle's moving into my apartment tonight. We already made plans."

Tanner met this with a few beats of silence. "Axle is moving in with you?"

"I talked him into it. I hate the idea of him living in that trailer park, and he'll share the rent." More silence. "Tanner! He's like my brother. He's ten years younger than me." Axle was eighteen and I was twenty-eight. Big difference. Of course, Ephraim was in his late thirties, and I didn't think he was too old for me. But wait, I didn't want to think of another man when I was on the phone with my boyfriend. "You can stop by if you'd like. I'll be moving boxes out of the spare room and helping Axle move in."

"Aren't you covering the towaway zones tonight?"

Tanner held contracts with the Main Street businesses to monitor their no-parking zones. He assigned Tuesdays and Thursdays to me, and he was responsible for Mondays, Wednesdays, and Fridays. Today was Tuesday. "Of course. Axle's moving in after I'm done."

"Hey, someone just pulled into my lot. I gotta go."

"Talk to you later." I shook my head at myself. Tanner needed to get over it.

By this time I'd driven home, so I parked in back of my apartment and called Nancy Abington from my truck. I was put through immediately, and Nancy asked, "What can I do for you, Delaney?"

"I talked to Bianca White, the owner of the BMW. She told me she's just starting out as a realtor and it's been tough, but she's got a closing in two weeks and can make the payment then."

Nancy chuckled low into the phone. "She told you that, huh?"

I flushed, a little taken aback. Nancy was a shrewd businesswoman, but was there no sympathy in her heart at all? "Two weeks isn't so bad."

"Delaney, we vet all the repos before calling you. Trust me, we know what we're doing."

"Okay…" I trailed off.

"Bianca White is behind four months. It's not like she missed one payment, she missed four. She's been selling houses for ten years, even named realtor of the year. You let her give you a sob story, but it's a lie."

My mouth flew open and I was too stunned to say anything.

"Look, we found out she has overwhelming debts from poor investments and real estate speculations. She needs to liquidate her assets and get out of debt, including her vehicle loan. You may think me harsh, but repossessing the car will eliminate one of her debts and get her on the right track."

"I see."

"Just capture the vehicles, don't talk to the owners from now on."

"All right, Nancy. I understand." We disconnected.

Boy, that Bianca White really had me fooled. In fact, I was losing my edge. I'd heard all kinds of excuses from people whose vehicles I'd hauled from the towaway zones, you'd think I would've learned to detect a lie by now. I'd messed up future opportunities to capture the BMW, because White would be on the lookout for my tow truck from here on out.

I ran inside my apartment and vacuumed all the rooms, including the spare room which would now be Axle's. I scrubbed the bathroom we'd be sharing and dusted the living room. The kitchen was already clean and in good shape. I scarfed down a hardboiled egg and a yogurt, then zoomed over to Main Street to begin an evening of monitoring the no-parking zones.

During the day the Main Street businesses called when a vehicle blocked their loading docks. After five in the evening, I trolled my truck up and down the alleys behind the old buildings to spot violators, and sometimes I towed three or four a night, generating a big piece of my income. I always captured the VIN on my cell and provided it to the police in case the owners reported their cars stolen, wasting police time. Most often the drivers figured out they'd been towed and didn't call the police, since the "No Parking - Towaway Zone" sign was a giveaway. *Ya' think?*

Tonight, however, there was only one violator, a Mini Cooper, red, two-door convertible, with the Union Jack printed on the vinyl roof. I gave the driver a break by leaving my business card under the windshield wiper with a warning. This wasn't like me. I didn't usually slack-off.

My record wasn't so good lately. I'd dented a customer's vehicle. I'd neglected the orange-tagged stalls on the side of the road. I'd screwed up the repo. I left the Mini Cooper blocking a loading zone.

That Impreza was the reason I'd lost my *mojo*. I needed to feel the magic once again...me, the high-heeled tow truck driver with my amazing self-loader, the Fulcan Xtruder. I had to be able to tow vehicles without damaging them. To recover abandoned or illegally parked cars or repos, all without fear. To sleep without nightmares. To get over this first responder trauma.

Solving the Mystery of the Dead Body in the Impreza would be a *win-win*. The crime had caused my epic fail. I couldn't say the murder was not my problem and just walk away.

Before heading to Byron's to leave my truck for the night, I checked messages for a text from Axle. That's when my phone rang, and I glanced at the caller ID thinking it might be Ax, but it was Tanner.

I answered, "Hey, Tanner. Did you decide to come over to my place after all?"

"Ah, no. That's not why I'm calling. I know it's late, but there's someone at my lot who wants inside the Impreza. Is it still on police-hold?"

"Yes, it is. I'm on my way."

Who could it be? I squealed my truck out of the parking lot to hurry over.

Chapter 5

A tall girl with choppy black hair waited in Tanner's lot. I could tell at a glance she was attractive, wearing a skimpy top and tight jeans with legs *up to here*—every man's weakness. And she was in a close discussion with Tanner.

I slammed the door to the truck, but neither of them turned to look. Her fingers clenched his tattooed arm, and his gaze was glued to her eyes.

Tanner usually gazed at me that way.

I gripped my keys until my fingers hurt and stomped over, stiff-legged. Without a doubt, my cheeks glowed as red as a stop sign. I asked her, "Are you here for the Impreza?"

She turned her blue eyes on me. "I'm Clem. Clementine Vargas. Quincy Davidsen was my boyfriend." Tears bubbled in her eyes and she held Tanner's arm tighter. *Oh, boy.* She played the *distraught girlfriend-dead boyfriend* card, laying it on thick, like she needed a strong shoulder to cry on. Tanner had strong shoulders.

"The police have impounded the vehicle. I'm sorry I can't let you inside." I hooked her elbow to steer her away from Tanner—and the Impreza. I didn't want her to catch a glimpse of the car's interior. That's all I was doing, okay? I'm nice like that, all right?

A tear ran down her face, but before she had a

chance to get a real cry on, footsteps sounded on the gravel behind us and we all turned around. Axle loped across the lot, his work boots treading heavily, his earbuds dangling from around his neck.

I felt my eyebrows shoot up in surprise. "What are you doing here?"

"Tanner called me. Said he wanted a word, so I had a friend drop me off."

I darted a suspicious glance over at Tanner. He gazed skyward.

Axle's chin pointed at Clem. "Who's this?"

"Clementine Vargas. Call me Clem." She turned her baby-blue witchy eyes on Axle, and it was his turn to go weak-kneed. Miraculously, when she gave him her siren smile her tears disappeared. She'd caught both men under her spell and had cast me out.

"Clem?" I waved my hands in front of her face. "Is there something you need from the Impreza?" I might've been a little harsh, but you have to understand, she almost licked her lips in the direction of my boyfriend, then did the same to my lil' cuz.

"I just wanted to see it." Her gaze lowered and her long lashes fanned against her cheeks. "I feel responsible. It's my fault Quincy's dead."

I put a hand over my mouth and stepped back. "What?"

"I told him he should take a drive up to the mountains, have a little break, you see. I'm the reason he was on that road, you know, where he got shot." Her bottom lip quivered.

Axle said quickly, "You can't take the blame for that."

Tanner added, "You can't hold yourself

responsible."

I thought, *why not, maybe she is,* but my sympathy gene finally kicked in. This young girl had lost her boyfriend and was going through a difficult time.

I patted her on the arm. "Let me have your phone number and that way I can let you know when the police-hold is lifted. I'll give you my card, too." And, yes, I had an ulterior motive. I could call and ask her some questions about the victim without the distraction of her fan club.

She recited her number and I'm pretty sure Axle's lips moved as if memorizing it. I rooted around in my bag for my business cards while Axle sidled even closer to her. The two of them had their phones out, both punching buttons.

I took Tanner aside. "What'd you want to talk to Axle about?"

Tanner's eyes darted around. "Just making sure he didn't need help moving."

Yeah, right. More like, just making sure he didn't plan to make any moves toward me. I looked up from my bag and forced a smile. *Girl,* I told myself, *a little jealousy is okay. It just means he cares.* Besides, I had on the *green-jelly* face a moment ago. "Tanner, he's as close to a brother as I've got. He's a good friend. He rides with me on tows."

"I can go with you."

I would love Tanner to ride with me and not have to work by myself right now, but he needed me to cover the shifts without his help. "You have tow jobs of your own."

"Really, Delaney, if you want someone to ride shotgun, call me."

I said, "I might just take you up on that, babe. I'll let you know." I strode over to Clem and handed her my card, then I turned back to Axle. "You ready?"

Axle and I climbed into my truck to leave. A Lexus LS Hybrid, rear-wheel drive, pulled up to the curb across the street with a man in a Bronco's baseball cap behind the wheel. The hat shaded his face and covered his hair. Axle and I watched Clem run across the street and get in.

When I steered my truck out of Tanner's lot, the Lexus pulled in behind us. Axle craned his neck for a last glance out the back window. He said, "Wow, that Clem's something, isn't she?" then turned his attention to his phone. I caught a glimpse of Clem's picture on his screen. He'd taken a photo of her! He had a bad crush already. Almost as tall as Axle and a good five or six inches taller than me, Clem was a beauty who resembled an anime character with sparkly, overlarge eyes and black, choppy hair, and I could see the attraction. All too well. *Ooooh*, I hated her.

I asked Axle, "Are you packed and ready to move in?"

"Yeah, swing by the trailer."

"Don't we need a pickup truck or something? I thought we might borrow Byron's." Byron drove a Ford F150, an all-terrain 4-wheel-drive.

"I only have a backpack of clothes."

"No furniture?"

"The trailer came furnished."

"You'll have to sleep on the sofa tonight." I spoke into my Bluetooth, "Call Mom."

She picked up right away. "Hello, Laney. How are you, hon?"

"I'm good. Do you have an extra bed, like in the attic or basement or somewhere? I want one for my spare room."

"Yes, dear. I've still got your old twin set. You want me to have Will drive it up to Spruce Ridge?"

"Does he have time to do that for me?"

"He'll make the time. You know how wonderful he is about everything." While Mom always had plenty of bad things to say about my dad, she never criticized Will.

"That'd be great." I turned my truck onto Columbine Court and entered the trailer park.

Mom said, "I'm sure he can run the bed over to you in a couple of days, at least by the weekend."

"Thanks so much, Mom. Talk to you later." I disconnected, trying to keep a smile off my face. I speared Axle with my right elbow. "You'll love the bed. So comfortable."

I glided my truck to a stop and Axle shoehorned himself out. He returned in moments with his dog and a ratty, black canvas backpack that he jammed onto the passenger side floorboard. Then he crammed his Rottweiler into the truck's backseat and we were off. So long, trailer park, not Axle's home anymore.

He carted the pack up the steps to my apartment—our apartment—with Boss padding along behind us, and I unlocked the door. Hello apartment, not exclusively mine anymore.

The extra key was in the junk drawer, so I fished it out and handed it to him. "You can help me move the boxes from the spare room to the back of my closet." It would be tight and I wouldn't have as much space for my shoe collection, but I'd made room at the very back and on the high shelves.

As Axle lugged the cartons down the hall, Boss nosed around the garbage can, so I set out a plastic dish filled with water and called out to Axle, "Do you have dog food?"

"In my pack. I'll get it." He found another bowl in the cupboard and loaded it up with kibble. The Rotty crunched the hard chow while bits flew out of his mouth onto the floor. Good thing I liked him.

"Good boy, good baby," I told Boss in my best *puppy-talk* voice. I grabbed clean sheets and blankets from the hall closet and passed them to Axle. "For you to sleep on the couch until the bed from my mom gets here."

"Sure, Delaney."

We ate popcorn and watched his favorite superhero movie. His phone pinged with texts all through the last scene.

He made my already comfy apartment feel even more like home.

****

Those cozy feelings evaporated the next morning because I'd tossed and turned all night with more bad dreams. And having to rinse Axle's whiskers out of the bathroom sink was a cheerless job, which didn't help the pain in my head. Then I had to fold the sheets and blanket Axle left scrunched up on the sofa. At least once I'd set up his bedroom, I wouldn't need to pick up his bedding again.

Note to self: talk to Axle about house rules. He was obviously raised in a barn.

I shoved my feet into yellow strappy sandals with cork platform heels. Yellow for happiness (I was trying to turn my mood around). After he gave Boss a quick walk outside, it was time to take Axle to work, so we tooled over to Byron's. After parking, I slammed the door to the Fiat, which sounded more like the *whoosh-click* of a toy car.

Axle said, "Thanks for the ride."

"You owe me, little cousin." I meant it this time.

Axle grumbled, doing the forehead wrinkle, but he went silent when we walked in on Byron's niece, Shannon, standing at the service counter.

An atypical teenager, Shannon loved everything vintage. She drove a VW Beetle with the fake flower in the dash. Her layered, light brown hair framed her face and black chucks peeped out from under her flared jeans. Oversized cat-eye sunglasses completed her style. She called Byron the "Old Man," the reason I took up calling him that, too.

I greeted his niece with, "Hey, Shay!"

Shannon lunged toward me and gave me a big hug. "I heard."

"News travels fast and all that."

She squinched her eyes at me. "You okay?"

I made shooing motions and rolled my eyes so she wouldn't detect my stomach was doing the rolling. "Natch."

"What's up with that new operator in town?" She raised one eyebrow in a question. "The driver with the long beard, drives a green tow truck."

"What about him?" I flipped my gaze from Shannon to Axle and back to Shannon. Axle acted like she wasn't there.

Shannon said, "I wondered what you thought of him. He seems the eager-beaver type."

I wasn't too happy about my competition, but I said, my words light, "I'm not worried about him. Should I be?"

"He's pushy. Kinda in your face, you know?"

"Why do you say that?"

The phone rang and Shannon popped on a headset. "Oberly Motors." Byron had hired his niece to handle the phones and filing. At one time I'd hoped Axle would get together with Shannon, but Axle was giving Byron's niece a wide berth. He hung back near the door to the auto bays while Shannon clickity-clicked on the computer keyboard.

I strode over to Axle. "Call me if you need a ride home tonight." I sounded like a bossy big sister. *Cripes.*

"Uh…okay, I'll let you know." Axle had his hands tucked into the back pockets of his jeans, a posture I now recognized as his *cool look.*

I saluted him with two fingers to my forehead. "See you later, then."

I unlocked my truck, climbed inside, and hit speed dial for Spruce Ridge Code Enforcement. After navigating my way through several menus—press 1 for one thing and press 2 for another—I could only leave a message asking if Del's Towing was still on the rotation for hauling stalled cars. I had to wonder if the green tow truck driver was getting all the assignments and whether the city had lost confidence in me as a tower after I'd fainted at the Impreza. They did ask me to remove it from the crime scene, I assured myself. But they hadn't called me since, and even I was losing confidence in my abilities, so maybe they were, too.

Just as I inserted the key in the truck's ignition, a call came through on the Del's Towing line. Was I ready to get back in the game? I wanted to be ready. I paused for a moment, shook myself, then sucked it up and answered. A customer needed a tow from his house to a repair shop.

A job. A paying job. *Come on. I could do this,* I told myself.

I arrived at the customer's address in about fifteen minutes. An old model Chevy Camaro, rear-wheel drive, sat in the driveway in front of a single-stall garage attached to a white one-story. A younger guy, not older than twenty-five, in torn jeans and dirty work boots, had his hands on his hips, impatient. He didn't seem to pay attention to me or notice my yellow sandals. My trademark heels nearly always generated a comment, but not from this man.

He asked, "How much is this going to set me back?"

The gas station where he wanted his car taken was near the business park on the other side of town, so I said, "It'll be $160, please."

He scratched behind an ear with several piercings, then threw out his arm in an *I-can't-believe-this* gesture. "That much?"

"That's the price." I gave him a firm smile, hoping for my best impression of a professional vehicle recovery specialist.

"All right, all right. Jeez. Let's do this." He brought out cash from his pocket and counted out the bills, stuffing the remaining handful back in his jeans. It wasn't like he didn't have the cash, but of course I didn't know if this was all he had in the world. As he handed me the money, the sun gleamed off one of his earrings. A lightning bolt, silver and dangly. I examined the backs of his hands. No tattooed letters.

His eyes gave me a vertical sweep. "I expected a man to show up." He waited a moment while I stared at him. "I thought I'd run into Del."

"I'm Delaney."

"You related to Del? You look like him."

"He was my dad. He died."

Surprise registered on his face. "I'm real sorry to hear that." His voice had gone low.

"Did you know him?"

He nodded. "Yeah. He was a nice guy, your dad. He helped a friend of mine, a single mom, well sort of a single mom. Her old man was in jail and Del fixed her car for her, didn't charge her anything."

This was satisfying to hear. Not knowing what else to say, I mumbled, "I'm glad he touched so many lives." A lot of people around this city knew Del Morran, but his daughter wasn't one of them. Me. I didn't know much about him at all. How fair was that? I said, "I'm sorry I have to charge you for the tow. I don't make a lot of money doing this."

He raised a hand. "No, no, I get it. But don't you work at the coffee shop?"

Small town. I was bound to be recognized, but I wanted to be remembered as the high-heeled tow truck driver now. "Not anymore. Stand back, please."

He shuffled over to lean against his garage door. I punched the keys on my remote to scoop up the rear wheels of his Camaro. I heaved a sigh of relief when my self-loader properly captured the wheels, then I secured the tow lights. I gave him one of my cards printed with *Del's Towing, recovery specialist,* and the logo of a black stiletto, and he sauntered inside his garage with a backward wave.

Without an audience, I had no trouble hauling his vehicle over to the gas station.

I went in to the auto bay to explain to the man behind the counter that the Camaro's owner would stop by later. Before leaving, I peered through the windshield for the VIN to make a record of the job. A black matchbook on the seat winked up at me. Scrolling gold letters spelled out: Centerpiece Tavern. I extracted my phone to take a snapshot of the VIN but lowered the phone for a second.

The guy had on an earring like Quincy Davidsen's, right? Like they both belonged to some kind of secret society, right? I knew it was a leap, but I was desperate for clues here. So, was this a clue? Would others with this same lightning bolt jewelry hang out at this bar? I didn't get a chance to ask the man if he knew Quincy, but maybe I'd get the opportunity to ask others at the tavern.

I raised the phone back up and took a picture of the VIN and also of the matchbook.

Back in the truck, I aimed for the coffee shop and brought my laptop inside with me. The soothing scent of roasting beans and the flavor of the month, French vanilla, filled the air. Kristen's Zen music played from wireless speakers. I couldn't score a better work environment. If I had to tackle spreadsheets and deal with business receipts, this was the most pleasant place to work on those most unpleasant tasks. Kristen was occupied with the bean roaster, so in spite of Guy's peeved expression, I made myself a double shot and zigzagged my way over to a table near the window.

Once my computer was connected to the internet,

instead of working, I queried lightning bolt symbols and went down several bunny trails before discovering something that made my jaw drop.

"Kristen!" I cried out.

She turned, startled, her eyes darting all around as if expecting to find a spill on the floor.

"Come here!"

She hurried to my table. "What is it, Delaney? What's the matter?"

"See this?" I swiveled the screen toward her. "See this lightning bolt symbol? It's the same as the earring the victim wore. It's a gang sign for the Thunder Knuckles. A gang out of Denver!"

Her eyes went round. "Nuh-uh."

"Yes. Look, see where it says members frequently tattoo gang symbols on their bodies. The B-O-L-T letters are for the Thunder Knuckles' symbol, the lightning bolt."

"A gang?" She made finger quotes. "Here in Spruce Ridge?"

My chin bounced up and down in a *yes*. "Quincy Davidsen was a member of a gang."

Kristen and I grew up in a nice part of Denver near Cherry Creek. My stepdad and her dad were both attorneys and our moms belonged to the country club set. The only memberships we knew about were golf memberships, not gang memberships.

"Gangs are everywhere, Kris." I said this like I was *in-the-know*.

"If you say so." She gave me a *yeah-right* look and disappeared back behind the counter. Guy raised an eyebrow and I returned one of my super-laser glares.

I sat back in my chair and punched Ephraim's

number into my phone. As soon as he picked up, I said, "Quincy Davidsen was a member of the Thunder Knuckles gang, wasn't he?"

Silence reigned for a moment. "Delaney, is that you?"

"Yes. The lightning bolt is the symbol for the Thunder Knuckles. What kind of a stupid, knuckleheaded...*ha-ha*...name is that for a gang?"

He chuckled. "Don't let them hear you say that." Then his voice turned serious. "Thunder knuckles means 'fast boxing,' as in punching out rivals. You don't want to be on the receiving end of that."

I shrank back within myself. "Is Davidsen's death gang-related?"

An intake of breath buzzed my ear from the other end of the phone. "We're aware of the potential connection and I've contacted the Denver Police Gang Unit. We're all over this, you don't need to worry. Please stay out of the investigation, all right?" His voice sounded stern when he repeated a little louder, "All right?"

"Yes, yes. I'm only curious, that's all." I cupped a hand under my chin to lean on the table. "I'm just trying to get some answers."

"Okay, Delaney. I'll let you know when an arrest is made."

We both said goodbye before hanging up. I looked around, but no one heard my conversation, so I searched the internet for the murder. Found a couple of articles and read through the news sites while I took gulps of my double espresso.

One of the stories included a photo of Quincy Davidsen, a young man with light brown hair, eyes light, too, like the color of wheat, and a prominent nose. Age twenty-two, occupation student, lived in north Denver. The same photo was on an obituary site. I downloaded Quincy's picture into my cell's photo gallery. The obit listed his parents, Gregory and Francine Davidsen, and a brother, Pierce, all from Spruce Ridge. So there was a link to this small town.

I phoned Clem, but only got voice mail, so I left a message and went back to my computer. I researched the name Francine Davidsen first and found nothing, then Gregory Davidsen second. I discovered a company in town that designed websites with Greg Davidsen as the contact. I assumed he was Quincy's dad and jotted down his number. Third and last, I searched for Pierce Davidsen. He had several social media accounts.

His profile picture showed a face I recognized.

I'd seen him before.

Chapter 6

I knew the victim's brother! Pierce of the video gamers who came into Roasters on the Ridge.

Since Quincy's family was from around here, there was a good chance Quincy had stopped in at one time or another, too, although I didn't remember seeing him. I got up from my table at the front window and showed Quincy's picture to two older men playing chess and to a young mother with a baby stroller, but no one recognized him, except for one of the men who remembered Quincy's photo from his obituary.

Zach strolled in and went up to the register to flirt with Kristen, so I quickly regained my seat and put my phone away. She handed him a drink and pointed to my table.

The Spruce Ridge officer slid out a chair and sat down across from me. "Kristen's taking a break and she'll join us in a minute."

I closed my laptop. "Sounds good."

He scrutinized me over the rim of his coffee cup and asked, his voice tight, "So, what have you been up to, Delaney?"

"Nothing much. One tow today." I shoved my phone under my laptop case.

"You know that's not what I'm asking." He knew me pretty well.

I scooted my chair closer. "Davidsen's girlfriend

showed up to see the Impreza."

Zach choked a little on his coffee and plopped his cup down. "You didn't open up that vehicle, did you? That Impreza's considered a crime scene, you know, and you promised me you wouldn't get involved."

"I didn't open the car. I know better than that. Besides, I don't have the key." I swished my espresso around, debating with myself, then I burst out with, "Davidsen was in a gang called the Thunder Knuckles. He had a tattoo of their gang symbol."

Zach shook his head, his big chin flying left and right, and he raised his palm in the air. "Don't jump to conclusions. Davidsen probably had nothing to do with the Thunder Knuckles. There are gang wannabees who wear the colors and the signs but aren't in the gang. His tattoo might not mean anything."

"Of course the tattoo means something." I narrowed my eyes. He gave me an equally intense stare, and I braced myself for more of the same *quit-investigating* speech I'd received from the sheriff.

Kristen had come up to us and taken a seat. "Are you telling Zach your gang theory? I hope it isn't true. They sound scary."

I blew air out, making my lips flutter. "They sound goofy to me. What kind of a gang is called the Thunder Knuckles?"

Zach said, "There are gangs called the Tiny Rascal Gang, the Maniac Disciples, and the Jousters. And the FDs. You don't want to know what FD stands for. Who knows where they come up with these names."

Kristen asked, "Why would Davidsen be murdered in Spruce Ridge if he's with a gang in Denver? Spruce Ridge is gang free and low in crime."

I said, "You don't know if it is gang free. Anyway, having relatives in town supplied Quincy with a reason to be on County Road 6."

"He has family here?"

"It said so in his obit." I waved my index finger in her face. "Although, that doesn't eliminate the gang connection. This is a rich town. Think about all those celebrities who live in the mansions up the canyon. Lots of money…and, I assume, lots of drugs. Drugs come from gangs. Ephraim told me the Gang Crime Unit in Denver is involved."

"Ephraim told you that? I wish I could be a part of the investigation." Zach's voice sounded resentful.

Kristen rubbed his arm. "I'm glad you're not. It could be dangerous."

His muscles stiffened and he stared at her hand. "It comes with the job, Kris. Do you have an issue being with a police officer because of the hazardous nature of the work?" His voice had shifted to worried.

Kristen's eyes opened wide and she pivoted in my direction. Zach yanked his gaze over to me at the same time. I tried to keep a knowing grin off my face. In an obvious attempt to change the subject, Kris asked, "So, Zach, are you coaching youth baseball this year?"

"You know I am." He gave her a quizzical glance, then his eyes traveled back over to me. "Oh, yeah, yeah, I sure am. That's right. Well, I'd better be going, coaching the kiddos and all."

They said goodbye, and Kristen headed to the backroom. I stayed at the table in the now-empty café, staring out the window, wondering if I should make another circuit around town for the BMW or look for stalled cars. But no, I opened my laptop again.

I couldn't help but think the Centerpiece Tavern might hold a clue, so I searched the internet for the taphouse, but found nothing in Spruce Ridge. I widened the search and located the establishment in Denver. The photo of the place looked rough, a building without windows fronted by a sidewalk with no landscaping. That had to be the place. How could I find out more about this bar? Who could I ask? Not Ephraim, he'd made it clear I wasn't to investigate. Kristen, of course, would have no idea. Forget Zach…

Byron would know. I'd ask him about the tavern.

But when I went to pick Axle up from work, I discovered Byron was out buying supplies for his mechanic shop. I'd have to catch the Old Man another time. On the way home with Axle, I swore him to secrecy, then told him about the lightning bolt earrings Quincy Davidsen had been wearing. We were roommates now, sharing the details of our day, and Ephraim couldn't expect me to keep secrets from either my best friend or my *roomie*. At least that's how I justified myself. I explained I'd handled a tow job for a man who wore those same earrings and added, "The guy didn't have the letters, B-O-L-T, tattooed on his knuckles, though, so I'm not sure he's with the Thunder Knuckles gang."

"Maybe the guy has ink somewhere else. It could be where you can't see it." Axle gave me a shove on my shoulder. "Like on another appendage." He laughed at his own joke.

"*Eeyeuuw!*" My lips curled back and I thought twice about sharing. "You came up with that on your own?"

"Hey, what do you know?" He rubbed his hip

where I poked him.

****

The next morning, while Axle ate cereal and I hung around for him to finish so we could leave, Mom called. She said, "Will can drop the bed off today. Are you going to be home?"

"What time?"

"He's getting ready to leave. He'll be there in an hour. Now, about your boyfriend. I'm going to fix a Mexican casserole tonight. I know how much you love my casseroles, Laney. Can you bring him over for dinner?"

"I'm sorry, Mom. I have to cover the tow-away zones." I narrowed my eyes. I hadn't heard from Tanner all day yesterday. In fact, I hadn't heard from him since Axle moved in. A long time to go without a call from my boyfriend. "We'll figure out another time soon and I'll let you know."

Axle gave me a grimace when I got off the phone. He understood about parents. I said, "Ready?"

He said, "Sure, just one sec," and poured another bowl, like the entire box of cereal.

"Seriously? How long will this take?"

He shrugged with his mouth full, so I walked Boss over to the park and back. Finally Axle was ready, and I ferried him over to Byron's to fetch my truck. After that, I steered back home to wait for Will.

I opened my laptop at the kitchen counter and checked my bank balance. I'd only had the two tows since hauling the police-impounded Impreza, and my income was down. I never should have ignored the orange-tagged Lincoln or the stalled-out Honda. Two opportunities I'd passed by.

A knock sounded on my door and I got up to let Will in. He said, "I can carry the headboard and footboard up the stairs, but I'll need assistance with the mattress."

"I'll help you." I propped the door open, but Boss started down the steps, so I had to block him with my feet.

"Where'd you get the dog?"

"The Rottweiler belongs to a friend of mine. So, you don't have to be at court today?" I asked, not really caring to know.

Will worked at a firm that handled mostly family law. He was average in every way. Five-foot-ten, lean at 175 pounds, thinning, dull brown hair, brown eyes. Not wearing a suit and tie. He said, "Lawyers don't go to court every day, Laney. It's not like a television drama."

"You don't say. Give me a second and I'll be right there." I coaxed Boss into my bedroom with a piece of baloney and shut him in.

I clattered down the steps to catch up with Will at the back end of his Chevy Tahoe, rear-wheel drive. The tailgate was open with a twin mattress and box springs wedged inside. He took one end of the mattress and I took the other, and we manhandled the squishy pad of foam and coils, bending this way and that, across the parking lot and up the staircase. While I fetched the sheets and blankets from the sofa, Will went back and forth, carrying up the box springs, the white headboard, the white footboard, a pink comforter, then the pink, frilly canopy for the top.

"You want me to set up the canopy, too?"

"Certainly." I couldn't wait for Axle to see it. Will

got busy assembling the girly bedstead while Boss scratched and whined at my bedroom door.

We both stood back and took in the pink monstrosity. "Thanks, Will. I appreciate you bringing this over." Will allowed me a doubtful look, gave me an awkward, one arm hug, and took off. For a lawyer, he wasn't very inquisitive. He didn't ask me who the bed was for or why I had a friend's dog.

I let Boss out of my room. The Rotty mix had managed to claw all the paint off the bottom of the door frame. *Oops.* I couldn't get mad. He'd been managing the change of scenery pretty well, considering he was home alone all day, and he'd even claimed the end of the couch as his own.

Note to self: Pick up some dog toys and dog bowls and a dog bed, too. The only thing Axle brought was a leash and a bag of kibble.

I made sure Boss had fresh water and took him for another quick walk before locking him back inside and climbing behind the wheel of my tow truck. Spruce Ridge's mini-rush hour had come and gone and traffic was at a minimum. I drove on autopilot around town past the BMW owner's office, down rows of parked cars at the mall, and past her home. No BMW. Bianca White was on to me and doing a good job of hiding her vehicle.

After parking down the street from her house to wait her out, I opened my cell phone and clicked on Greg Davidsen's website which included an address. The link to the location showed a house on the canyon road outside of town, so the victim's dad likely worked from home.

Starting the truck back up, I headed toward County

Road 6. Sunshine warmed the spring air, the way it does in Colorado, and I let down the window to enjoy the passing scenery and mix of floral and evergreen scents, an aroma you only get in the Rockies. Tall, straight pine trees with lower branches denuded of needles marched up the vertical mountain slopes. Yellow blooming potentilla bushes dotted the meadows of waving grasses.

The turnout where Quincy met his death came into view. I'd completely forgotten it was there until the memory smacked me in the face. I rolled the window up and sped past the spot.

His parents' house, a sand-colored stucco structure in the Spanish style with a broad front porch, was located at the end of a long gravel driveway. I turned off the ignition and sat there gathering courage to approach the door. Someone had parked a Lexus, rear-wheel drive, near a closed garage. Okay, that meant one of the family was probably home. I climbed out of my self-loader and slogged up the walk to the door, but nobody answered the bell. Should I leave a note? *Nah, better not. What would I say? Greg and Francine, I found your dead son. Wanna talk about it?*

Ouch, huh?

I retreated to my truck and after making my way back to town, I took one more circuit through the labyrinth of lanes and side streets, then called Patrick Crump on my cell. "Any luck locating the BMW?"

"I'll contact you when I find it. You'll be the first person I call." He hung up.

Alrighty, then.

Five minutes later and I was once more inside Roasters staring out the window at the blue sky. Today

75

the horizon was bare of clouds and the leaves on the aspens fluttered from a soft breeze. I waited for calls that didn't come, played on my phone, and consumed two espressos until it was time to close and the place was deserted.

Kris said, "I'm locking up." The two baristas, Guy and Sierra, had completed their shifts at noon and Kris had been working by herself.

"I'll help you." Good thing I wasn't busy on a tow.

I wiped the top of the tables with a rag soaked in vinegar, then sponged off all the chairs, all the way down the chair legs. I squeegeed the windows and mopped the floor. Kristen scoured out the coffee machines and microwave, then tallied the receipts, and prepared the bank deposit. I lugged the garbage bags to the dumpster and swabbed down the trash bins with another rag.

Kristen didn't bother to stock at night. That was a job for the morning. An hour before opening, the crew would refill the beans, cups, lids, napkins, straws, cane sugars, and organic creamers, and place orders, including the green coffee beans Kristen roasted. She was a purist and that's where Roasters on the Ridge got its name. Closing chores only took an hour and we were quick, having done them a million times.

I tossed the dirty rags in the laundry bin on the way out, and when Kristen flicked off the lights, she said, "I wasn't able to balance the register."

"What do you mean?" I waited beside her as she locked the door.

Her dark eyebrows pinched together, a knob of skin nudged out between them. "Money's missing."

There had never been a short register before.

"Could it be a mistake? Someone gave out the wrong change?"

"Too much is missing, and I counted twice."

"What do you mean, too much? How much is that?"

"A little over a hundred."

That was a lot when you sold coffees for five bucks a pop. "Really? Who do you think…?"

A deep frown crossed her face. "I don't want to accuse an innocent person."

"All right, but are you okay?" I grabbed her arm.

"I'm fine." Her lips trembled and her tone of voice indicated she wasn't. We climbed the exterior stairs to our apartments with the doors across the landing facing each other. She stopped on the top step and inhaled a deep lungful of air. "At least I have some good news. The gamers want to hold a tournament at Roasters."

"Go, sister." I raised my fist to give her a fist bump. "Some sweet D&D money headed your way. That'll help with the loss."

She bumped back. "D&D? I'm not sure that's the game they play. I've never paid attention."

I scrunched up my nose. "I didn't know gamers held tournaments at coffee shops. I thought they stayed home so they can play on their big-screen TVs. High def and all."

"You got me. I have no idea. Maybe I should ask them." She lifted her shoulders and let them fall back down. "But, it's not a sure thing. They're also going over to the coffee shop on Main to check out that venue, too."

"Jump on this, Kris. Tell them your place is the best. 'Cause it is."

Kristen unlocked her door. "They want to hold it on a Saturday, our busiest day of the week. Will they crowd out our regulars?"

"Our customers would understand. And I can help out. I'm here for you." I meant it, too. Kristen was always there for me.

"Thanks, Delaney. We'll talk more later." She went into her apartment.

When I turned the key in my lock, voices carried through the closed door and I froze. Someone was inside my place! A red-hot bolt of fear ran through my body and I almost stroked out.

Chapter 7

Wait, no. I had a roommate now. Axle had probably caught a ride home and was in there watching television. I needed to settle down. Maybe drinking that second double espresso wasn't such a good idea.

The door swung open and Boss ran up to me, placing his big paws on my chest. In the other room, Axle and Clem jumped apart. They'd been snuggled close together on the couch. That was my spot to snuggle Tanner!

Thrown off stride, I made a show of setting my purse on the counter, acting calm and collected. "Hey, guys. Whatcha doing?"

Axle hesitated for a split second. "Clem came by to hang out."

"How'd she know where I, um, we live?"

Clem poked her head over the back of the couch. "Axle texted me the address."

I strolled into the living room and lowered myself onto the seat across from them. This was an interesting development, but it's not as if I didn't see this coming. Axle was all gooey-eyed, crushing on Clem. I might as well find out what I could, now that the victim's girlfriend was right in front of me. "Clem, I'm glad you're here. I want to ask you about Quincy."

Axle drew his eyebrows down and gave me a quelling glance, but Clem said, "What do you want to know?"

"What was he doing in Spruce Ridge?"

She picked at her nail polish. "He has family here. His parents live here."

Heh, heh. I knew this already. "Right. Does his dad own a website business?"

Axle's hands circled the air behind Clem's head making *what-are-you-doing?* gestures that distracted me for a moment.

"Uh, I don't know what his father does." Clem glanced up at me, her choppy black hair sliding along her cheeks.

I touched my coarse, red plait. What I wouldn't do for her shiny smooth hair. "How long did you go out with Quincy?"

"Only for a little while." She giggled. "I get asked out a lot." Her big, blue-eyed gaze traveled over to Axle.

He said, "Clem's pretty broken up about everything," and he gave her a puppy-dog look.

Fat chance of that. I ignored him. "Was Quincy in a gang?"

"Of course not," she said with a frown.

"If a gang is involved, you need to tell the police."

"I know, I know," she went into a singsong voice. "But he wasn't."

"Did he have a fight with anyone? Anybody threaten him? Any enemies?" I avoided looking at Axle who mouthed, *shut-up, shut-up.*

Clem answered, "No, nothing like that."

"In the news it said he was a student?"

"He dropped out."

"What did he do for work?"

"He had help from his parents. They still thought he was in school." She laughed as if this was funny.

I made a pucker-face. It's not as if my folks never assisted me, but a lot of trust-fund kids in Spruce Ridge lived off their parents, and I never belonged to that group. I asked, "Who do you think killed Quincy? You must have some idea."

Axle glared at me behind Clem's back. He waved his hands around frantically and mouthed, "*No, no*," then held up his left palm to hide his right index finger pointing me toward the kitchen. He twitched his head as if to say, *in the kitchen now*.

"I-I don't know." Clem's whole demeanor changed. Now she blinked as if trying to dredge up a tear or two.

I wasn't going to get anything else out of her, so I conveyed with a glance to Axle, but not out loud, *No, I'm the one who wants you in the kitchen*. We both twitched our necks, *you-in the kitchen!*

I glanced at the time on my phone and rose from my seat. I said, all *little Miss Polite*, "Axle, can you give me a hand?"

We crammed through the kitchen doorway at the same time, but I got through first. I pried open the refrigerator and examined the contents.

Axle poked me in the back. "What are you doing questioning Clem like that?"

I twirled around. "Why is she here?"

He said in a quiet voice, "She needs a friend right now."

I sighed. "No doubt." I grabbed a hard-boiled egg from the container I kept on the refrigerator door. "Ax, be careful, she could be dangerous." I bumped the door shut and grasped his shoulder, giving him a little shake.

He hissed, "Shut it, do you want her to hear you?"

I said back in an exaggerated whisper, "I mean it. She could be involved in that guy's death."

He hooted, "No way," then clapped a hand over his mouth.

It was my turn to say, "Shhhh, be careful, Clem can hear you," like we were a married couple trying to argue with our child in the other room.

His eyes cut back to where Clem sat typing on her phone. "Don't worry, I'm always careful." Axle followed me to the living room and we pretended we weren't just talking about her.

I said cheerfully, "I'm off. And Clem, I'll give you a call so we can talk some more."

She squinted at me as if unsure at first, but I presented a reassuring smile. Her eyes focused on her nail polish for a second or two, then she looked back up. "That's fine, Delaney."

"You'll return my call next time? I left you a message the other day and you didn't phone me back."

Axle gave me a serious pout to communicate, *leave her alone*. My gaze went back to Clem and I caught the triumphant grin on her face, a look that said, *he's wrapped around my finger*. Our eyes locked, and she knew that I knew. She said, "Sorry."

I ripped my jacket off the hook by the door, and Axle and Clem cozied back together on the sofa. What was I going to do about him? He was out of his depth.

After parking in the alley next to one of the towaway zones, I peeled the hard-boiled egg into a paper napkin and chewed while searching the web on my phone.

A Buick LaCrosse, which came in both front-wheel and all-wheel drive, pulled in behind one of the fashionable boutiques, and I alighted from the truck. I leaned against the back of my truck, trying to look like a professional vehicle recovery agent, and said to the driver, "You'll have to move your car, please."

He glanced at the towaway warning sign and back at me. Red crept up his neck, but he said, "All right."

"Thank you." Before he buckled himself back inside, I pulled Davidsen's photo up on my phone screen. "Do you recognize this man?"

He stuck his nose out his window and studied the picture. "No. Why do you ask?"

"I'm trying to get information on him."

"He skip out on you?" He must not watch the news.

"Something like that."

He shrugged. I handed him one of my business cards and asked him to consider me if he needed a tow.

I'd asked around the coffee shop. I'd asked this random person. Nobody I'd asked knew Quincy Davidsen so far. Time to step up the investigation, but where could I look next? I didn't have time tonight to check out the Centerpiece Tavern down in Denver, but Tanner had told me a while back that he got his ink done at Spruce Ridge Body Works right here in town. Those lightning bolt tattoos had to hold a clue and maybe the tattoo artist knew others who had the same design. The tat shop was near Main and Fifth in one of the old buildings just a couple blocks away.

The door jingled behind me as I walked up a narrow staircase to the second floor, my flat green sandals making loud clomping noises on the ancient stairs. Behind an empty, scratched wood counter, drawings of tattoos adorned the walls. Cartoonish renditions of naked ladies, the well-endowed kind. *Ugh.*

A man opened a door to my right and called out, "I'll be with you in a minute."

I caught a glimpse of Tanner sprawled on what appeared to be an old dentist's chair. The tattoo artist held a needle attached to a machine that made a whirring sound. The door shut, so I leaned up against the counter to wait for Tanner and the tattooist to come out. Tanner talked frequently about getting another tattoo, but I didn't know he'd planned to get one tonight.

A signed consent form had been left carelessly on the ledge. I flipped the page to the diagram below it, fancy letters spelling out the name, Annie. I eyeballed Tanner's signature, then went back to the sketch of the tattoo.

Who the hell was Annie?

There was Annie Sullivan who owned the flower shop. And there was an Annie who came into Roasters all the time, but she was married with a couple of kids. *What the heck?*

I stole a glance at the closed door, then wiggled off my sandals and tippy-toed silently down the stairs with my shoes in one hand and the railing in my other. Back on the street, I shoved my feet into my sandals and hightailed it to the truck.

Being distracted, waiting for nine o'clock to roll around, I didn't even notice if there were any more cars parked illegally. When the clock struck nine, I drove straight to the autobody shop and caught Byron working late.

I marched up to him. "Do you know a girl named Annie?"

Byron peered at me from behind a Ford Ranger truck, rear-wheel drive. "Can't say I do." His deep voice was soothing, but not soothing enough.

I plonked onto a stool and dropped my purse on the floor. "Tanner's getting a tattoo with that girl's name on it." I'm sure my face went bright, tomato-soup red.

Byron's hazel eyes narrowed, crinkling at the corners. "There's gotta' be an explanation. Why don't you ask him? Or, do you want me to ask him?"

"No, I will." I chewed on my lip.

Note to self: grill Tanner about Annie.

I asked Byron, "Why you working so late?"

"Just need to finish a job, then I got paperwork ta' do."

"I won't keep you then." I reached for my purse, but asked as I straightened up, "Have you heard of the Centerpiece Tavern? It's a bar in Denver."

His eyes narrowed once again. "I have. Why?"

"I want to go there, show Quincy Davidsen's picture around, ask a few questions." I clapped my hands together as if imparting something exciting. "Come with me, Old Man." I called him that as a ploy to get what I wanted. It usually worked.

"Now, Delaney, you know I can't go to a place like that."

I gave him my brightest smile. "You don't have to drink anything or you can just get a glass of seltzer water with a lime. That's what Kristen does at bars. Come on, we're in this together, both of us being crime scene witnesses and all."

"Not a good idea."

I had to respect his decision since Byron had trouble with alcohol in the past. "Of course, I understand." I dragged myself off the stool and hooked my purse over my shoulder.

He used his fingers to massage his temples. "Wait. Are you goin' ta' go by yourself anyway?"

I had no one else to ask. Axle was too young, Kristen wouldn't feel comfortable, and on the nights I was free, Tanner was busy working the private property lots. Or getting tattoos. And when Tanner was free, I had to work the towaway zones. We didn't often have a night off together.

"What are you thinkin', Delaney? Now you aren't plannin' to go, are ya'?"

I averted my gaze and pinched my lower lip between my teeth.

Byron swiped his hand across his brow. "I know I'm going to regret this…" He closed his eyes and his Adam's apple bobbed up and down. He opened his eyes back up. "Okay. I'll go with you."

I gave him an excited smile. "For real? Cool!" But, would this be like going to a bar with my dad? Would that be weird? I asked, "Will we stand out from the crowd, you and me?"

"Because I'm an old man and you're a young gal?" He chuckled, "No, not there."

"How about tomorrow night?"

"I guess that'll work. We'll be takin' my Harley."

"*Oka-a-ay?*" I drew out the word in a question.

"It's a biker bar."

My thoughts went straight to what shoes to wear. I had a great pair of chunky black boots with lots of buckles.

Oh, boy. This was going to be so much fun. I couldn't wait!

Chapter 8

Axle leaned on his bedroom door with his mouth hanging open. " Are you fricking kidding me?"

"You just now saw this?" I stood next to Kristen who'd followed us inside his bedroom. We both covered our mouths, our shoulders shaking, fighting the giggles. "So, do you like?"

Axle gave me a withering look. "I'm just waiting for the hilarity to end."

I'd collapsed against the wall and had to go sit down. Boss caught on to the fun and tried to jump in my lap. "Axle, you need to take your dog for a walk."

He inhaled crossly. "Right, Miss Bossy, and I'm referring to you, not the dog." Axle harnessed up the Rottweiler and they disappeared out the door.

"You got him good," Kristen said.

I bit my lip to stop myself from splitting a gut. "When Will offered to put up that pink, frilly canopy I couldn't resist."

"Don't be surprised if Axle takes that top down."

"Okay by me. I never liked it either."

Kristen snickered. "Thanks for the laugh. I needed that."

Too late I remembered my friend had problems at work. "You all right, Kris?"

She flapped her hands. "I'm fine. No worries. See ya' later."

After Axle and his Rotty returned, I headed to my room to get ready for bed, calling over my shoulder, "Sweet dreams, Axle. Sleep tight in your cloudy pink bed."

He didn't answer me, but I heard his bedroom door slam shut.

After I kicked my shoes off and stripped out of my clothes, I shimmied into pajama bottoms and a tank top. I climbed in bed and pulled the covers up to my chin. Grabbing my cell, I texted my boyfriend about dinner tomorrow night. It would be his turn to monitor the towaway lots, but he could come over for an early meal. He texted me back that the plan was a go, so I replied with a kiss emoji.

I fell asleep contemplating how to ask Tanner about his new tattoo—he must have a good explanation—and I smiled, looking forward to our time together. Surely I would have pleasant dreams falling asleep with Tanner in my head, but a good night's rest was not for me.

Quincy Davidsen visited my slumber. Once more his hands were tied to the steering wheel. I stood outside the car's window and leaned in for a better look. He slipped his wrists out of the ties and turned to face me. His hands flew up and punched the glass with a bang and I jumped back. Lightning streaked across the sky like skeletal fingers, illuminating Quincy's face, and he mouthed the words, "Watch out!"

Dark circles marred the skin under my eyes the next morning. After turning on the coffee maker, I stood in front of the freezer with the door open, shivering, waiting for inspiration. Got it. I mixed garlic, basil, and soy sauce into a gallon plastic bag and added a couple of extra-thick rib-eye steaks from the freezer, then put it all in the refrigerator to marinate.

When Axle came down the hall with Boss, I told him, "Tanner's coming by for an early dinner tonight."

"You want me to make myself scarce?"

"No, you live here now, and I just wanted you to know, that's all. We're roomies, we talk about stuff like this."

After I dropped him off at Byron's, I waited until he entered the auto bay. He tugged on a pair of safety glasses, a safety mask, and repositioned his knitted cap on his head. He got busy, the paint sprayer making whooshing sounds, so I climbed in my truck to start my rounds for the day.

At two in the afternoon, I gave up on the BMW— and I hadn't even looked for stalled cars—and after a quick check of the impounded Impreza in Tanner's lot, I ended up at Roasters. *Yet, again.*

Two guys and two girls came through the door, the same time as me, talking loudly and laughing; the girls in artfully torn designer jeans and fancy loafers and one of the guys in an anorak jacket paired with mid-washed jeans. They seized a table on the other side of a wire rack holding Roasters on the Ridge coffee mugs and immediately opened their smartphones to begin texting.

After I set up my laptop, I couldn't help but overhear one of the girls say, "Oh, Alison's parties are so boring. Do we have to go?"

The guy to her left said, "We can kick it up and make some money, too. I know a dude who lives not too far from here who can get us something."

My bored ears went on the alert. This was interesting. I opened my PC and ducked behind the screen.

The four observed each other, as if in agreement. The girls dug around in their leather handbags while the guys pulled cash out of their pockets. It appeared as if they'd all chipped in some bills, and one of the guys folded the cash into a napkin. I couldn't tell the denominations, but it measured up to be a good-sized wad.

The guy said, "I just sent my man a text. He's coming over."

I might as well stick around, right? I could spy out the scene unfolding in the middle of Roasters and report back to Kristen. She should know what was going down in her shop.

About ten minutes went by, and right when I debated sending Zach a text about my suspicions, a guy breezed through the door, aiming for the rich kids' table. He had big blue eyes and straight black hair…good-looking, but not as well dressed as the other four. So, I'm thinking, he's the drug dealer. Proof that Spruce Ridge has a drug trade. Wait till I tell Kristen!

The dealer did a head nod to the rich kids and snatched a fifth chair up to the table. He grabbed the napkin where the group had hidden the cash. He reached his hand into his jacket pocket. His eyes skimmed around the other tables before he took his hand back out and held a little plastic baggie against his leg.

A deal was happening, right next to me. Ecstasy? Since small amounts of pot were legal in Colorado, there was no point in selling marijuana on the down-low. But in Spruce Ridge, ecstasy might be the go-to-choice. I'd heard about a Rich-Teen Party once where things got out of control and a couple of teenagers died because someone laced the drinks with ecstasy. Just imagine, Axle might attend one of those parties! I wanted to keep Kristen's cousin safe from scary things like this. *Ohhhh, yeah*, I'm the big sis' now.

One of the guys in the group put his hand under the table. With their eyes riveted on each other, the two men made the hand-to-hand exchange. I acted like I was playing with my phone and snapped a picture.

The dealer got up. "Hey man, great to see ya'. I gotta go." He slinked out the door.

The group leaned in and whispered together while glancing around as if expecting to be busted. When they all knocked their chairs back, I shot up from my table behind the mug rack. "I saw everything and called the cops. How fast can you run?" I hadn't, but everyone's jaws dropped as if they believed me.

The guy with the bag of pills started to say something just as Kristen walked over. "I saw what you did, too."

"They didn't even buy any coffee," I added.

Kristen told them, "You need to leave. But think about this, Jesus can give you an abundant and fulfilling life. You don't need drugs."

One of the girls tossed her hands up in the air. "Oh, no. A Christian."

The others laughed, and the guy who bought the baggie said through clenched teeth, "Leave us alone, you weird freak."

I knew my face turned red with outrage. Kristen was nothing but good, kind, and caring, never judgmental. After all, she had me as a friend, right? "You can't talk to her that way!"

The one holding the bag pivoted on his heel and strutted toward the exit, the other three following behind.

I clenched and unclenched my fists, my chest heaving in indignation, but Kristen had remained calm. She patted my back. "It's all right Delaney. They can't hurt me. I've got on the armor of God." I glanced at her, not sure what she was talking about.

"I snapped a picture of that drug dealer." I opened my camera app. "But the photo isn't very clear."

Kristen pulled out her cell phone. "We should call Zach."

"Yes, definitely." I gave my friend an *I-told-you-so* look. "See, there *are* drugs in Spruce Ridge."

"I guess so." Her face paled. "And right here in Roasters, too."

"Kris, everybody in town comes into Roasters."

She nodded and headed to the backroom, cell in hand. "I'll let you know what Zach says."

I called, "See ya' later," to her back and went out the door to climb the stairs to my apartment. The drug deal had distracted me, and I still had to prepare dinner for Tanner.

Boss exploded into barking when I unlocked the door. After I'd walked and fed him, I pulled out the two humongous rib-eye steaks from the fridge. Axle showed up just as I switched on the oven to preheat.

He held up his palms. "I know you have plans and I'm not staying. Clem's coming to pick me up."

"Wait." I stabbed my hands onto my hips. "I'd like to talk to her."

He shouted, "No way," then cleared his throat and said in his fake-nice voice, "We don't want to be a bother." He scurried down the hall to his bedroom and returned in moments wearing a clean shirt, cloying aftershave, and the knit cap on his head. "I'll just wait outside for her," he said over his shoulder as he bustled down the stairs.

Darn. Well, some time alone with Tanner would be okay, too. More than okay.

I sliced a couple of fat potatoes and arranged the thin slices in my largest cast-iron pan with a little olive oil. Boss nosed around at my feet, so I made sure his bowl of kibble was once again full. The marinade contained spices, but I drained the juices and added fresh garlic and green onion to the steak before sliding the skillet in the oven.

Tanner knocked and came in. "Something smells good."

"I just diced up an onion." I stared at the large white bandage on his forearm. "What's that?"

"Got a tattoo last night."

I acted like I was surprised. "Oh? What's the design?"

"You'll see when I take the wrap off."

"Give me a hint." I inched closer and nuzzled my nose against his warm neck. His arms went around me and I snuggled tighter. He gave me a deep kiss and I forgot my question for a couple of minutes. Somehow my braid loosened and my long red hair hung down my back and we were on the couch in a clinch.

The oven timer dinged and I extracted myself. "I need to set the table."

He said, "Interrupted again!" He must have been hungry, for dinner that is, because he let go of me.

I sorted out two plates and some silverware. "So,

about your new tattoo…"

"I'll show you later." He gave me a wink to indicate he had something else to show me, too. A steak knife fell from my hands onto the floor and I bent to pick it up.

I said, "Um, my mom wants to have you over for dinner, but I think it's too early to meet the family, don't you?" Tanner knitted his brows. I asked, "What's the matter?"

"Nothing."

"You look like you've just been pulled over for speeding."

Footsteps pounded up the stairs, then Axle and Clem came through the door, and Boss ran over to them. Clem was wearing a black leather jacket with fringe, and Axle had a bulging duffel bag slung over his shoulder, causing him to list to the right.

"Clem, it's good to see you." I *was* glad she was back so I could ask her some more questions. "Uh, good to see you, too, Axle. Are you hungry? I have plenty."

"Sure," Axle said, sniffing the air. "I'll be right back." He headed for his room and returned in a moment without the bag.

Tanner made space for the two extras at the table.

I asked Axle, "Can you get out two more plates?" The rib-eyes were more than enough for four people, even when one guy was as muscular as Tanner and the other was a growing boy like Axle. I took the pan out of the oven, spooned the potatoes into foil to keep warm, then pan-seared the meat in the hot cast-iron skillet.

Tanner watched over my shoulder. "What are you doing?"

"It's called reverse searing, and it creates a beautiful crust." I cut each steak in two, and after Axle got out the extra plates, we all sat to eat. There was even enough for Boss to have a small taste. He'd already been fed plenty, but I couldn't help spoiling the little monster.

Hardly taking a bite himself, Axle admired Clem while she sliced into her rib-eye. Tanner's gaze jumped between the two of them and a knowing smile appeared on his face. *Good. Tanner knows he has no reason to be jealous.*

A silver chain dangled around Clem's wrist. "See the bracelet Axle bought me."

Tanner said, "Nice."

I looked at Axle, but he wouldn't meet my eyes. I sure hoped she wasn't taking advantage of my little cuz'.

By the time we finished dinner, it was close to five o'clock and Tanner had to leave to monitor the towaway zones. We said our goodbyes on the landing outside the door, then I came back in.

Clem shoved her half-eaten dinner away. "I feel like an old person, eating this early at night."

"Tanner had to go to work," I explained. "Did you have any lunch?"

"No."

"Breakfast?"

"No."

"Well, you needed to eat." After saving the uneaten meat for the dog, I scraped the plates into the garbage can, Boss's eyes following my every move. "I love your jacket, Clem."

She slid her arms out of the sleeves. "Feel free to

borrow it anytime. It might be a little big, but it'd look real cute on you."

"Really? Are you sure?"

She hung it on the hook by the door. "I hardly ever wear it myself."

"That's sweet of you to offer." I wiped my hands on a dishtowel, then pointed my cell toward her face. "You ever see this guy before?"

She took a quick peek at the picture of the drug deal going down, then grabbed the phone and appeared to study the dealer's face. After a drawn-out moment, she shook her head. "No. I don't know anyone from around here except Quincy's family."

I was disappointed, but it was a long shot the drug dealer from Roasters on the Ridge was involved, and I couldn't start suspecting every stranger I met.

Axle said, "Come on, Clem. Let's see what's on TV," and they vanished into the living room. I finished loading the dishwasher, then paused in the doorway to give them a moment, you know, to give them a little more time to themselves. *Yeah, right.* I was eavesdropping. But as hard as I tried, I couldn't hear a word they said. Maybe they weren't talking. I'd better get in there! I walked into the living room and took a seat on the couch, and they both got up.

Axle said, "We're taking off. Thanks for dinner."

"Oh, I guess I need to get going, too." I snagged my keys and slung my purse over my shoulder. We all traipsed down the stairs together.

My mind churned with questions for Clem as I motored my tow truck over to Bianca White's house. I stationed my self-loader in the alley across the street and fiddled around on my phone wasting time.

Just then that ugly green tow truck barreled past me with an orange-tagged Hyundai Elantra, front-wheel drive, trundling behind. That bearded man who ran the green tow truck operation sure seemed to be getting a lot of city jobs. Why didn't I receive those calls, too? I should be notified when the city needed a car hauler, but Code Enforcement had never returned my message asking if I was still on the rotation. Did I want to tow the abandoned cars? Yes, I guess I did. It was work and I needed the income. So I left another message with the city and waited some more for Bianca.

This is the fourth or fifth time I'd tried to catch the BMW at the owner's house. I was not having any luck. But it was time to forget the BMW and head out for my exciting Friday night with Byron.

****

Parked in Byron's lot was a shiny Harley Davidson motorcycle, black with gold fenders, a gold fuel tank, and lengthened forks for a stretched-out appearance. Dressed in his leather chaps, his jacket tight across his belly and black boots on his feet, Byron looked the part. He handed me a gold helmet that matched his.

I admired my reflection in the shiny chrome, posing in Clem's black leather jacket with fringe I'd gone back to the apartment for, along with my own black jeans and black, buckled boots. Twisting around with my hands in the pockets, I felt the weight of the jacket. It was a little big on me, but in it I looked like a badass tow truck driver, extraordinaire.

I said, "Oh, my God, Byron. This is going to be so much fun!"

"Fun? You think it'll be fun?" He scowled at me. "This is serious. Where we're goin' is not a nice place."

The smile fell from my lips. "Yeah, yeah, got it."

"Have you ridden a motorcycle before?"

"Absolutely! I even have a motorcycle license because I had a boyfriend once who had a bike and he let me drive it." I cooed over Byron's chopper and the custom paint job he explained he'd done himself.

I climbed onto the back and wrapped my arms around Byron's substantial middle. My stomach felt queasy with nerves as we sailed at full throttle on the main artery that cuts east through the mountain canyons to the plains, the two of us leaning into the curves with each bend in the road. We raced up, then down, Floyd's Hill past the turnoff for Evergreen and the old Chart House restaurant overlooking the interstate. At nine at night, the usual gridlock had disappeared from I-70, and we moved along at highway speeds through Golden, into Lakewood, then Denver.

Byron lined up his bike next to a row of other wicked-looking Harleys in front of the Centerpiece Tavern. I swung one stiff leg over the seat and hopped off.

He said, "Don't get too friendly with anyone."

"I won't. I came in with you, I'm leaving with you, Old Man." I gave him a saucy grin, but he only frowned back at me, a concerned look in his eyes. I caught my braid from under the helmet and finger-combed out the plait.

First off, the bar was dark and ear-splittingly loud. Second, it smelled like sour sweat and whiskey. I stuck close to Byron's heels. He strode the length of the counter over to two empty stools as if he belonged there. My jaw dropped when he ordered two shots. The bartender carded me. He didn't card Byron. No need for that.

I whispered out of the side of my mouth, "What are you doing, Byron?"

"What?" He couldn't hear me over the blaring sound system.

I leaned closer to speak into his ear. "Are you drinking?"

"I'm not goin' ta' drink this. But we need ta' blend." He put cash on the counter and shouted to the bartender, "Keep the change."

The whiskey tasted smooth, yet it burned going down and I gagged. Even though I'm Irish, whiskey's not my drink. Big, hefty men with loud voices played pool, as rough-looking women—their bitches, I guessed—watched them. It seemed sexist to me, but I wasn't going to jump on any tables and pull a Beto O'Rourke routine. I shoved the shot glass away. I'd like to play my part here, but I wasn't going to be able to keep it up.

I yelled in the direction of the customer sitting to my right, "How's it going?" One open beer bottle sat in front of him and an unopened one waited in line. An inviting smile crossed his face. I brought up Quincy's picture from his obituary on my phone screen. "You ever see this man before?"

The guy with the two beers gave me a disbelieving snort. "What are you, a narc?" He pointed toward Byron and back at me. "You with that geezer?"

Nodding, I glanced at the Old Man. His eyes mirroring disappointment, Mr. Two Beers turned his face up to the big screen television. Should I spear him with an elbow and show him the drug dealer's blurry picture, too? The trouble was, that snapshot did look like a narcotic sale going down.

I swung off the stool and ventured around the room to search for Thunder Knuckles tattoos or lightning bolt earrings. Suspicious eyes followed me. One man, bent over the table with a pool cue aimed toward the pocket, glanced up from his game. His upper arms were as big around as my upper thighs, his head was bald with nicks and cuts as if he'd shaved it himself, and his eyes were sharp and mocking, the very picture of a murderer's eyes. A single teardrop tattoo was inked under his right eye. Didn't that signify he'd killed someone?

My skin prickled with goosebumps and my stomach muscles clenched like grinding gears.

I popped down the hall to the women's restroom where the loud music went silent behind the thick, closed door. Thankful to be alone, I dripped some water from the faucet onto a paper towel, then pressed a wet corner under my eyes and across my forehead. It took a while to study my makeup, finger-comb my hair, adjust my bra straps higher on my shoulders and the cuffs of my jeans over my boots, and make sure there wasn't anything in my teeth. Once again I admired my reflection—Clem's jacket was mighty fine—but in the mirror my saucy look had disappeared, replaced with a scared shitless look. With nothing more to delay me, I came back out.

Byron waited for me in the hall. "Where'd ya' go?"

My cheeks burned. "Just the restroom."

He shook a finger in my face. "You worried me, Delaney. Don't disappear again. Stick with me." He wended his way back to the bar and I boosted myself onto the stool next to him. Byron's glass was half-empty and mine half overflowed on the countertop.

He said something to the bartender, then to me, "I'll be right back. You stay put. I mean it."

"I will." My voice squeaked.

He moseyed over to the billiards table and struck up a conversation with the shaved-headed pool player. Trying to read their lips, I came up with, "I swallowed an ice cube," and "You are like a small tree." I doubt that's what they were talking about.

Alone now at the bar and feeling conspicuous, I struggled to keep my surge of panic at bay and thought about checking-in on social media just so I could pretend to be occupied, but that wouldn't be a good idea since Kristen and everyone else would know where I was.

A hand on my back made me jump. Byron said, "Time to go."

I sprang off my stool and beat him out the door. When the brisk air hit me, I realized the noise had receded by several hundred decibels, and my ears reverberated like the ringing sound of tires on blacktop.

I stretched out my jaw a couple of times. "What did you talk to the pool player about?"

"The Thunder Knuckles gang."

He kick-started the motorcycle and motioned for me to get on behind him.

Chapter 9

Off we flew down the highway where we exited at an old-fashioned, all-night diner, with an interior that looked like every other all-night diner across the country, complete with a pie case, booths, and the aroma of burning, stale coffee.

We ordered two cups. The brew tasted pretty bad, so I dumped several tablespoons of creamer into mine.

After Byron threw down a gulp of the hot stuff, he said, "That pool player, he rides with the Thunder Knuckles, and he knew Quincy Davidsen."

"He did?" My ears still rang.

"He claims the gang had nothin' to do with Quincy's death. The gang's huntin' for the shooter, too. And he has no reason ta' lie. Lots of gang members brag about shooting somebody, at least when they think there aren't any cops around. This guy did nothin' like that. He sounded mad at the killer."

"Why? Was he friends with Quincy?"

"Gangs are like, well, like brothers. They defend each other. If someone takes out one a' their own, they retaliate."

"Was Quincy killed by a rival gang?"

"No, that man said he wasn't."

"Not a territory war?"

"Nope. None a' those things. I asked the guy 'bout all that. There's no word out on who did it." Byron's voice, deep and rich, made his words difficult to distrust.

"A drug deal?"

"Not involving the Thunder Knuckles."

I sat back and crossed my arms. "Are you sure that guy wasn't lying to you?"

"Hard ta' know, but I don't think so." Byron said, "Look, the police woulda' checked out the gang angle, don't cha think? Gangsters are obvious suspects."

"Just because that's everyone's first thought doesn't mean they couldn't've done it."

"Sorry I wasn't more helpful."

"Don't be sorry. This is better information than I had before. The Denver Gang Crime Unit doesn't have a thing on you." I tapped my front teeth with a fingernail.

Byron put his head in his hands and shook his head from side to side. "What you thinkin' now?"

"I'd like to know more about the tattoo I saw on Quincy's fingers. It was simple, just letters on each finger spelling out "B-O-L-T.""

"Draw 'em on a napkin. I want ta' see what the letters looked like." He handed me a pen from his inside pocket.

I sketched the tattoo onto the soft paper. The inscription was on the gothic side, and I did the best I could. I added a facsimile of the lightning bolt earring, too, and pushed the napkin across the table. "Does this help?"

He studied the drawing for a moment, then shook his head as if stumped. "I don't recognize these designs."

"Did you think you might?"

"Doesn't seem like a prison ink job ta' me. Those are usually simpler." Byron had served time for manslaughter years ago. The other guy started the fight and had died after Byron threw an unlucky punch. My dad gave ex-felons jobs, and Byron had been one of his employees—one of the good guys, sorry for what he'd done, a reformed alcoholic, and a substitute father to me. I was glad he was here with me.

I pushed my coffee cup away. "You ready to go?"

"I worry about you, kiddo." His hazel eyes crinkled at the corners. "I can tell you're makin' other plans. Whadda ya' goin' to do next? I hope you're done investigating after tonight."

I scrunched my forehead. "I don't have any more leads, Old Man, so you don't need to worry." That was truth.

He swallowed the last of his coffee, and we took off out the door.

Now that we'd left the dangerous bar behind and were on the journey home, I appreciated the beast beneath us much more. The wind in our faces blew cold, but Clem's jacket felt heavy and warm. The night turned dark. The pine scent was thick and the wheels on the pavement smooth, with just me and the Old Man and an adrenaline rush. The best way to navigate the mountain passes.

After Byron dropped me off at the autobody shop, the drive back to my apartment in my Fiat felt strangely confining compared to the long motorcycle ride in the cool, open air. A random claustrophobic fear hit me, like my jacket was clenched too tightly around my neck. I'd gotten a good bead on one of the Thunder Knuckles, the one with the teardrop tattoo, but he'd zeroed in on me, too. A scary thought. Should I be worried? Had it been foolish to show up at the tavern? The gangbangers knew about us now…knew we were asking questions. But the teardrop-tattooed guy claimed Davidsen's death was not a gang hit and Byron seemed to believe him. So, maybe there was nothing to be concerned about and it was time to pursue Quincy's killer elsewhere. There were sure to be a lot more people to question if I could only figure out who.

When I pulled my Fiat into the apartment's parking lot behind the coffee shop, Tanner was waiting for me at the bottom step.

"Tanner! What are you doing here?" I ran over to sit next to him. I snaked his arm around my shoulder and snuggled close.

"I drove by, noticed your car gone, and thought you might be out on a late tow." He held me tight. "How was your night?"

"Boring." If Tanner only knew the truth! I unzipped my jacket and let the cool air in. "What are you doing out so late?"

"I was on a tow myself. It never ends." He chuckled.

"I'd invite you up, but I'm afraid of what's inside my apartment." Axle was such a slob.

He sniffed. "You smell like cigarette smoke."

I tried to hide a guilty look. "It's this jacket I borrowed from Clem." I tugged his sleeve. "Are you going to show me your new tattoo now?"

"Not yet."

"What's the big secret?"

"Why do you want to see it so bad? You haven't been interested before."

He had me there. "I am now. What's this one mean?" I pointed to the geometric pattern on his forearm.

"That's a Sak Yant design."

I reared my head back to stare at him. "What's a Sak Yant?"

"I had it done in Thailand on a trip there a year ago."

I was still getting to know Tanner and I did not know about this. "You went to Thailand?"

"Yeah, they have beautiful beach resorts. I'll have to take you there." He hugged me to his chest and gave me a long kiss, but all the time I couldn't help wondering who he went with. Was it Annie? Irrational fear went through my heart. Did he have another girlfriend? Was he cheating on me?

His arms went slack as he sat back. "Hey, one of the business owners stopped me tonight and said there was a car blocking their loading zone last night. Didn't you see it? A Ford Fusion."

I felt the blood rising in my cheeks. "No, I didn't."

"They said it was there for at least half an hour, you had to have seen it behind the art studio."

"Oh, no. Did they miss a delivery?"

"The guy had to carry in the art supplies and picture frames through the front door."

I blushed scarlet under his gaze. "I'm sorry."

"Where were you?"

I couldn't tell him I was at the tattoo parlor spying on him! "I'll be more careful next time, I promise." If I didn't keep the owners satisfied, Tanner could lose his contract for the towaway zones.

Tanner said, a bit reluctantly, "I should let you get

inside. It's cold out here."

"I'm not cold."

He snuggled me tighter against him. "Am I keeping you warm?"

Actually, the jacket was hot, but I let him believe he was the one who warmed me up as he gave me another kiss, his lips soft but pressing hard over mine. We said goodnight, and I hitched myself up the stairs and let myself in the dark apartment. I went straight to my room and collapsed into bed.

My dreams that night included a skeleton with long, white, bony fingers holding a pool cue saying, "I didn't do it, it wasn't me." He smacked the long stick in the palm of one bony hand. "But I'll kill whoever harmed my bro' Quincy."

I woke up in a sweat. I thought I'd heard voices, so I ducked under the covers, shivering and willing myself back to sleep. But, a couple of hours later, I still tossed and turned with my eyes open. Finally, a call for a tow came in at two in the morning, the time when the last of the bars closed, and I took down the information, relieved to finally have a job to do and a reason to get up.

My bedroom was chilly, the floor on my bare feet even chillier. I tugged on my jeans, pulled a hoodie over my head, and stumbled out to the living room…to find Axle asleep on the couch.

He opened one eye. "What's the matter, Delaney?"

"What are you doing out here?"

He rested a finger against his lips. "Put a sock in it. Clem's in my room."

"Whaaaat?" I wasn't sure I'd heard that right.

"Clem needed a place to stay. She thinks that pink

bed is cute." He threw off his blanket. "I'll go with you." He still wore his baggy jeans and a tee-shirt.

"Glad to see you're dressed and ready."

He picked up a stinky tennis shoe and paused with the shoe in his hand. "You aren't going to scratch up another car, are you? And get all teary about it?"

I winced. "Ouch! No, I am not!" At least I hoped not.

Clem plodded down the hall, wearing one of Axle's indie band tee-shirts. Beneath the hem, her long legs stretched to the floor. "I want to go with you. I don't want to stay here by myself." She spoke in a whisper, but there was no need since we were all awake. The Rotty thumped his tail as if he wanted to be in on the action, too.

"Fine. Let's everyone go." I stuffed my feet into shoes and snagged my keys. "Not you, Boss."

Axle and I waited by the door in silence for Clem to put on more clothes, then we gallivanted down the steps. "How are we all going to fit in my Fiat?"

Axle said, "Clem can sit in that teeny back seat. We've got three people in there before."

"Yeah, I can do that." Clem squeezed inside the back, then Axle got in the front, and I slammed the passenger door after them. When I opened their door at Byron's lot, they tumbled out onto the ground. We climbed into the tow truck, followed Fifth to Main, and rocked to a stop behind Main Street Brewery.

A man in his late twenties, about my age, met us at his Mazda Tribute with its hood up. "My girlfriend is on her way to pick me up. Can you tow my car to my house?"

I nodded, and he gave me his address and credit

card. I ran his card through the reader and handed it back. "Is your Tribute front or all-wheel drive?" The vehicle came in both.

He rubbed his chin along his five o'clock shadow. "I don't know."

Wow. A young guy who didn't know what kind of car he drove. Get out! I took a photo of the VIN on his dash and ran the numbers through an app on my phone. This Tribute was front-wheel drive. I stepped close to his side and showed him the picture of Quincy Davidsen. "You ever see this person?"

He appeared unnerved by the question, but shook his head no, then plucked his credit card out of my hand and turned his attention to Clem. Both my customer and Axle crowded around her so I went back to the truck.

The cloudless sky with stars bright and infinite illuminated the darkness. A nice night to be out if I had to be. The last time I brought Axle with me on a tow in the middle of the night was a disaster. Not his fault, of course. That was mine alone. I'd had a few successful hauls since then, so I told myself *easy peasy. Nothing to worry about.*

I hit the buttons on the controller and watched as the claws scooped the Tribute's front wheels off the ground. I never got tired of seeing my truck perform its magic. The guy's girlfriend pulled in a few minutes later. I gave her my business card, since her boyfriend was busy, and asked her to tell her friends about me. She elbowed her way between her boyfriend and Clem, and they took off.

After the three of us got into my self-loader, I hung a right and rumbled down Prairie Falcon Street to drop off the Tribute, then bustled back to the apartment. It was too late, or rather too early in the morning, to bother with storing my truck at Byron's lot. Axle clumped his feet up the wooden stairs with Clem following, complaining loudly about how tired she was.

I was worn out, too. I said, "Shush! Don't wake up Kristen."

Rotty kisses and the scent of dog breath greeted us at the door.

"Sorry you bothered to come along on the tow, Axle. You, too, Clem. It was an easy job this time. I could've handled it on my own."

"You couldn't've done it without us." Axle punched my shoulder, and we all headed back to our respective beds.

My head hit the pillow for a few more hours of shut-eye, but those same nightmares kept intruding—except this time an anime cartoon character with black, chopped hair was caught in a storm, fighting and clawing to get into my truck. Clem invaded my dreams now!

When morning arrived, my head pounded from lack of sleep, bony fingers poked the back of my eyeballs, and pain radiated over the top of my skull. It didn't help that I had to wait for my turn in the shower. After we were all finally ready, I transported Axle, Clem, and Boss in my truck over to Byron's and dropped them all off—Clem said she wanted to hang with Axle at the autobody shop. I felt a little sorry for Byron, what with Axle's love-sick face, Clem's smug expression, and Boss's sloppy drool.

Once I'd said hello and goodbye to the Old Man, I moseyed over to the strip mall and parked outside Friendly Finance, a small loan company that used

Tanner for repos. I'd done a job for them one time, which caused some friction between Tanner and me, showing how little I understood about the towing business.

"Good morning, Hailey," I greeted the woman behind the metal desk. She looked professional in a herringbone blazer and a starched white blouse. Her short hairstyle showcased her high cheekbones and mocha skin tone. Hailey was Friendly Finance's office manager, loan officer, and repo agent, all in one—and I suspected she was the owner of the finance company as well.

She answered, "Hey, Delaney. What are you doing here?"

My gray heels caught on the industrial carpet that covered the cement floor. As I flung myself into the chair at her desk, I answered her, "I stopped by for a smoothie from next door. I need an energy booster. You want one, too?"

"No, I try to stay away from that place. It's too convenient, you know?" She smiled. "Tanner's still handling all my repos if that's what you're here for."

"That's not why I came in. I just thought I'd say hello. Well, that's not true, actually. I need your expert advice."

"What about?"

"I'm working on a repo for Nancy Abington over at Abington Auto Mart, and I can't ever seem to locate the vehicle. The repo agent can't find it either or he would've called me."

"A lot of times the owners hide their cars until the finance company gives up searching for them."

"That's what I'm afraid of. I thought you might

have a better idea for me other than trying to spot the car on the street somewhere."

"Sounds like you need a court order to open up the owner's garage to check inside." She sighed, "I have four court orders pending myself right now, so I feel your pain."

"Four? Wow. You work too hard, Hailey." I stood. "You sure you don't want a smoothie? I'm buying."

She weakened. "Well, okay. Thanks."

I wrenched the door open. Hummingbirds flitted from one giant planter to another on the sidewalk along the storefronts. I strolled past the temp agency and a consignment shop and went in the smoothie place. This was a treat I sorely needed after the sleepless night and my bleak gray mood. A few minutes later, I ducked back inside Friendly Finance with two strawberry banana blends. I set Hailey's on her desk and slouched back into the chair I'd just vacated.

She put the straw to her lips. "Mmmm. Yeah, I remember why I like these so much."

I slurped down a cold mouthful and rubbed my hand to my temple. "Brain freeze."

"Ha. I know! So, sounds like you're keeping busy?"

"Busy trying to locate the repo." I nodded. "I'd like to have an impound lot of my own eventually like Tanner has. I'd like a second truck, a flatbed, someday, too." That way I could accept jobs that required a flatbed, like ones involving overturned vehicles. Maybe I would get more calls for tows if I had a flatbed with a winch.

"You have a business plan?"

"No. I should've taken some business courses in

college." Another thing to put on my to-do list.

"There are a lot of on-line programs from some good schools."

Hailey's phone rang. "I should get this." When she picked up, I mouthed, *call you later*, holding a thumb to my ear and little finger to my mouth. Hailey was not only a business contact and networking opportunity, she gave good advice, too. I genuinely liked her.

Intending to get back on the job, I eased myself up into the truck cab and phoned Patrick Crump.

He asked me, "Were you able to seize the BMW?"

"No. That's why I called you. Have you located it?"

"Still hard at it."

In the past, Patrick had left me hanging trying to capture a vehicle from an angry owner. Now that he worked for Nancy instead of her husband, he didn't have as big a chip on his shoulder.

He said, "I have some more info. Next of kin's listed on the loan application, plus a reference." He gave the names and addresses to me, and I entered the information into my phone, and we disconnected.

The BMW owner's mom lived in the historical district, a pricey although transitional area, so I threw the truck's gear into drive and cut across town to her address. Bianca had parked her black BMW 5 series, rear wheel, in the driveway. Yes! I jammed my smoothie into the cupholder and flew out of my self-loader to compare the VIN against the number Nancy had given me. It was the same. *Gotcha*!

I texted Patrick, "I found it," adding some happy emojis.

I sprang back inside the cab to operate the remote.

The BMW rose into the air with a squeak and swoosh, and I hurtled my truck down the street, the BMW sailing behind, the passing scenery a blur.

Repo work felt a little bit like stealing, *I know, I know*, but remember, people who didn't pay were swindling the financing companies. It seemed like a moral gray area to me, too, but the rest of us make our payments so they should as well. And if I didn't do the repo work, someone else would, like the new guy in the green tow truck, that man with the long beard, a few car-lengths ahead of me.

I stomped on the brakes. An orange-tagged Dodge Charger—in both rear-wheel and all-wheel drive—was angled off on the shoulder. Even though the city had not called me to pick it up, no one told me I couldn't, and in fact the impound tag gave me the authority to tow it. That green tow truck driver was sure to have seen the tagged Charger, too.

In the next alley was the perfect place to stash the BMW, so I turned in and lowered the car behind the building. The green tow truck operator doesn't know about this BMW, so he has no reason to haul it away. The owner doesn't know I've repo'ed it yet. And neither of them knows I've stowed it in this back street. I'll snag the Charger and come right back for the BMW. I'm not going to miss this tow opportunity. I'd lost out on too many already, and I wanted to grab it before my competition did.

I circled back around to the Charger.

Should I tow from the front or back end? Since it came in both rear-wheel and all-wheel drive as options, I got out to take a peek at the VIN through the windshield but did not find FW, RW, or 4W mixed in the jumble of letters and numbers. I grabbed my phone from my pocket and searched the internet for Chargers, but no clear answer was there, either.

Family sedans, compact cars, and minivans were usually front-wheel drive. Trucks, full-sized SUVs, and sports cars were mostly rear-wheel drive. The Charger appeared sporty. In all likelihood, rear-wheel.

To make sure, I should scope out underneath for a rear differential. Don't know what that is? Now that I'm a vehicle recovery specialist, I do! If I found the differential, the Charger was rear-wheel. At least, that's what Tanner had explained to me. I'd never had to do this before. Just a quick scan, and if I still couldn't figure it out, I'd go ahead and use the dolly wheels, but that took extra time. I scooched underneath the front end of the Charger, the heels of my shoes digging into the dirt.

I could do this! Yes! I was so full of baloney trying to convince myself.

Muffled rumblings from a diesel engine sounded from somewhere nearby. I froze and listened closely. Then a squeak of metal joined the traffic noise.

All of a sudden I felt dizzy, hit with a weird sensation like I was sliding feet first along the pavement, and next thing I knew, daylight blinded me, and I let out a hair-raising shriek.

Chapter 10

I propped myself up on my elbows as the Charger pulled away, its rear hitched up on the back of the bright green tow truck!

Unable to move for a full thirty seconds, I stabbed my heels into the gravel to get up. Had anyone seen me in this ridiculous situation? The big, bad tow truck driver in her gray stilettos lying in the dirt as the competition swooped off with the target vehicle. I started to grapple my way up to a stand when I felt hands under my arms giving me an assist.

"Delaney, what are you doing? You okay?" Ephraim misjudged my weight and slammed me into his solid chest. His citrus, jasmine, and musk scent filled my nose, and a jolt of electricity went through my body.

"Now, now, hands off," I said.

The sheriff released me, and I tottered back a few steps. He repeated, "What were you doing?"

There was no good answer to that. "Um, I was just trying to see the differential, er, checking for, uh, I mean, trying to estimate the length of the average size car…" *As if!*

His eyebrows bent down toward his nose. He seemed as confused as me. He said, "Cars are all sizes and lengths."

I gave a nervous laugh and dusted off my butt.

"Thanks for the hands up."

He crossed his arms and considered me while my fingers played with my shirt sleeve. My heel hit a rock and I just about fell over. What a klutz!

Ephraim reached out to steady me.

My phone buzzed from my pocket and I recognized Mom's number on the screen. I'd call her back, but this was as good an excuse as any to get out of there. "I need to be going. See you later." I tottered back to my tow truck and clenched the steering wheel with white knuckles. Ephraim got in his sheriff's vehicle and took off.

The faint smell of motor oil combined with a woodsy scent rose from my seat. I imagined Dad leaning back in the same spot, his hands on the same wheel. It was almost like he was there with me. What would Dad think of me right now? He would've known how to tow that Charger.

Note to self: just get out the dolly wheels next time. Forget about differentials!

But that green tow truck driver was something else. Stealing the Charger right out from under—or rather, over—me! That tower was everywhere, sometimes showing up first and beating me to the stalled vehicles, but this time I'd gotten there first. Here's a thought. Did the green tow truck driver stop to check the Impreza with the gunshot victim inside? Hard to believe he would pass up the opportunity. If he'd seen the Impreza, did he also see the murder victim? Or the murderer?

Maybe I should question the green tow truck driver.

I turned my truck in a circle to retrieve the BMW. I

missed out on the Charger, but at least I'd made a good job of recovering the BMW for Nancy Abington.

But when I drove back to the alley, I couldn't find the car. Maybe I was in the wrong place. I zipped through all the alleys in the area, and returned to the first, getting my bearings. That's when I remembered the *No Parking - Towaway Zone* sign with Tanner's number.

I dialed up Tanner. "Did you tow a black BMW 5 series from behind the furniture store?"

"I did. So, you put it there?"

"Yes," I admitted.

"When I called the cops to let them know I'd towed it, I found out the owner had reported it stolen. She swore she didn't know how it got parked in the towaway zone. She was so adamant, I let her have the car back without paying the fee. How did it end up in the alley, Delaney?"

Jeez, this was one of those days! Embarrassing didn't begin to describe it. I tried to make a joke. "Well, ha-ha, I couldn't tow two vehicles at once."

"Tell me what you did." After I explained, he asked, "A repo? Is this for Hailey?"

"No, no, this is for Nancy Abington."

"So, she's running the dealership now." His voice turned gentler. "I'm glad you're still getting work from them."

"What's up with that green tow truck?"

"Owen Eckerd. He's a go-getter."

"How'd you know his name?"

"I had a run-in with him at an accident scene. He let me know he beat me there by just a few minutes even though we arrived at the same time. He wasn't very nice about it."

"I'm not surprised. He towed a vehicle just when I was about to hook up to it. I was trying to figure out the drive wheels when he drove away with it!" All that outrage came back in full force.

"If you got there first, he should've let you have the car. He violated the unspoken rules between towers."

"Is this town big enough for so many tow businesses? I don't think so." I sounded like a Wild West gunslinger. Owen Eckerd seemed to be on every street, scouting out the orange-tagged vehicles before I spotted them. Except that Charger. I found it first.

"Sure it is. There's enough work for everyone. Look in your rearview mirror." My boyfriend had pulled in behind me.

I angled myself out of my truck and climbed into his passenger seat. As I propped my shoes on the dash, I got a good view of my pointy-toed heels, the suede torn and dirty now.

Tanner tugged on my elbow where my shirt had ripped. "Check you out. How'd this happen?"

"I was crawling around on the ground." No need to mention how Ephraim helped me up.

He rubbed my back. "Forget about Owen. Maybe he didn't know you got there first."

"Not likely. He had to have seen my tow truck at the other end of the Charger."

He knew I was there. Couldn't miss me. But now that I had his name, I'd give him a call. Boy oh boy, would I give him a call. But when I did later, I only got his voice mail.

Owen Eckerd, the creep.

****

Axle's blankets had fallen off to join his dirty clothes and work boots on the living room floor. He snored on the couch in a tee-shirt and gym shorts, so I shielded my eyes with one hand as I entered the kitchen to make the coffee.

Unwashed plates filled the sink. Dog chow caked Boss's food dish. Clem and Boss had the second bedroom, and I dared not go in there, not wanting to know what state that room was in.

After a bracing cup of joe, much muttering and swearing, then showering, I left my hair loose to dry around my shoulders and returned to the living room. Axle had disappeared. While I was slumming on the couch, scrolling through news on my phone, Axle rambled back into the kitchen fully clothed.

"I need a ride to work. Can you take me?"

"Of course, but it's Sunday."

"Yeah. Byron has a paint job for me to finish."

"All right. Make sure Boss has a walk before we leave."

"Okay." Axle leaned over my shoulder and caught me staring at Quincy Davidsen's photo on my screen. He asked me, "Why do you have his picture? The dead guy, right?"

"I've been showing his photo around. Some people in this town must've known him. Hey, they might recognize Clem, too. Can you forward me your photo of her?"

"No can do." Axle shook his head and indicated with pinched eyebrows that he was seriously unhappy with my request. I matched his gaze with my own mean-big-sister glare. He goggled at me. "What?"

"Nothing, nothing." I didn't press him because his expression had changed to that dimwitted, love-sick look.

We climbed in my Fiat and zipped over to Byron's. I parked *caddywhompus* to the door and Axle jumped out. My fingers beat a drum solo on the wheel until he disappeared inside. Once back home, I ran into Kristen in the parking lot and was all set to complain about her messy cousin who was proving difficult to live with, when she said, "It's so sweet, Delaney, you letting Clem and Axle stay in your apartment." It was the sort of thing Kristen herself would do.

The tip of my nose turned red. If she only knew how annoyed I was with the two of them. I imagined for a second giving them the *clean-up-after-yourselves* and *this isn't a pig pen* parental speech before kicking them out. I shook that thought out of my head and told Kris, "Sure."

"Really, Delaney, you're a saint." I was about to agree when she said, "Well, I need to get going or I'll be late for church." I watched her get into her Prius, then I headed up the stairs to my apartment.

Clem had not yet made her way out of the bedroom. I glanced at the clock, then muttered under my breath, "Screw it," and "Take *this*, Anime Lady," while I switched on the vacuum cleaner, loud enough to wake the soundest sleeper. Except it didn't wake Clem. Next, I tackled the kitchen, washed and put away all the dishes, mopped the floor, and even cleaned the oven and stovetop. After I gave Boss some fresh water and kibble in a fresh bowl, I walked him to the park across the street. He raised his leg against a bush and sniffed around the bench. Walking his dog and doing the chores took all morning. That little turd, Axle, would pay for this.

Note to self: Grow a pair and tell Axle and Clem to clean up their own mess.

Moving on...moving on. I returned the Rotty to the apartment and got ready to head out.

Before leaving, I searched for open houses on my phone. *Bingo.* Found one listed by Bianca White, the BMW owner. Just as I took hold of my keys to leave, Clem wandered out from her bedroom, stretching as if she'd had a nice sleep. "Morning, Delaney."

"You mean afternoon."

She yawned and slid onto a counter stool. "What are you doing today?"

"I'm trying to find a repo."

"Can I come with?" Before I could answer, she said, "Let me grab a shower." She jumped off the seat and hurried to the bathroom. I considered leaving, but still hoping to pry more info out of her, I waited with foot tapping while she put on makeup, did her hair, and primped in the mirror. Wasn't I a sap?

When she finally said she was ready, I asked her for her photo with the excuse that I wanted to add it as an avatar to my contacts. She forwarded a picture playing up her straight, razor-cut, black hair, her enormous blue eyes, panda-face makeup, and red lipstick. A female anime character come to life.

We collected my truck, picked up Raspberry Passion Lemonade teas from the smoothie place, then headed to the golf course community. I braked across from a home with an *Open House* sign but no BMW, so I hit the gas and circled the block. *Nada.* No BMW anywhere. Maybe Bianca White had sent another agent.

I parked around the block and told Clem to follow my lead.

We left our drinks in the truck and approached the house. Bianca greeted us at the front door. "Welcome. Come on in." She acted like she didn't remember me as she politely took us on a tour, and when I asked to see the garage, I spotted the BMW in one of the stalls. A car locked in a garage cannot be towed without consent unless you have a court order.

Clem inquired about the square footage, whether there were HOA fees, and if the home had a water softener system, just like she was ready to close on escrow. When we walked out, she told the realtor, "Love the house. I'll be in touch." Then Clem asked me, "What next?"

We could hang around until the open house ended and follow the realtor home, but the event was scheduled to last three more hours and I was too impatient. Besides, I had Clem alone and captive in my truck. Now was my chance.

I would've rubbed my hands together, but I was clutching the steering wheel, getting ready to turn onto Pine Street. "So Clem, tell me what you know about Quincy."

She poked the straw in and out of the lid to her iced tea. "What do you want to know?"

"Everything. Like who were his friends?"

She frowned while gazing out the passenger side window.

"Come on, you want the guilty person found, right?"

"Why do you care about Quince?" She turned her baby blues on me, and I must admit, they affected me, too. My sympathy gene kicked in.

"I discovered him, Clem. I saw what the killer did to him and I've been having nightmares." I slowed the truck as we rolled down Main Street with the expensive boutiques and marked-down ski clothing hanging on sales racks on the sidewalk under the blooming crabapple trees…hoping she couldn't see the moisture behind my eyes.

She turned to face me, seeming to consider me for the first time. "Nightmares? His death bothered you that much?"

"Of course it did. I need closure like you do."

"What do you want to know?"

"Who he hung out with."

"They all had nicknames. There's Haxxed and there's Demented."

"What? That sounds like something out of a scary movie. Do you know their real names?"

"Haxxed means 'badass gamer,' and his name is really Jack. Demented is Lance Palmero. I don't know Jack's last name."

"Did Quincy have a nickname, too?"

"Just Quince."

"What about his family?"

"He had a brother, Pierce."

I smiled, pleased with myself for knowing this already. "I've seen him around. He's been in the coffee shop."

Clem keyed into her phone, both thumbs tapping. "Here's Pierce's picture."

I glanced at the screen. "Yes, that's him." Another connection to the victim. If I'd shown the gamers the photo of Quincy, his brother would have recognized him. But I didn't even think to ask them at the time. I told Clem, "Pierce comes into Roasters with a couple of other guys to play video games on their laptops. Now they're thinking of having a tournament there, too."

Clem nodded. "That sounds like him."

Spending time with Clem reminded me to check on the impounded Impreza, so I pulled into Tanner's lot and put on the parking brake. We both stared at the death vehicle. It had signs of dust, as if untouched. The *police-hold* stickers were all over the windows, intact and undisturbed.

She asked, "Is the car still locked up? Axle told me you can't get inside."

"The police have the keys."

She graced me with the smile she usually reserved for the guys. "How did you learn how to operate a tow truck anyway?"

"Mostly just by doing the work, but Tanner helped me a lot."

Her eyes lit up. "How'd you meet him?"

"I know, he's hot, isn't he? And we're dating." If that sounded like a warning...well, it was. I wanted her to know I was on to her. But I didn't feel like sharing more details about my boyfriend with Clem.

While we sat there watching traffic flow by, she told me about her life. She'd been raised in a foster family. And now she didn't know where she would live, since she'd been staying with Quincy. She ended with, "His folks moved his stuff out and closed up the apartment already."

"Do you know his parents very well?"

Clem whipped out her cell phone and showed me a picture on the screen. "This is Quince's dad." A close selfie of the two of them…Clem and *Quincy's dad*? In the photo, she gazed at the man with her bewitching expression. The handsome man pushed fifty, with dark, trimmed hair, and he had on an uncertain smile.

"Why isn't Quincy in the picture, too?"

"He wasn't home at the time."

I wagged a finger at her. "You were alone with his dad?"

"Just for a minute. He stopped by the apartment looking for Quince." She put the phone away. No big deal to her.

"Why do you need inside the Impreza?" I shrank back in my seat as we both gave the death car another glance.

"Quince gave me a ring, not an engagement ring, but a gold band in the shape of a feather. I was able to get my clothes out of his place, but I forgot the ring and when I went back for it, they'd locked the door and I never had a key. I thought maybe his keys were with his car."

"We can ask the police if they found the ring. They'd have searched his apartment." I started the engine back up. "We can ask right now." I pointed the truck toward the sheriff's station.

As we walked in the door, we ran into Ephraim heading out. "Delaney, I was going to call you." He gave Clem a thoughtful glance, but her blue eyes didn't seem to have an impact on him. Since Ephraim was known as a ladies' man, this was surprisingly satisfying.

"You were? We have a question for you, too." I had to tilt my head back to catch his eye.

"What's that?" He motioned us to the side, away

from the door.

"This is Clementine Vargas. She was Quincy's girlfriend." I pointed a thumb toward Clem.

"I know." His gaze darted to Clem and narrowed back to me.

I cleared my throat. "She's trying to find a ring that Quincy gave her. She might've left it in his apartment. You searched his place, right?"

He asked Clem, "What does the ring look like?"

She gave him the full-on, vampy, blue-eyed treatment. "A circle of leaves that went around my finger, gold."

I asked, "Wait, a circle of leaves?" Hadn't she just said it was feathers or something?

"Yeah, leaves and stuff."

Ephraim said, "I'll check the inventory and photos, but I don't recall a ring."

Clem wanted to know, "Can I get in the apartment?"

"It's not a crime scene, so it's not up to the sheriff's department. We don't have a key. You'll need to ask the tenant or the owner of the building." He turned to me. "Can I talk to you?"

"Sure." I fixed my gaze on my black high tops— for once I wasn't in heels— and twirled my braid, coquettishly. Yes, I know I'm with Tanner, but I had a certain attraction to the sheriff. Besides, I was trying to distract him from the *leave-it-to-the-police* lecture. What can I say?

Taking my elbow, he led me down the steps past the scrappy yucca plants and potentilla bushes on either side of the walkway. Above the building, thin white clouds streaked the dusky blue sky. I wished I could escape into the blue yonder, but Ephraim asked, while resting a hand on his duty belt," Where'd you get a photo of Davidsen? I know you've been showing his picture around the coffee shop."

"Downloaded from an internet news site. How'd you know?"

"Zach told me." He crossed his arms. Yep, Kristen must have spotted me and told Zach who told Ephraim. Brothers in blue. Ephraim said, "Look, you shouldn't hang out with Clem, she's a suspect."

"I suppose you're right." I darted my eyes past Ephraim and gave her a weak smile.

A muscle jumped in his cheek. "You're investigating the murder, aren't you?"

Ah-ah! The warning I expected. I put my hand on his arm and felt his muscles relax. "Clem came to me, I didn't seek her out. She wanted inside Quincy's car to find her ring, but don't worry, I didn't let her close to the Impreza."

His eyes bored into mine and a tingle went up my spine. He couldn't possibly know Byron and I had gone to the Centerpiece Tavern, could he?

After a long moment, he said, "All right. But police work is dangerous. I'm going to keep my eye on you. Consider yourself warned."

"I don't mind your eyes on me." The words came out of my mouth before I could call them back. *Whoops*. Playing it down, I said, "I understand you're trying to keep me out of harm's way and I appreciate that. But you don't have to worry about me."

He grunted a laugh, like *yeah-right*, and my face heated. I waved Clem over and she followed me to the truck.

Ephraim climbed in his sheriff's vehicle and took the exit. As he drove past us standing in the parking lot, he stabbed two fingers toward his eyes, then at me, like *I'm watching you.* Clem and I stood still, not moving a muscle, like rabbits stalked by a coyote.

After the sheriff's vehicle disappeared, I let out a pent-up breath. "Let's go ask Quincy's folks for the key. Or maybe they have the ring."

Clem's eyes darted all around. "I'm not sure that's a good idea."

"Why not? Doesn't hurt to try." I wrenched open my door to climb in, but Clem stopped with her fingers on the passenger's door handle. I asked, "What's the problem? Let's go."

"Maybe we'd better not."

"I'm going." I hopped inside. "You coming?"

Clem shrugged and got in my truck, looking as nervous as a fluttering aspen.

Chapter 11

I recognized Pierce when he answered the door. Thin, still growing and not yet filled out, taller than me—but that's not saying much—wearing man-sized sneakers, baggy jeans, a tee-shirt that read, "Die and Retry," and a pale complexion. Typical for a video-gamer.

Pierce said, "Hi, Clem. You doing okay?"

She flashed her big, blue eyes at him, and Pierce's eyes blew up wide. She made all the guys gaga. I wished I had that same influence. She said, "Well…."

He stepped out the door. "Let's sit down." The two of them took seats together on an old-fashioned porch swing, while I grabbed a wicker chair.

The scene from the stoop fanned out into a spectacular view of the mountains in every direction with the valley spread out beneath us. The green aspens waved their spring leaves among the dark pines. I never tired of that landscape.

"Ask about your ring," I urged Clem.

She swung her gaze over her shoulder toward the picture window before turning back to Pierce. "Can I get the key to Quince's place?"

"We don't have it. I'm pretty sure Mom returned the key. What'd you need it for?"

Clem fiddled with the end of her sleeve.

"The ring," I reminded her.

She stared in her lap, her lashes lying against her cheeks, the picture of innocence. "Quince gave me a ring. It had bird's wings all around it."

Didn't she remember what the ring looked like? How significant could this ring be to her?

Pierce deflated. "I didn't know he gave you a ring."

"Well, I left it at the apartment and I'd like to get it back."

"I'll track it down and call you, okay?" He reached for her hand, and the porch swing gently rocked back and forth. She didn't seem to notice Pierce had taken her hand in his. He didn't appear too broken up about his brother's death. It looked as if he tried to comfort her, not the other way around.

I jumped in. "Pierce, was Quincy on his way here when, uh, right before, you know…"

Pierce turned his face toward me. He didn't resemble his brother. In his picture Quincy had light brown hair, hazel eyes, and a big nose; Pierce's hair seemed darker, his eyes browner, but he had the same nose and a protuberant Adam's apple. He asked, "Who are you, again?"

"I used to work at Roasters on the Ridge. You know me."

He raised his upper lip. "That place where the cops hang out all the time?"

Woah-kay. I got the impression he wasn't fond of the police. "Yeah, that place. You might be holding your video game competition there. One of the gamers talked to Kristen about it. Maybe that was you?"

"Roscoe is handling that. He thinks it'd be a good idea for the guild to meet up in person, so he's putting together this tournament. The only reason anyone other than *noobs* will show up is for the prizes."

Guild? Noobs? I must have had on a blank face since he seemed to dismiss me and turn back to Clem.

I still asked, "Do you know what Quincy was doing on County Road 6? Was he on his way here?"

His jaw tightened. "Who knows?"

"Did your brother have any enemies, Pierce? You must have some idea who could have done this."

"Step-brothers. Not brothers. Same Mom, different Dad."

I wrinkled my nose. "But, you have the same last name?"

His almost bored voice shifted to angry. "Dad adopted Quincy, so, yeah, we have the same last name."

"Were you close?"

"Hardly. Quince got mixed up with some bad dudes and they got him into trouble. I didn't want anything to do with him after that."

I sat forward, my hands on my knees. "What bad dudes? What kind of trouble?"

"Money trouble. There, is that what you wanted to know?"

I willed for him to go on, but he seemed to have difficulty keeping his eyes off Clem. She stood, glancing at the front door. "Well, we need to get going. Good to see you, Pierce. Keep in touch."

I jumped up. "Hang on a minute. Who were these dudes?"

Pierce said, "What's it to you?"

It took restraint not to react to the jerk and I had to remind myself he'd just lost his brother. "Have you heard of the Centerpiece Tavern?"

"I don't know. Maybe." He said, "Clem, I'll call

you tomorrow."

"All right." She hightailed it down the driveway and his gaze followed her. I came along in her wake and we both climbed into the cab. Clem said, "Let's go."

The gravel kicked up as I sped the truck out of the driveway onto the paved road that led down the canyon. I gave my passenger a sideways glance. Why was she in such a hurry to leave? How well does she know Pierce? They must be familiar enough with each other since they parted on a *call-me* moment.

"Clem, did Pierce seem angry to you?" She only shrugged and stared at her phone. I asked, "Did Quincy hang out the Centerpiece Tavern?"

She faced the window, showing me the back of her head. "I dunno. He never took me there."

I tried to be upbeat. "Well, at least Pierce will dig around for your ring, right?"

"I suppose." She checked the time on her device. "Do you think Axle's done at work?"

"Probably. I doubt he has to work the whole day. He might be home by now." I gave up a big sigh as we came around a bend. "Clem, please be careful with Axle's heart. He's sweet and I don't want him hurt. I see how you flirt with Pierce and the rest of the guys."

She splayed her hand across her chest and fluttered her eyes. "Who me?"

"Yes, you. I mean it, Clem."

She gulped in a sob. A fake-sob, I was almost sure of it. "Believe it or not, I'm still trying to get over Quincy's death. You're not the only one upset about it. I keep thinking about him, I can't stop. I loved him. Don't you understand that?"

Sitting at the traffic light at Industrial Lane and Main Street, I observed the young woman beside me. She had her fist to her mouth, but no tears in her eyes. Way out of Axle's league, Clem was surely going to let him down. A slow boil simmered in my blood. It was hard to stay neutral.

I was done with her. Yes, the murder had to have affected her more than me. Yes, the death had great ramifications on Quincy's family and friends. And, yes, she'd had a rough childhood, I got all that, but Clem used her witchy superpowers for evil, not for good, playing on the emotions of the opposite sex. Axle and I aggravated each other and we did a bunch of pushing and shoving, but if she made him suffer, I'd punch her out.

When I pulled into the parking lot behind Roasters, Axle was standing next to a dented, black Jeep with a cloth top talking to a man with a baseball hat perched at a right angle on his head. The man's pants bagged low on his hips. A body piercing in his neck reminded me of a miniature barbell stabbed through his skin. Between his thumb and forefinger he clinched a cigarette. But most importantly, silver lightning bolt earrings dangled from his lobes.

My whole body tensed. Clem and I both dove out of the truck at the same time.

"I want what's mine." The man flung his arms around, then poked Axle in the chest with his finger. Axle's hands formed into fists and he took a few steps forward. Axle could come off as intimidating, too, with his knit cap covering his hair and his black tee-shirt with the picture of a heavy metal band.

I marched up to stand next to Axle. "What's going

on?"

Clem had followed me. She said, "Delaney, this is Demented."

I didn't get it. "Demented?"

"He was a friend of Quincy's. Remember, I told you about him."

I squinted at the guy as my brain cells careened into each other, trying to recall exactly what she'd said. Then I remembered. "Oh, that's your nickname. You're Lance Something."

The obvious gangbanger turned to face me and growled, "Call me Demented." A tattoo of a lightning bolt across his forehead peeked out from under the brim of his hat. I could see where he got his nickname.

Whatever confidence I had crumbled like a day-old cheese Danish. I squeaked out, "I will." A handle easy to remember. I couldn't recall his real name anymore, anyway. Larry? Lars? A cold breeze blew in from somewhere and I swallowed convulsively several times.

Demented dropped his cigarette on the pavement. "I need to talk to you, Clem. Call me. You got my number."

All business now, she said, "I'll phone you tonight."

He lifted his knees over the Jeep's half door, shoved his long legs into the space under the wheel, and drove off.

The leaving of the gangster caused a collective release of tension from all of us. Still a little in shock, shivering slightly, I asked Axle, "What did he want?"

Axle shrugged. "I don't know. He didn't say exactly, but he wanted to talk to you, Clem."

I sucked in my lips. "He's one of the Thunder

Knuckles. He's dangerous." A bad criminal element right here in Spruce Ridge. I'd need to tell Kristen.

Clem said, "I can handle him." She wouldn't meet my eyes.

Why did he show up at my apartment? What does he want with Clem? Is he involved in Davidsen's death? Of course, he was. Not only would I have to warn Kristen, I'd need to get Axle off by himself and give him a lecture to be careful, too, but now was not the time. He'd hate me for preaching to him in front of Clem. I could bring up something else, though.

I weaved my finger back and forth between them. "I have a bone to pick with you two."

Clem turned on her smile. "I'm sure Demented won't bother you again."

"I certainly hope not, but that's not what I'm talking about. I want you guys to clean up after yourselves." I turned abruptly and trudged up the stairs, Axle and Clem trailing behind me. "I spent all morning straightening up the apartment."

Axle replied, "Sure, cuz', whatever you say."

"Don't cuz' me." I swiveled around and fake-punched him in the arm.

"So, you're what, my mom now?" He rubbed his shoulder as if it hurt and pinned me with a scowl.

"Mom? Gack, no. And your evil-eye won't work on me." I opened the door and Boss dashed out, jumping for joy at the sight of his three humans.

I had to admit to myself I was glad not to be alone after the encounter with Demented. It was nice to have the company, even if it meant battling over household chores. We were like a little family. I was fond of Axle and Cl—well, I was fond of Axle. Snapping at each other was all part of the *fammy* experience, right?

We trooped inside, me first, then Clem and Axle, and Boss came in last. The four of us recoiled to a sudden stop, and Clem screamed, "What the…"

Garbage coated the kitchen floor—empty soda cans mixed with lettuce and tomato and yesterday's lunch. Scraps of tissues created a pathway to the living room where white batting from the sofa pillows piled up like snowdrifts in a mountain landscape.

Axle said, "Looks like Demented searched our place before I got home." Ice filled my chest and my blood ran cold. Clem swayed and clutched Axle's arm.

I took a moment to breathe until my wits returned and I got a good look at the dog. "Yes, this is the work of a deranged animal all right, but it was only Boss." Tale-tell pieces of batting hung from his upper lip.

The Rotty-mix capered around in agreement, trying to explain he'd been hungry and bored and wanted outside for a walk…and didn't mean to make such a mess. I'd seen the funny dog videos on *YouTube*. Not so humorous when it happens at your house. And I'd left the apartment so clean this morning!

My phone rang but I let it go to voice mail. I held up one finger. "These are the rules. One, feed and walk Boss in the morning. I'll try to swing by at lunchtime and check on him." I raised a second finger. "Two, take him outside as soon as we get home at night." I gave Axle a stern scowl. "Rottweilers need lots of attention. Three, you two need to clean up after yourselves and your dog."

Axle said, "Sorry, Delaney. We'll do better." He headed to the bathroom.

Once he was out of sight, I pulled Clem aside and

asked in a quiet voice, "Do you know what Demented wanted?"

Clem closed her eyes and tucked her chin down low. Scared.

I grabbed her elbow. "Tell me!"

She shook her head. "I don't know."

Axle stormed back down the hall. "Give her a break, Delaney." He put his arm around Clem and she laid her head on his shoulder.

Give *her* a break? *Jeez!* Give *me* a break! But Axle was making me feel pretty rank, like the mean redheaded stepsister. He began to replace the couch cushions while Clem went into the kitchen and came back with a broom and dustpan. They were actually cleaning. Miracle of miracles! Like making all the cups in beer pong.

I scooted down the hall to my bedroom. Mom had left a message, so I listened to her voice mail. She'd cooked broccoli and chicken casserole for dinner, would I like to invite Tanner? This being Sunday, it would be the best opportunity, since neither one of us had to monitor the towaway zones and I certainly didn't want to help Axle and Clem clean up. Been there, done that. So, I texted Tanner asking if he was up for dinner with the parents. He replied that he'd pick me up in a half-hour.

I tossed my phone on the bed and ran to my closet. What shoes should I wear tonight? The red stilettos would aggravate Mom the most, so I grabbed those, then picked out a yellow chevron-patterned sweater to go with my jean skirt. I left my hair in the long plait that fell over the front of my shoulder—no time for hair styling. I brushed some concealer lightly over my cheeks to try to disguise my freckles.

When I came out of my bedroom, Axle had the vacuum running, but the television news blared louder with a headline banner across the screen, so I asked him to shut the machine off.

The headline read, *killer sought in roadside shooting*. A middle-aged woman, thin, with expensively colored blonde hair, heavy makeup, and a honking big nose, stood at a microphone, pleading, "If anyone has information on the death of my son, please call this hotline." She rattled off the number. A man with dark brown hair and eyes, in a collared shirt and tie, towered behind the woman.

Clem said, "That's Quincy's parents."

The dad, Greg Davidsen, I'd recognized from Clem's selfie. He seemed angry on television.

Our eyes remained glued to the screen until the news alert came to an end.

Clem threw an arm out wide. "Gee, Pierce didn't say anything about his parents being on the news. Weird he didn't mention that."

Axle said, "What's this?"

Clem answered, "I'll tell you later."

I said, "So, they're asking for tips to see if anyone knows something. Very interesting." My need was nothing in comparison to Quincy's family's, but I wanted answers, too.

And closure for my traumatic *found-a-dead-body* experience.

Chapter 12

"So, you also drive a tow truck?" Mom regarded my boyfriend over the rim of her wine glass.

"That's right, Mrs. Sharpton."

"Call me Eve." Mom handed the big spoon to Tanner and indicated with a nod of her blonde head, her hair styled in its usual short bob, that as the guest he should serve himself first. We ate in the formal dining room, away from the kitchen nook where we ate when we didn't have company.

After Tanner scooped out a big portion, I plonked some of the steamy chicken and broccoli onto my plate. I mentioned, all-casual-like, "Tanner has a fleet of trucks." I'd fallen into Mom's trap.

Will asked, "How many?"

I answered, "Three."

Tanner peeked over at me. "Even if you only have one, it's called a fleet. That's a technical term."

"Right. That's what I meant," I said. Didn't want Mom to think I didn't know what a fleet was. Who doesn't know that? Me.

"Laney has a degree in social work. She's a social worker." Mom's voice held a touch of pride. That came out of the blue, and yet was not unexpected.

"Was, Mom. I *was* a social worker." I stared out the dining room window of the house where I was raised, a beige and white two-story, nestled in an older neighborhood with giant, gnarly cottonwoods, red maple trees, and green, long-needle pines. Snowball bushes held big, puffy white blooms and lilacs displayed light purple flowers. This was a home where kids grew up to be school teachers or dentists. Not tow truck drivers.

Mom always reminded me that I was underemployed. She felt my former career gave her bragging rights. But after five years of working for Social Services, I'd realized I was the tender-hearted type, tearing up at every sad case, and not suited to the profession. That's when I went to work for Kris. Then after Dad left me his tow truck, I thought fate had intervened with the perfect opportunity to be my own boss.

As if reading my thoughts, Mom said, "I have no idea why Del handed that truck down to you. Driving a truck isn't any kind of a job for a girl. It's a man's business." Her eyes cut to Tanner.

My boyfriend gave her a charming smile. "There are a lot of women tow truck drivers. And, Laney's doing well. She has quite a following on social media. You should read her reviews."

Actually, I was the only female tow operator in Spruce Ridge. "Tanner's the one who taught me how to operate the self-loader." I nudged him with my knee under the table.

Will asked Tanner, "How did you get into the towing business?"

"By starting out working for someone else." My boyfriend didn't mention his college degree or that he owned his own home or that he belonged to the Spruce Ridge Chamber of Commerce. I'd feed Will that intel via a conversation with Mother later when Tanner wasn't around. Yes, I was caught up in seeking their approval, but too embarrassed to let on.

Mom didn't seem impressed, though. She went on to share some gossip about the next-door neighbors, then we talked about shopping over the following week or so. I may have my dad's red hair and his name, but I had my mom's love for shopping. She asked me, "So, anything new with you?"

"No." I would not admit to my mother that there was anything wrong. Like how deep I was immersed in a murder investigation or that gang members had shown up at my apartment. No way! She'd go on and on about it if I did. I threw a warning glance at Tanner, hoping he wouldn't bring up all the craziness that was my life.

Tanner finished his second helping when both our cells beeped with texts. He had his phone out first. "Friendly Finance has a repo."

By this time, I'd found my phone, too. "Hailey sent me the same message." I read it out loud, "Urgent repo, Infiniti hardtop coupe convertible parked at the curb at Second and Sims."

Tanner shoved his phone back into his pocket. "She's anxious to get a capture right away and that's why she texted us both. I'll reply that we're on it."

"You're taking this one, Tanner. Tell her *you're* on it." Hailey preferred Tanner. I had a bite left, so I dug in for one last nibble before screeching my chair back. "Thanks for dinner, Mom. We need to get going."

"No time for dessert?"

Tanner said in his polite way, "Sorry, Eve, but it'll take us an hour to get back and we should be on our way."

I laughed and slapped Tanner's arm. "We could never get married because we'll both be on-call all the time, and who will take care of the children?"

Will's and Mom's eyes opened wide as they sat frozen in their chairs, bouncing glances between me and Tanner. I turned my head toward Tanner who also stared at me. *Awkward!*

Saying goodbye was always a long process with Mom and Will. First, Mom made me promise to call her soon to make plans. Then, we embraced at the door and again on the front step while Tanner fidgeted with nervous energy.

Once in Tanner's car, I said, "Sorry that was so uncomfortable. It might've been too early for you to meet the parents after all. But Mom pressured me to invite you, plus I'd like to get to know your brother and sister someday, so I guess I thought it'd be okay."

Tanner kept his eyes on the road.

I babbled on, "When will I meet your brother and sister?"

"It's a little soon like you said."

My face flushed hot. He must think I'm pushy.

He asked, "Is Axle still living with you?"

A startled bark of laughter came out of my mouth. Could he really be jealous of Axle? "Of course. He just moved in. He sleeps on the couch and Clem has the spare room. There is someone I share my bed with once in a while, though."

I felt Tanner stiffen in the driver's seat. His voice had a hard edge. "Who's that?"

"Boss."

His glower deepened. "Is that his nickname?"

"Axle's dog. And he hogs the bed, too." I giggled,

but Tanner didn't seem amused.

I fell silent and watched the mile markers fly by. What would Dad think about me and Tanner being together? Dad and Tanner had known each other as most people did in the small town of Spruce Ridge. Would Dad have had an opinion? Tanner's headlights illuminated the mileposts, the numbers shining out in the dark, drawing my attention as always. Marker 419, then 420, then 421, where Dad went off this very road. His hit-and-run accident remained unsolved.

I didn't want to think about that, so I asked, "Do you need me to help with the capture? Rear-wheel drive is standard on the Infiniti convertible." I smiled to myself, happy that I knew this.

"I'm familiar with this Infiniti. It's a rear-wheel. I can manage on my own." His words were curt. He pulled through the parking lot behind the coffee shop and reached across me to pop open the passenger door. I nailed him with a look as if to say, *what've I done?*

He blinked, then shook his head, like he needed to clear his mind. "Sorry, Laney. I don't mean to be in a bad mood. I'll call and explain later. I'd better get that Infiniti for Hailey."

I did a brush-off flap of my hand. "It's all right." *Not.* I stepped out and slammed the door shut behind me. *Cripes.* What an awkward *faux pas*.

Still fairly early, I knocked on Kristen's door. She answered in a sweatshirt with a steaming mug in one hand and pulled me inside. "I can tell something's wrong. What is it?"

I made short work of how I botched the evening. "I can't believe I brought up marriage and children! I was only joking. And then I tried to tell Tanner his business.

I expect that put him over the top and now he's mad." My face scorched hot. I'm sure my cheeks shone as rosy as a little red wagon.

"He's being awfully sensitive." She took my side as she always did. "You want some hot tea?" She set her mug on the coffee table.

"No thanks, Kris." I relaxed into her gray chenille sofa with the black and white afghan draped over the back. Kristen's apartment was all black and white. Soft piano music was playing and something like lavender scented the air—like an aromatherapy infuser. "I haven't even asked how things are going with you."

She fiddled with the afghan's fringe, twisting the ends into knots.

I could read my good friend like she could read me. "You figured out who's taking the money from the cash register?"

She gave up a big sigh. "Yeah."

I thought about Guy, a recovering alcoholic, and Sierra, who had lived on the streets… "Is it Guy?"

Her mouth gaped open in astonishment. "How did you know?"

"There's something sneaky about him, that's all." Besides the fact he'd taken over my spot in Kristen's crew. "How do you know it's him?"

"I'm the one who was sneaky today." Worry pinched her face. "He didn't know I counted the money in the drawer after the last customer left and that I counted it again after I cleaned the coffee machines. Almost two hundred missing. He and I were the only ones closing Saturday."

"Oh my God! That's quite a bit." Roasters only had about a couple hundred customers on a good day. With an average receipt of five bucks, sometimes more with pastries, do the math. Profit margins were small in this business and the loss would be painful. "Why did he take the money, do you know? I thought he was on the up-and-up with his recovery."

"He's had a relapse."

"Drinking again?"

"Worse, Sierra told me he's been taking drugs. I thought he would stick to his ten-step program."

I rubbed my forehead. "Do you think that's why that drug deal went down at Roasters? Did it have something to do with Guy being there?"

"Good question. I have no idea."

"Kris, one of the Thunder Knuckles gang showed up here."

Her face went white and her gray eyes widened so far her top lashes touched her eyebrows. "What! Did you call the police?"

"No." Part of me wished I had called the cops, but what could I have complained to them about? Demented hadn't threatened anyone. "Did you call the police to report the theft?"

"Uh-uh, I'll handle it."

"I want you to be careful. Having Clem here might be bringing in a bad element."

She clutched the afghan tighter to her chest. "I can't believe there's a gang around here."

"I hear ya'." I didn't appreciate the gangbangers showing up on my turf, either. "Do you think Guy knows Demented? Guy could be getting drugs from that gang, right?"

Her body caved in on itself, and she spoke slowly, almost in a whisper. "I'm planning to fire Guy tomorrow. I feel bad about it, but I can't keep him on. I'll give him my pastor's number because he works with people with addiction issues and can get Guy into one of those programs with supervised employment."

My friend was hurting and needed me. "How can I help?"

Kristen elbowed herself up straighter. "Can you take some of Guy's shifts? He's the only one who knows how to open and close beside me and you. I haven't trained Sierra yet."

"Of course I will, on one condition."

She glanced at me in surprise. "What's that?"

"You're not paying me. I'm helping you, not working for you." One thing I'd learned from my best friend, doing a good deed felt awesome and was a way to get over yourself. I could use some of that awesomeness. "I'll see you at the coffee shop in the morning."

She smiled for the first time since I walked in the door and gave me a side hug. "At least something good's come of this. We get to work together again. But I'll need you for the afternoon shift, not the morning."

****

I didn't have any nightmares that night, only good dreams. I was back in Roasters on the Ridge, pulling espresso shots, breathing in the soothing scent of the beans. Kristen and I laughed together behind the counter. Inspiring music played, the tables were all full, no one waited at the cash register. All the orders were filled.

Then loud banging on my apartment door woke me up. My feet hung off one side of the bed and my head off the other. Half asleep, I rolled off the mattress, then rushed out of my bedroom and threw open the door.

"Ephraim?" I was glad to see him, a nice, safe officer of the law. Then I stiffened. What if Demented had been at the door? I needed to be more careful.

"Good morning, Delaney." His eyes swept over me in my sleep shirt and little else.

"What time is it?"

"Seven."

I would have to get used to waking up early again if I was working at Roasters. "Come on in. I'll be right back." I rushed to my bedroom and pulled on a few more layers of clothes. When I returned, Axle rose from the couch and gave me questioning glances. I asked the sheriff, "What do you want?"

"Is Clementine Vargas here? I need to talk to her."

I wheeled toward Axle. "Clem's here, right?"

A sliver of fear passed over Axle's face. He said, "I'll get her," and disappeared down the hall.

"What is it, Ephraim? Do you have news?"

"Just routine questions." His dark eyes behind those long lashes didn't give anything away.

Clem crept down the corridor after Axle, and they both came to a stop at the kitchen doorway. Her straight black hair was in a bed-head state, but she still showed every sign of being adorable. Sweatshirt hanging off one shoulder, stretchy short-shorts, sagging socks, tennis shoes. I wish I came off that good. My red hair was snarled and wild, my sleep shirt poked out from under a stretched-out sweater, my jeans were the same ones I'd worn the day before, and my feet were bare-toed with chipped polish.

"Ms. Vargas, I'd like for you to come with me to the sheriff's office. I have some questions."

"Do I have to go?" Clem turned her baby blues on me like I was in her corner or something.

"You should go. Sheriff Lopez is not arresting you," I said, glancing at Ephraim, "or he would have said so."

Her head fell on her chest as she surveyed the floor, her shoulders in a resigned slump. "All right."

Ephraim held the door open for her, but before he followed her out, he said to me, "Delaney, thanks for your help." His gaze flicked to my red hair. "And you're looking fine this morning."

"I am?" Maybe I was still dreaming.

He stepped outside, and Axle shut the door after him. "He has the hots for you." Axle shook out his hands as if they'd been scorched.

"Me? I'm a mess!" I stretched out my sweater to show him the coffee stains.

"You're really pretty, Delaney, and low maintenance. You should wear your hair down more often." Axle sidled over to the coffee maker to suss out the situation. He opened the cabinet and got out the beans, then filled the pot with water.

My cheeks warmed, I hoped in a pretty way. "I'm stunned."

"Well, don't expect any more compliments. Don't want it to go to your head." He made a duck-face with flat lips.

I swatted his arm. "No, I'm stunned you're making the coffee."

He pushed me back and I gave him a body slam, shoulder to shoulder. He grabbed the sink sprayer and gave me a full blast of cold water.

"I give up! You win!" If I wasn't fully awake

before, I was now.

"What do I win?"

"You get to take the dog out for a walk."

"Okay. Boss!" he called. The Rottweiler had been asleep on the couch in Axle's warm spot. "What do you think Lopez wants to ask Clem about?" he asked as he snapped on Boss's leash. He pretended nonchalance.

"She'll tell us when she gets back." I pushed the "brew" button on the machine. "You forgot to turn it on. I knew you wouldn't be able to make the coffee right."

"Just waiting to take Boss for a walk first. Pour me a cup when it's done and I'll be right back. By the way, I don't have to work today, since I worked over the weekend."

"Suh-weet." I gave an air kiss to the tips of my fingers, then Axle and the Rottweiler cleared out.

Once they got back, we drank two pots of coffee and stared at the clock. He couldn't sit still and kept asking me what Ephraim wanted with Clem. By the time she returned at nine, Axle was in a state. She came through the door with an attitude, flipping her hair around, her eyes sparking.

He asked her, "Well, what happened?"

Clem said, "That sheriff only asked me the same questions as before. What a waste of time." She went into her room and shut herself inside.

Axle and I held each other's questioning gaze. Not knowing what else to do, he sat shotgun with me when I had to go out on a tow. A Toyota Yaris, front-wheel drive. The $160 charge would edge my bank balance up to black. When we got home twenty minutes later, Clem had packed up and left. Her satchel of clothes.

The stuff hanging in the closet. The shoes. The makeup from the bathroom. All gone.

At least she'd made up the pink canopy bed and straightened the room.

But she'd messed up Axle. He was tight-lipped with a deep scowl.

"It was only a matter of time, little cousin. She was never going to stick around." I gave his shoulder a clip.

He didn't punch me back, a sure sign he was upset. He only slouched onto a chair in the kitchen. Instead of giving him another jab, I stood behind him and wrapped my arms around his shoulders. He hung his head, sad.

He texted Clem the rest of the morning, likely blowing up her phone. She must've replied because he told me later she'd moved in with Demented. The gangster!

Not to honk my own horn, but I totally saw that one coming.

Chapter 13

After dropping Axle off at a friend's, I parked my truck next to the white cross on the side of the road at mile-marker 421. I was glad he had a buddy to talk to. Maybe another guy could help Axle mend his broken heart. Male bonding and all.

So, I'd been okay with everything that happened and I felt guilty. Yes, *moi*. I didn't like Clem and I was glad she was gone. Axle could take the bedroom and I'd have my apartment back to semi-normal. *Petty, right?* What kind of a selfish SOB feels that way when their friend is suffering from a heart-stab? I wanted to say, *good riddance*. I wanted to say, *I told you so* and *you're too good for her*. I wished I'd said *don't let the door hit you on the way out, Clem*. But I couldn't voice any of that.

Axle hurting and in pain was the last thing I wanted that day. Or ever.

Unsettled and unhappy with myself, I hated this guilty feeling that left a nasty taste in my mouth.

I got out and picked my way down the verge, slipping on pine needles in my leopard-print heels. I trudged up through the trees on the other side of the shallow ravine and stopped at the rock outcropping where the mountain vista offered a hundred-mile view of pointed peaks spearing the sky, sharply in focus in the thin, clear air. The sight made my heart soar and my world feel large and at peace.

Axle was the closest thing I had to a brother, and I had no experience dealing with a brother. I wished I could ask my dad for some advice. What would Dad have done with a son? Would he have slung his arm over Axle's shoulder or punched him in the arm and talked about sports? That's what Dads did on TV. I was good at punching Axle, at least.

"Dad?" I asked the mountains. "Are you there?"

The breeze stirred up a dust devil. As the wind moaned through the pines, I inhaled the dusty wood scent. A cloud passed over the sun, leaching the warmth from the air, and I became aware of the crash of the water runoff in the mountain stream far below, the chatter of black and brown-faced chipmunks, and the harsh *skreeka! skreeka!* of the Steller's Jay. Peering down from the cliff edge made me dizzy. I turned around and hiked back to the truck, my heels stabbing into the dry needles. Once inside, I slammed the door closed, insulating myself from the cacophony of sound on the other side of the glass.

Not for the first time did I wish Dad were here with me. But he'd been forced off the road at this very spot. I had so many questions, including what caused his accident and why he had to die right now when I still had so much to figure out. How could I help anyone else when I couldn't sort through my own confusion?

At least, I'd learned a few things about my dad. Byron had told me how he'd helped ex-cons get jobs, and I'd run into some of his old customers who had nice things to say about him, too. Someday I'd like to solve the mystery of my dad's death. But right now, Quincy Davidsen's homicide was on my mind, and it felt like, maybe, I was getting somewhere with that.

I knew the time, place, and means of Quincy's death. Just not the why and the who. I'd questioned Clem, his girlfriend. I'd questioned Pierce, his brother. I knew his parents' names, Francine and Greg, and where his family lived in Spruce Ridge. Pierce had told us his brother was mixed up with bad dudes and needed money. Did he need the cash for drugs? Were the bad dudes drug dealing gangbangers? Quincy wore gang symbols and was a member of the Thunder Knuckles gang. He had to be. Why? Because the gang wanted revenge for Quincy's death. But Demented was after something. What did he want to talk to Clem about?

There were so many questions. Maybe I'm not the best tow truck driver in town, but I'm not too bad at digging around for clues. The gang connection was obvious, and the drug tie-in a strong possibility. But there was likely more to it, and it was time to pursue new leads.

Funny, I never even thought of asking Tanner for help. Or Kristen. Or Axle. You'd think so, but no. Sometimes I bounced ideas off them, but I needed to do this on my own and keep my friends out of harm's way.

It was time to work a shift at Roasters on the Ridge, and I barreled into the coffee shop just before noon. I toed off my heels in exchange for the comfortable sneakers I still kept in a drawer, then whipped the café's black apron embroidered with a swirl of steam over a coffee mug around my waist, nipping it down to ride low on my hips.

Afternoons were typically slow, but there was still plenty that had to be done, so while Kristen counted the inventory, I wiped the shelves, emptied and cleaned the cooler and the ice machine, and straightened the stockroom. The soothing smell of the brew, the serene music, and the uncomplicated work had been my life for seven months before I took on the towing business. The coffee shop was familiar and safe, that is until Zach showed up right before closing, his eyes tight at the corners, looking distressed.

He took a chair with his back to the wall at the table near the window. Kris and I both came out from behind the counter and walked over.

"Guy overdosed last night. He's in the hospital." The Spruce Ridge officer appeared to dislike imparting the news.

"Oh, no." Kristen collapsed into the chair across from Zach. Tears rolled down her cheeks, and I felt sick with concern for my friend whom I'd hardly ever seen cry. She blotted a tear with a napkin. "It's all my fault! I shouldn't have let him go."

"Don't say that. This is not your fault, Kris." I thought Guy was tougher than that. "How did he take it when you fired him?"

"I thought he took it well. I had no clue he would do something crazy. He wrote down the name of my pastor and seemed open to contacting him. I thought we parted on good terms. I've only fired one person before, and that went much worse."

"See, this has nothing to do with you, I'm sure." Zach took her hand.

A couple walked in, so I got up to take their orders. While I pulled the shots and lidded the containers, Zach and Kristen remained at the table, their heads together in close conversation. A call for a tow came in, but Kris needed me at the coffee shop, so I referred the call to

Tanner. After Zach left, Kris went into her closet-sized office to take care of paperwork, or so she said, and I remained stationed behind the counter waiting for the next rush of customers.

I texted the news to Sierra: —*Guy overdosed.*

Sierra called me back right away. "So, is Guy dead?" she asked, her voice wobbly.

"No. No, no, but he's in the hospital and I guess he's stable." I'd overheard Zach tell Kristen as they prayed quietly together for him.

I asked in a near whisper, "Did you know Guy very well? Does he have family?" I wanted assurance he had a support system in place.

"I only know him from Roasters, except…"

"What?" The phone was scrunched to my ear as I wiped down the counter with a rag.

"This isn't a surprise to anyone but Kristen and she should've fired him a long time ago."

"Is that so?" I wasn't the only one who didn't care for him.

"He's been doing drugs for a while. Cocaine."

I gasped and the dirty cup I'd picked up from the counter sloshed and spilled over onto the floor. I cast a look over my shoulder, but Kristen remained in the backroom. I knew she was still upset about Guy. I was, too, actually. "How do you know?" I placed the cup in the sink.

"He had some on him one time and asked me if I wanted any."

"Has he been dealing? Here at Roasters?" I shoved a hand on my hip.

"No, nothing like that. But I know where he gets his narcotics." She gave me the name of a bar off

Industrial Lane. One I'd never visited. There was a reason I'd never been inside that place. I thanked her and hung up.

Three o'clock closing time arrived. After we locked the coffee shop and Kristen left for the bank, I hightailed it upstairs.

The black leather fringed jacket still hung on the hook where Clem had forgotten about it, so I wiggled into my blue jeans and plum-colored cowboy boots and donned the heavy, oversized leather. I finger-combed my hair out of my braid and it tumbled over my shoulders. Should I wear it down more often as Axle suggested? But I couldn't while working at the coffee shop, and it would get in the way if I had to bend over and roll out the dolly wheels from under my tow truck. *So, no.* But, I could right now, though. I added some thick black mascara and big hoop earrings.

It was early for a drink, but the bar opened in the afternoon and was, in fact, open right now. If not too busy at this time of day, perhaps the bartender would agree to answer a few questions.

Despite the cowboy songs that played when I entered the door, the bar customers called to mind the clientele at the Centerpiece Tavern. Bad-mannered brutes competing at pool. Belligerent bitches watching their men.

I took a stool at the counter and asked the man sitting next to me about Guy, but the man didn't know him. The bartender brought me a craft beer, and I asked her about Guy. She didn't know Guy, either. I wandered through the tables with my drink when a tall, handsome dude in a checkered shirt, blue jeans, and cowboy boots asked me to dance.

It was a slow song, the perfect opportunity to talk! I set my beer on a table and he took me in his arms. I asked him if he knew Guy. *Nope*. Did he know Quincy? *Nada*. I asked him if he scored cocaine in this bar. He didn't. But he did say he wanted to score with a freckled redhead.

A strong arm grabbed me around the waist. "She's with me." He spun me around, my chest hitting his in a close embrace.

"Ephraim!" A flash of heat went through my entire body.

He'd left his light blue sheriff's uniform at home and had on cowboy boots, tight jeans with a western belt buckle, and a blue-jean shirt, but he still had his military bearing and straight posture. A can of chewing tobacco wore a circle in his back pocket. I let him lead me around the dance floor, taking in his citrus, jasmine, and musk aftershave.

"Do you come here often?" I asked. Not an original line, but I couldn't come up with a better one.

"No. Do you?"

"No. What did you question Clem about?"

"You know I can't tell you." The song changed. Ephraim, the cowboy Casanova, smoothly led me into a two-step. "I saw your Fiat parked outside. This is a known hangout for people who want to purchase illegal drugs."

"You're joking." I acted all *Miss Innocent*.

"What are you doing here by yourself?"

"I like to dance."

He twirled me around. "Anytime you want to dance, you call me."

"Just when I want to dance?" My heart pounded

and I was short of breath.

"What else would you like to do?"

"Talk about Clem. What'd you want with her?"

"Delaney, please quit trying to investigate."

"All right. I'm busted. You want to get out of this place?" I smiled up at him.

He held my hand as we went out the door. I hoped my palms weren't sweating.

I asked, "Meet me at Roasters? The coffee shop's closed, but I have a key."

"See you there." He clambered into his pickup, not the sheriff's vehicle, but a black F250, rear-wheel drive.

It was still early evening, so after I unlocked and we went in, I made espressos and we sat at my favorite table near the front window. I hung the leather jacket on the back of my chair, thinking he might ask me about the cowboy bar some more, but he didn't. He asked, "Are you still seeing Tanner Utley?"

"Yes, but I don't think he's speaking to me at the moment."

"What happened?"

"I took him to meet my mother. It didn't go well."

He chuckled. "My mama would love you."

I flushed warm, the tip of my nose red, as I took a sip of my coffee. "I should mention Tanner's the jealous type." I sneaked a glance out the window as if he were watching us through the glass. My eyes went back to the handsome sheriff with the thick dark hair and tantalizing brown eyes and lashes. "I feel so young next to you, talking about jealous boyfriends. It's silly."

"Does my age bother you? I'm thirty-nine."

"No. I'm twenty-eight. I know you're divorced." I blushed even more. This hot guy probably thinks I'd been checking up on him.

"I've been divorced for eight years."

"How long were you married?"

"Four years. Law enforcement is hard on marriage."

"I heard that. Zach told me all about how police and paramedics get PTSD from seeing all that violence…like homicides."

"The worst are the car accidents on the mountain roads in winter. Spruce Ridge doesn't have that much crime, let alone homicides."

"It doesn't feel like that lately." I wound a red curl around my finger.

He scooted my chair closer to his with the toe of his cowboy boot, causing my body to press against the back of the chair. "If Tanner ever singles you up, let me know." He gazed into my eyes with an intense look.

Yeah, what was going on with Tanner? He so easily ignored me, he didn't want me to meet his family, and maybe he was more important to me than I was to him. Feeling disloyal, I gave myself a mental shake.

I hadn't learned a thing at the cowboy bar, but maybe the sheriff could help with that. "Ephraim, do you know who Demented is? He's with the Thunder Knuckles gang."

"Yes, why?"

"He showed up here, like he was nosing around for something."

His dark brown eyes went a shade darker and his hands formed into fists on the tabletop. "What did he want?"

"I never found out. He left right after I arrived, but

Axle spoke to him." Now I felt bad, *sic'ing* Ephraim on my lil' cuz'. Not what I intended. "You said if I saw anyone with tattoos or earrings to let you know. Well, Demented had on all kinds of gang symbols, plus I had a customer who was wearing those same lightning bolt earrings." I got out my cell to scroll through and find his name and address.

"Someone from the coffee shop?"

"No, someone I met on a tow. I'm texting you his contact info."

He checked his phone for receipt of my text and stood to leave like he had somewhere to go in a hurry, all serious now. I grabbed my jacket and purse before following him to the door and locking it behind us.

****

Tanner must have decided not to single me up, because he came by the coffee shop the next morning. So many customers waited for drinks that we could only exchange a few words. He appreciated the referral I'd sent his way and I assured him I was still covering the towaway zones that night. After I gave him a vanilla frappé on the house, he left to go out on a tow.

Once the customer line emptied, Kristen said, "The video game tournament is this Saturday. They chose our place after all. Will you be able to help me? We're going to be swamped."

I rubbed her back. "Of course. Remember, I said I would." The tournament would make up for the loss from the theft. "So, you doing better?"

"I am a little bit. You can leave now if you want, Delaney. We won't have another rush today, and Lord knows you need to rest before you have to monitor the towaway zones tonight."

"Thanks, I think I will head out in a minute. I need to walk the dog."

Kris prepared a batch of coffee beans for the roaster, so I finished wiping down the espresso machine and looked around for anything else I could do before leaving.

"I've been meaning to ask, I haven't seen Clem around lately." Kris pressed a button on the roaster and the popping sound of the beans began to accompany the quiet jazz music playing over the speakers.

I hung up a damp rag. "Oh yeah, you don't know the latest. She's moved in with Demented."

My friend's eyes went to the ceiling. "Who?"

"One of the Thunder Knuckles gang." I made a *gag-me* face.

Kristen puckered her mouth in agreement. "Oh, that's too bad."

She went to load the dishwasher while I exchanged my sneakers for my street shoes. I grabbed my purse, ready to take off. When I came out from the office into the kitchen, Kristen straightened herself up to a stand, one hand against the small of her back, the other rubbing her forehead.

I jolted to a stop. "What's the matter?"

"Now the dishwasher's broken." Kristen was *way* calmer than I would have been.

"Oh, no! Are you sure?" I bent to examine the controls. The button panel flashed and water pooled on the floor. "Uh-oh." We gave each other panicked looks.

Kristen scanned her phone for an appliance repairman, while I put my sneakers and apron back on. I carried the dirty cups and plates from the broken dishwasher to the industrial-sized sink and filled the tub with hot water. I squeezed the sprayer to create a layer of suds and submerged the dirty silverware.

Kris came bustling back. "The soonest I can get a repairman here is next week and if he has to order a part the repair will take even longer."

"It'll be okay. So what, we have to wash the dishes by hand? We can do it." I plunged my arms in the water up to my elbows to prove my point. This was not a good time, though, with the tournament coming up.

"You're right, but I'm short-staffed."

"I'll call Axle."

"To wash dishes?"

"No." He was not that much help in the kitchen, as I knew all too well. "He can fix anything. He's very mechanical. Don't you know that about your own cousin?"

"That's right, he is." Her voice rang with hope.

I wiped my wet hands on a towel, then got Axle on the line. "Kristen's dishwasher broke at the coffee shop. Can you check it out? She can't get a repairman until next week."

Axle said he would come down, but his voice sounded flat. Maybe if Axle helped his cousin, that would take his mind off his own problems.

Kristen turned the "Open" sign to "Closed" at the same time Axle came through the employee entrance. Following behind him and excited to be allowed in, the Rottweiler waggled his tail every-which-way.

I asked, "Did you take your dog for a walk? I was going to do that."

"Yeah, I took care of it. I let Boss loose in the parking lot for a minute."

Kristen said to Axle, "You fix this and I'll buy you

a steak dinner."

I said, "*I* never got a steak dinner."

Kristen pointed to me then up toward the ceiling. "You need to take that dog upstairs."

"All right." I grabbed the Rottweiler by his collar and pushed his heavy body through the door. I led Boss over to the park and threw him a tennis ball for fifteen minutes. A trip around the parking lot with Axle wasn't much of a walk for the big guy. He could've played for longer, but my arm became tired. The two of us returned home and plopped together on the couch. Not too much time passed before Axle came through the door.

"Well, is it fixed?"

"No. Needs a drain pump. I ordered one." The few words he spoke were lackluster. We all seemed to be in a funk, including Kristen, the most upbeat person I knew.

I asked, "You want to ride along with me tonight?"

"Is it Tuesday?" Axle scanned his phone. "Clem's been gone two days. I hope she's okay."

"The Clems of this world know how to take care of themselves," I assured him. "Let's grab some dinner, my treat."

We drove through the fast-food place for chili dogs, not steak, but our favorite dinner, and milkshakes which we quickly devoured. Then we cruised through the alleys behind Main Street. The aroma of sautéed onions and French fries coming from the back of the brewery tickled our noses. The kitchen smells attracted scavengers, and the harsh *wock-a-wock* cry of the magpie came in through our open windows as the birds picked around the dumpsters.

A Mini Cooper, red, two-door convertible, with the Union Jack printed on the vinyl roof, front-wheel drive, blocked the loading dock. "Oh, no." I pointed to the car, one that I'd seen parked here illegally before.

"Let's tow it!" Axle was all for making off with the convertible.

"We'll double back in ten minutes. Let's give the driver a chance to move the car." I circled a few blocks and turned back into the alley just as the young driver, looking like one of the blonde rich kids in this upscale town, pulled out. I whirled down my window and shook my finger at her. "I've seen your car parked here before. Next time I catch you, I'll have to tow you."

"Sorry. Won't happen again." Her eyes went to my name on the door. "I know you could've towed me before and you didn't. Hey, read your reviews." She sped off with a wave and a beep of the horn, and I hit the gas to proceed down the alley.

Axle thumbed his phone and found this on the internet: *Tow truck drivers can be nice people, too, like Del's Towing. If you need a tow, call Del. Signed, Coop.* "That's her."

"A good review won't keep me from towing her Mini Cooper if she does this again." I spoke big but was all bluster, secretly pleased.

"You're such a car shark," Axle teased. "Here's another one...oh, never mind."

"What? What does it say?"

"Nothing."

"You can tell me. I'm a big girl."

"No, you don't want to know."

I stood on the brakes and we lurched to a stop. "Give me that." I snatched the phone out of his fingers before he had time to react. I read the review: *Delaney is one incompetent tower but she's tits on wheels...check out her shoes.*

I tossed the cell back in his lap. "Whatever. Doesn't bother me in the least."

Note to self: figure out how to get reviews taken down. And this reviewer blocked! I'd had some abusive comments in the past and still hadn't learned how to get them removed.

Axle said to me, "Yeah, don't worry about it. You da' tow queen."

I squealed my self-loader out onto Main Street, putting the jerk reviewer out of my mind, then made the towaway zone circuit one more time. "Axle, remember when we saw Quincy's mother on television asking for information?"

"What about it?"

"I wonder if anyone's called that hotline. She might have received some news."

"How are you going to find out?"

"I know where she lives." I added, "Maybe she's heard from Clem."

"All right, let's go." Axle thumped the dash.

I turned the truck around to head up the canyon. *I know, I know*, I was supposed to be working, but we could zip over and back in a matter of minutes. But once we arrived, I had reservations. What if she didn't want to talk to us, complete strangers trying to horn in when she was grieving? I sat there with my hand on the keys, but didn't switch off the ignition.

Axle said, "What's the matter?"

I waved my palm. "Give me a second."

He nudged my arm. "Come on. We're here. We

might as well see if anyone's home."

I turned off the motor. "Okay, fine." I hitched my bag onto my shoulder and followed the curved sidewalk up to the wide porch of the Spanish-style house, the red roof tiles sparkling in the slanting evening sun, Axle shuffling along behind me.

I rang the bell and Pierce answered the door. This time his shirt read, "Born to Frag." Axle had on a tee with a skull-and-crossbones and the name of a popular band, "Badflower." Kittens and hearts embellished my powder blue, stretchy top.

"I remember you." Pierce craned his neck to scope out behind me. "Where's Clemmy?"

Axle said with a hitch in his voice, "She's gone."

"Pierce, is your mom at home?"

"Yeah, come on in."

We followed him through a massive foyer to a kitchen with a double island showcasing miles of granite countertop, a gourmet oven, and a wall of windows with striking views of virgin forest and snow-draped peaks. The air smelled like a mix of carnations and overripe bananas from fruit baskets. Quincy's mom stood at the sink staring absently out a window.

She turned and gave me the false smile one gives strangers.

Maybe now we'll get some answers, but I needed to tread carefully.

Chapter 14

"I'm sorry for your loss." I held out my hand. "I'm Delaney Morran and this is my cousin, Axle Guttenberg." I didn't bother to explain we weren't really cousins. Too much information…and who cared? "I was the one who found your son."

The wooden smile on her face crumbled and she reached for a stool to sit down. Middle-aged and thin, her bones stood out, making her appear gaunt along with grief-stricken.

Pierce said, "Mom, you okay?"

She gave a stiff nod.

He asked, "Where's Dad?"

"With a client," she answered, before turning back to me. "My husband wouldn't let me view my son's body. But you saw him, right?"

"Yes."

Her eyes sharpened and she appeared suddenly eager. "The police didn't give us any details. Tell me, did he suffer?"

Pierce stood in the doorway resting one hand on either side of the frame. "Mom, why do you want to ask that?"

"I want to know what happened in his last moments." Her face showed conflicting emotions…hope, fear, and shame. Nothing is worse than what we can imagine, so I'd bet she'd been thinking about this every second of every day.

I blinked a few times and took one or two breaths to compose myself. "I don't think he suffered." I was sure with those injuries he died instantly, but I didn't say so.

She pressed, "Was it bad?"

How do you respond to that? "Um, this has to be extremely difficult for you." I pretended to study the view out the window while tears gathered in the back of my throat. Swallowing hard, I asked, "Did anyone call the hotline?"

"The police told me there have been calls, but no new leads." She gave me a droopy-eyed look, her eyes full of pain. "Why do you want to know?"

"Your son's death has upset me, so I can't even conceive how you feel. I thought if his killer was caught and we could get justice for Quincy, it would help. Maybe help both of us."

"You're upset?"

"I've been having nightmares," I admitted. "I'm sure you're having a hard time sleeping, too."

I felt Axle's gaze on me, but couldn't take my eyes away from the grieving mother.

Quincy's mom covered her face with her hands for an uncomfortable moment, then dropped her fists to her lap. "You're absolutely right, my son needs justice."

Somehow, I made myself ask, "Did Quincy talk to you about any problems he was having? Something he was worried about? Anyone threatening him?"

Her arms crossed in front her, hugging herself against the horror, and she stared off in the distance before answering. "He called here that night, said he was stopping by, didn't he, Pierce?" She turned to her younger son for support. He nodded, sucking his lips in until they disappeared.

I studied Pierce's expression. "I thought you said you didn't know where Quincy was headed."

He shrugged. "He said he was coming here, but who knows?"

His mom said, "We expected him, but he never showed up." She started to sob, putting the brakes on further conversation. I felt at a loss as to what more to say, anyway.

The sky faded to dark outside the windows, reminding me I needed to get back to work. I addressed Pierce, "Did you find Clem's ring?"

"No, I didn't." He placed his hand on his mother's back. "Mom, Clem asked about some ring she says Quincy gave her. Have you seen it?"

His mom's head snapped up. "I'm sure he never gave her a ring. Clem's nothing but a gold digger and a thief."

"No, Mom. Clem's not like that." Pierce gave me a head-shake and held up a hand as if to say *we're done here*. I backed away and knocked into Axle, who felt like a rock wall, stretched tight, tense, behind me.

Pierce said, "Come on." He hurried toward the door, I followed him, and Axle brought up the rear.

I stopped at the threshold and peered over Pierce's shoulder to make sure his mom wasn't anywhere close. I lowered my voice to ask, "Was your brother involved in drugs?" Bad taste, I know, but when would I get another chance to question him? "The reason I'm asking, we're worried about Clem. Axle and I are." I flapped a hand between Axle and me while Axle gave me a sharp look.

Pierce blinked and darted a glance around. "It's possible he was."

Bingo. Some real information. "You told me before that Quincy was having money troubles?"

Pierce's jaw tightened and he bristled. "He was always hitting Mom up for cash, but please don't ask her about it." The tone of his voice sounded resentful as he threw open the door. "If you see Clem, tell her the funeral is tomorrow. Tell her I'd like to talk to her, would you?" He had that familiar wistful look in his eyes.

There was only one mortuary in Spruce Ridge, so I asked, "Is it at Mountain View Funeral Parlor?"

"Just a graveside service at the cemetery right next to the mortuary. Closed casket. Ten in the morning."

"Thanks, Pierce." I stepped onto the porch but glanced back. "Are you going to be at the video game tournament on Saturday?"

"I planned on it."

I wouldn't judge him. The teen was young and self-centered. Too immature to realize the total import of death, even though this was the death of his brother. He might also be trying to distract himself, with all that noise and social interaction.

"See you then." I retreated to my truck, Axle tracing my steps. Once inside with our seatbelts fastened, I turned toward him. "You were quiet in there."

"Nothing to say." He unwound the earbuds attached to his cellphone.

"Do you want to text Clem about the funeral?"

His face lit up. "All right." His thumbs flew over the screen, then he popped the buds in his ears, but he pulled one out to ask me, "You've been having nightmares?"

Last night Quincy had chased me through a lightning storm, shouting, "Help me!" I wanted to help him, but I couldn't stop, I had to keep moving. I kept running and the thunderbolts and flashes would not cease, and I found myself thrashing around, my legs tangled in the blankets.

A lump in my throat refused to budge, and I croaked out, "Zach said it's like a post-traumatic thing from seeing a dead body, you know? It'll pass." Axle had enough on his mind, so I didn't go into details. I didn't want to sound like a little kid afraid of the dark. Which I totally did feel like.

I turned the truck out from the noisy gravel driveway onto the smooth blacktop and the tires went silent. Even if my towing business turned into a huge success, what peace would I have? I'd witnessed the aftermath of a violent crime. Would I be subjected to even more gruesome situations down the road? Accident scenes? Deadly disasters? I knew the best way to get over this brutal death was closure. But what about the next time? And the time after that?

We returned to the alley behind the brewery, and while I was tempted to duck inside for a cold one, I idled the truck beside a Chevy Bolt, front-wheel drive, that blocked a cargo bay. A glance at my watch reminded me a regular delivery of kegs was about to arrive, and here someone had planted the Chevy's nose against the dock. I needed to capture the front wheels the truck couldn't reach, not the exposed rear wheels the truck could reach. Axle and I gave each other a silent stare.

"I should ask Tanner how he hooks up vehicles that are parked like this." I tapped the bottom of my chin. "I've seen *YouTube* videos showing how to capture the front wheels from the side with a Fulcan Xtruder like mine, but I've never done it that way. I've only used the claws from the front or the rear."

Axle offered me a palms-up shrug.

After climbing out, I stood back and gave it a long thought, but I'd simply have to pull the car away from the building by the rear wheels until I could grab a hold from the front. I hustled to my truck just as a man started around the side of the building. He quickly stepped out of sight.

A moment later he popped back out with a ski mask covering his face. The masked man stomped toward his car, while I remained frozen in place. He plowed right into me, pushing me to the side, and I stepped down funny on my left foot. *Ouch.*

Axle slammed the truck door and stormed over with clenched fists. "You *asshat*." He shoved the masked man up against his Chevy Bolt. "You're one rude dude."

The tip of my nose flamed red with anger. "We can find your name and address from your license plate. Or from the VIN." I don't know why I thought it important to tell him that. The dummy had to know we could ID him through his vehicle registration.

Brilliant, huh?

He raised his hands in the air. "I just want to get in my car and leave."

Axle squinted at me. "Your decision."

Technically, if I hadn't yet hooked up the vehicle, he was entitled to do just that. I pointed my finger at him. "I could have you arrested for assault. That's a criminal offense, a felony. You'd end up in jail." I tugged at Axle's arm and he released the man, but not before he snatched off his mask. The three of us went into a stare-down.

"I'll let you go this time. Don't ever let me catch you here again." My voice had gotten high and loud. "I'd better not see you near these loading docks, ever," I added with a confidence I didn't feel.

Axle took a few paces back, and the man leaped into his car, reversed out, and sped away. Axle and I wrenched open the truck doors and swung ourselves up into the cab. I started up the motor and revved the engine.

"Delaney, he pushed you. We could've called the cops on him."

"I need to be able to do the job without help from the police. They'll take me off the city rotation if they think I can't protect myself." That reminded me I still needed to get in touch with Code Enforcement since they'd never called me back. All the city jobs were going to the green tow truck driver. "And I'm not sure I could prove actual assault. Plus, you pushed him back and I kinda threatened him...so let's just let it go."

"Are you hurt?"

"Nah." My left ankle throbbed, but that would go away.

"Why don't you buy a flatbed? Then you won't have to figure out how to position the truck in front of the car." My self-loader was the type without a winch.

"Front-loaders like mine are supposed to be safer. If I'd known how to grab from the side, I wouldn't've needed to get out of the truck." That, and if everything lined up just right, including all the stars in the sky and all the luck in the galaxy. Those old doubts came back, making themselves heard. Was I tough enough for this job? That nasty reviewer had called me incompetent.

"Look up his name and address like you said. I can show up at his house with a few friends and rough him up." He raised his hands in a boxing posture. "We shouldn't have let him get away so easily."

I wasn't sure if Axle was teasing this time or not. I lifted my palms in mock surrender and sang, "No, no! Please don't hurt him, Axle."

We both lowered our hands.

I said, "Well, it was worth bringing you along just to hear the names you called him. *Asshat*? Rude dude?"

He gave me a sober once over. "I'm glad I was here. Hey, if we're done, can you drop me off at the trailer park? I'm going to meet up with some people."

I'd already put my truck in gear, so I hit the brakes. "You aren't serious about ganging up on that masked guy, right?"

"No, course not." He twirled his hand in a *speed-it-up, let's-go* gesture.

I pointed the truck in the direction of the mobile home park. "I worry about you, Axle. Are you going to be okay?" His friends at the trailer court were mechanics who had been involved in an illegal chop shop. Sketchy guys I didn't want Axle to hang around with, but it was his life, his decision.

"I'm over Clem. I'm fine." He was slightly hunched, seeming tired and depressed to me. I'd forgotten all about her, wrapped up as I was in the moment. But now that I did think about her, I didn't really believe him. So, I had two things to torment me when it came to Axle. His friends. And Clem.

There was so much to worry about, including rude dudes like the masked man. What an idiot. But, I had to laugh at myself, too. I may be a *badass* tow truck driver, but if I did see that man again I'd do nothing! *Nada. Zero. Zilch.* Just being honest.

****

The four-inch black stilettos were not the best choice for a graveside ceremony in the wet spring grass with a sprained left ankle. But they went well with my black skirt and black raincoat.

Axle dressed for the occasion in all black, too— baggy black jeans, a heavy metal band tee-shirt, and a trench coat a few sizes too large that he'd borrowed from Byron. We both wore dark shades. The raincoat disguises were overkill, but not the sunglasses since a bright sun greeted the morning.

The Davidsens seemed to have a lot of friends and relatives, all arriving in nice cars. Represented were Lexus, Maserati, Land Rover, Jaguar, and BMW. I stared hard at the BMW, then scanned the mourners' faces, searching for the realtor. I'd once tried to repossess a vehicle at a funeral, an unlikely time to do it, but I had to take what opportunities came my way. I didn't spot the BMW owner, though.

The service started. A young pastor, dressed in black pants and black shirt with a white clerical collar, read the liturgy in front of the closed casket. I watched Quincy's parents. His stepdad supported his mom with a hand on her back while she quietly sobbed. Her tears made my eyes water and I brushed them away. Pierce stayed subdued in a dark suit on his thin frame. Clem didn't show up. Neither did anyone who gave the impression he belonged to a gang or dealt drugs.

The pastor announced that refreshments would be served at the Davidsens' home, and everyone picked their way across the grass toward their cars. I limped a little, trying to keep the weight off my injured left foot as I stepped in line behind the Davidsens.

Mrs. Davidsen glared at Pierce. "You are, too, coming to the reception."

"Do I have to?" His back stiffened under his suitcoat. "I can't believe you didn't want Clem to come."

"She's a terrible person, Pierce. Greg, talk to your son." Her eyes were glued to the ground as she avoided rows of flat grave markers.

His dad slung his arm around his son's shoulders and their heads gravitated together. See, that's what dads did, gave their sons manly hugs. My dad would probably have done the same. Greg spoke in an undertone and Pierce nodded, then the three of them disappeared into a black limo.

Axle and I folded ourselves into my car, and the Fiat came to life when I turned the key. "You want to go to Davidsen's house?"

"No, I'm with Pierce on that one. Besides, I should get to work."

"Okey-dokey." After stopping at home so we could change clothes, I dropped Axle off at Byron's autobody shop, unlocked my truck, and heaved myself up into the cab.

Death was hard to think about on a superb spring day like today. To me, everything seemed vibrant.

The striking snow-topped peaks were truly majestic, with sturdy pine trees and graceful aspens swaying in the breeze. Two women zipped by on their mountain bikes. Runners in jogging gear, moms pushing strollers, and teens chatting together crowded the sidewalks. My beautiful red tow truck was mighty fine and life was good. I felt grateful to be alive.

But it was a strange feeling. Death happened, yet life went on.

The graveside ceremony reminded me I hadn't checked on the Impreza in a while, so I drove over to Tanner's storage lot. I could see Tanner from a block away, messing with the tailboard chains on the back of his flatbed. I was a little nervous about running into him. We hadn't really cleared the air and I'd only seen him once at the coffee shop since last Saturday night at my folks'.

While still halfway down the street, I spotted Hailey walking around Tanner's flatbed. She ran her hand down Tanner's arm in a familiar way.

What the…?

A spike of jealousy cut through my heart. Hailey was beautiful, her dark bronze skin perfect, her short, coal-black hair setting off her high cheekbones. She had large, almost-black, eyes and long curly eyelashes to die for. Her tight jeans and sweater made her come off as younger than when she wore her usual skirt and jacket at Friendly Finance.

I shook myself. Her hand on Tanner's arm meant nothing. They had a working relationship, that's all. Tanner captured repos for Hailey. She was only giving him an encouraging caress—*er*, pat—on the arm. I was getting all paranoid because of that time when Clem hit on Tanner.

My right front tire scraped against the curb when I

pulled into the lot. *Shoot.* So much for me passing as professional. Hailey and Tanner kept talking while I remained in the cab. Should I simply leave? Or have a look at the Impreza as I'd intended? Have a look.

I threw open my door and slithered down to the ground, being careful of my ankle.

Hailey spoke a couple more imperceptible words to Tanner, then turned in my direction to give me a wave. "Hey, Delaney. Good to see you." I waved back. She strode over to a red Saab, got in, and took off.

After I did a quick walk-around of the Impreza while avoiding the windows, I made my way over to Tanner. He smiled at me, so I asked him, "Are you busy?"

"Just finished a repo for Hailey. What's wrong with your ankle?"

I'd exchanged my funeral dress for a pair of jeans but still had on the black stilettos. I pointed my toe and stretched my foot around in a circle. *Ouch!* "On-the-job injury. I should make a worker's comp claim with my boss," I joked.

"You're crazy for wearing those shoes. How'd you get hurt?" He wrapped an arm around my shoulder and hugged me to his chest.

I leaned my head against Tanner and felt his heart pulsing against my forehead. "Stepped wrong." I angled backward and gazed up at him. "Hey, I haven't seen you much lately. Everything okay?"

"Sure." He rubbed my back. "How's work going?"

"I have a question and you're just the person to ask. I know that I can grab the tires from the side of a vehicle with my self-loader truck, but I'm not sure how. Can you show me?"

"Sure." He gave me a quick squeeze, then let go. "It's not too different from what you're doing now." He went into teacher mode. "You need to be more parallel to the target vehicle so the wheel cradles can contact the tires from the side. The only difference is the claws slide under the vehicle laterally and pull the car out that way. You can even pluck a car right out from a tight parking spot between two other vehicles."

He directed me over to a Nissan Altima, front-wheel drive, stored in the back corner of his lot. "Stand back. Don't let your feet anywhere near the lifts."

I shuffled farther away, my eyes glued to the smooth performance by the experienced tow man. Tanner's ability with the truck made him even more attractive than ever. Next, it was my turn. I tried the side-extraction while Tanner watched.

He said, "Move your bumper closer…no, too close. Now you're too far."

When I finally captured the Nissan's tires from the awkward position and managed to get the whole front end up on the hydraulic lift, I was jackknifed. But I got it straightened out and released the Nissan down to the ground.

Tanner leaned in my window while I admired his good looks and competent moves. Tow moves, I mean. His sky-blue eyes stared into my soul. Having this easy-on-the-eyes man helping me was a bonus on this job.

"I'm sorry dinner with my parents turned into such a disaster, Tanner." I gave him a weak smile, still wanting to make sure there was nothing sour between us.

"No, it was me, not you." He laughed, so I did, too. He said, "I'm cautious about meeting family. I'm very protective of my little brother and sister, ever since they got close to my last girlfriend, and then she dumped me. She never said goodbye to them and they were hurt, maybe even more than me."

"I understand, but I would never do that." What more could I say? He wasn't ready for the *Brady Bunch meet and greet*, and maybe I wasn't either. My eyes drew to his muscular arms, but his tattoos were hidden under a long-sleeved tee-shirt. "When are you going to show me your new ink?"

"Do you have a couple of hours?"

"It'll take that long?"

Tanner leaned forward into my space, a naughty expression on his face. "I can make it last."

My heart rate quadrupled. I fanned my face and labored to breathe.

Tanner's phone chimed, so he picked up the call. He said to me, "I need to get going."

Yet another interruption! "Way to get out of it, Tanner. Nice try, but this isn't over."

"You're right." He flashed me his sexy grin, before half-trotting to his flatbed. He wheeled his truck out of the lot and disappeared down the street. An experienced tow man like Tanner was constantly busy on tows. I wasn't at that level yet.

Was Tanner just a flirt, toying with me? Perhaps he wasn't serious about me. Intense about work, absolutely, but not about me. He gave some pretty good reasons for keeping his family life separate for now, which I got, but despite that I still had doubts he was all-in.

I sent Kristen a text seeking her opinion on the conversation and included a pouty cat face emoji. She sent me a surprised face back. She must agree with me. I wasn't important enough to meet *The Fam*.

Chapter 15

I sailed down Main Street toward Pine, past the Spruce Ridge Police Station, radio blasting, brooding over my boyfriend, when I sighted the drug dealer coming out of the city building housing the police department.

Clem walked next to him. And she wore my yellow suede heels with bows!

At least, they resembled mine, and I realized I hadn't seen that pair in my closet for a while. I found a parking place and nosed into it, my right front tire bumping against the curb—again!—and sat there with the engine idling and my mind stewing about those shoes. Maybe Clem didn't *steal* them, maybe she *borrowed* them without letting me know. After all, I still had her leather jacket, although she'd given me permission to wear it.

I beat my forehead with the palm of my hand. I should get a grip on what's important here. Clem was with that drug dealer. And she'd claimed she didn't know him when I showed her his picture. The one I'd taken at Roasters on the Ridge of the suspicious encounter that looked to me like a drug deal. This had to be an epic clue.

They had almost reached my truck, so I threw the gear into park and got out. I hollered, "Clem!"

The traffic noise drowned out my words as the

couple kept going, jaywalking across Main Street. I limped to the corner to cross over, my right foot in the stiletto landing solid, my left foot quick-hopping, but by the time I'd caught up, they'd nipped inside a Chevy Malibu, front-wheel drive—formerly rear-wheel, but current models are front-wheel—and sped off.

Wasn't Clem with Demented? Or was she with that drug dealer now?

Neither was a good choice, and I felt for Axle.

My shift was about to start, so I headed to the coffee shop.

As soon as I walked into Roasters, I said to Kristen, "Looks like you've been busy." I could tell from the state of her apron and the spills in the workspace that they'd had nothing but rushes. I felt bad, even though I'd arrived at the time she'd asked me to.

She answered, "It's all good," as I hurried to tie on one of the store aprons.

I waited on the office workers and sales clerks here for their afternoon breaks. After the line disappeared, I wiped down tables, stopping to chat with one of our regulars, Rory Rearden, whom I always teased about his hard-to-say name. I hadn't had a chance to show him Quincy's picture before now, so I whisked my phone out of my pocket. "You recognize this guy?"

He nodded and leaned back in his chair. "Went to high school together, but I'd lost track of him. I read about the shooting in the papers." Rory pointed his finger at me. "How did you know him, Delaney?"

"Long story. Small town. What was he like in school?"

"A stoner. Had a little brother who was a nerd.

They hated each other, but actually I think they were step-kids. Different mothers or fathers or something." He rubbed his chin.

"*Reeally*." I stretched out the word. "They hated each other?"

"Yes. And Quincy ran away from home a couple of times. He'd be missing from school for a bit. He hid out with a friend of mine, that's how I heard about it. I wonder how he ended up dead on County Road 6, though, ya' know? How in the world did he end up getting killed?"

"It's terrible, right?" I wasn't ready to go over the scene details again, even with one of Kristen's regular customers. "Did you ever hear why he disliked his brother so much?

He shook his head. "No idea. Sad he died, though. Jeez, someone I went to school with, dead. Weird, you know?"

"I do know." My eyes threatened to water. "Too young, I agree. I need to get back to work. Take care, Rory." Three men had come in and stood at the counter to order.

Soon it was time to close. Kristen left to make the deposit, and I swabbed the tables and chairs with vinegar water and washed the windows. I locked up behind me, tossed the garbage into the dumpster, and jumped in the truck to pick up Axle.

I was worried about the teen. Was he doing better? Still down in the dumps? I knew what it felt like to be stuck in the blues, and he was still at the age when emotions were hard to control. He probably hadn't yet learned how to ride the wave.

When I arrived, my little cuz' was finishing up a

paint job, so I went inside the office to visit with Byron. "Hey, Old Man. What's up?"

He rubbed his fingers on a red rag and asked in a serious tone, "Any news on the police investigation?"

"Nothing. *Bupkus*." I wagged my finger from side-to-side. "And you mean *our* investigation."

"What do you mean, *our* investigation? I thought you were goin' to drop it after I went with you to the tavern. You aren't still investigating, are you? You haven't been back to the tavern, or done any more nosin' around, or anything else risky, have you?" A formidable look crossed his face.

"No, of course not."

"All right, then."

It wasn't the best lie I ever told but he bought it.

He leaned on his elbows. "I might have some info for ya', but you have to promise me something before I tell ya'. Promise you won't go running around trying to figure out what it all means. It's not much. Just a little info."

I plopped onto the stool in front of his service counter. "What is it? Come on, you should've led with this."

He hesitated and his eyes bulged out. "Promise."

"Yes, yes. I promise."

"All right, then. The bartender called from Centerpiece Tavern."

"What did he say?" My words came out high and eager.

"He wanted ta' know if they caught the murderer yet. He says the gang's still askin' around, and there's a hit on the killer."

Prickles of alarm went up my spine. "What! A hit?

What do you mean?" I was afraid I knew what he meant.

"Gangs have their own way a' meting out justice."

We both thought about that for a second. I asked, "How'd he know your number?"

"I gave it to him. Told him ta' call me if he found out anythin'."

"Was that wise? Aren't you concerned he knows who you are?"

"Nah." He shook his big head.

He may not be worried, but I was scared out of my wits thinking about that rough crowd. "If a guy has a teardrop tattoo, does that represent a kill?"

"You referrin' to the man playin' pool?"

"Yes."

"It can mean a couple a things. In prison, it can have a whole lotta' meanings and one of 'em is that he killed somebody. Or it can mean one of his friends was murdered and he's seeking revenge."

"Which do you think it is?"

"Hard ta' say."

I blurted out, "I ran into one of the gang members, Lance Palmero, and his nickname is Demented. Can you believe that?"

Byron's face went stiff. "What'd he want with you?"

"Nothing that I know of. He only wanted to talk to Clem." I patted Byron's hand. "It's all good. He left right away. Did Axle mention to you Clem's moved out of our apartment? Since she's gone, I doubt he'll come back." I hoped!

Byron said, "Shhhh, quiet, here comes Shannon." His niece strolled inside and a guilty feeling washed over me. I'd put Byron in a situation he wanted to keep from his family. He'd never want them to know he'd been to a bar.

I said, "Hey, Shay!"

"How are ya, Delaney?" Shannon deposited her pocketbook behind the counter and gave Byron a quick hug. "And how are you, Old Man?"

"Good, good, just fine."

Right then Axle banged through the door. "I'm ready to go." He skidded to a stop when he spotted Byron's niece.

I jumped off the stool, favoring my left ankle, holding my truck keys in my hand, but Byron waved Axle over to the computer. "There's two appointments for collision repair double-booked at the same time tomorrow." Byron clicked on the mouse, and they both reviewed the screen with their foreheads scrunched up.

"Shannon." I tugged on her sleeve. "Have you seen that green tow truck again? Remember him? The guy with the long beard?"

"Sure. He's all over the place. He's been here, asking the Old Man for work."

I sucked in a deep breath and the tip of my nose turned red. "What did Byron tell him?"

"Don't worry. My uncle would never give tow work to anybody but you."

"I'm not worried." Now I just had to repeat that to myself, like a thousand more times.

"No kidding? You're not freakin' out?"

I tried to relax my face. "No. Byron never told me the guy had been around here."

"Uncle Byron didn't want to say anything."

Axle sidled up to me, evidently having resolved the

schedule. "Ready?"

I said, "See ya' later, Old Man, Shannon," as we headed out, my mind still stuck on the green tower, Owen, the *buttinsky*. The city was sending all the car hauling business his way. Did he have to go after Byron's business, too?

I asked, as we buckled our seatbelts, "So Axle, are you any closer to getting your driver's license back?" I couldn't quit with the big sister routine.

"I sent in the money for reinstatement, just waiting to hear."

"Oh, gosh, soon then." On the one hand it'd be nice not to have to ferry him around town, but on the other hand I'd miss our car time together. "You have something to drive?"

"Nah, I sold my car to pay the fine when I lost my license. But I'm looking around for new wheels." Axle tapped on his cell phone. "Let's search for that BMW."

"You want to help me find the repo?"

"Don't have anything else to do." He seemed deflated, so I decided not to mention seeing Clem with the drug dealer. I loved to tease Axle, but not to put salt on the wound. I needed reinforcement to cheer him up, someone who would know what to say. "Call Kristen for me, would you? Ask if she wants to do a little surveillance with us tonight?"

Axle called his cousin and we drove by the apartment to pick her up, then set out for the fast-food place for burgers and shakes. *Yes, again!* After picking up bags of food, I parked half a block down the street from the realtor's house, but my red tow truck with "Del's Towing" and the drawing of a black stiletto on the door was hard to hide. I should've thought of that when I asked Byron to give my truck a new paint job. We unwrapped our burgers and dug in, the sweet and tangy smell of onions and mustard filling the cab.

Kristen leaned her head back against the headrest. "Whew. Long days lately."

"Are you going to hire somebody to replace Guy?"

"Working on it."

"How's he doing anyway? Heard anything?"

"He's still in the hospital. I went to see him, and he promised to go back to his AA meetings." She sat up straighter and took a slurp of her shake. "Hey, you haven't said anything for a while now about the Quincy Davidsen case. What's up with that?"

Axle snorted. "Case? Like you're detectives."

I gave him a shoulder bump. "I've solved a murder before, but don't say a word to Byron. He's not to know we're investigating." I'd decided that was for the best.

"You're just trying to get it on with Sheriff Lopez. Pass me a napkin."

"Whaa?" I gave him a bug-eyed look.

"Come on, you want to do the *cha-cha* with Lopez. Can I have one of your napkins?"

Kristen choked on her milkshake. "Axle! Watch your mouth."

"That was a joke." He shook his head.

I said, "*Ish*," and passed him a wad of napkins from the bottom of the bag. A green tow truck turned onto the street and coasted past us. Owen Eckerd! He seemed to be everywhere.

Kristen asked me, "Where's Tanner tonight?"

"Wednesday night. He's covering the towaway zones."

"Oh, yeah."

A black BMW 5 Series whisked by, then turned in the realtor's driveway. The garage door rolled up, the BMW motored in, the door wound back down.

"Hand me the binoculars in the glove compartment, would you?" I asked Kristen. She opened the box and gave them to me. I held the lenses over my eyes to peer through the front window. The woman had a pair of binoculars up to her face pointed back at me. *Gack! Busted.*

I phoned the repo agent, Patrick Crump. "About the BMW, we're going to need a court order to break into her garage. She knows I'm after her car. She's keeping it locked up when she's at work *and* when she's home. We're never going to find it out in the open."

"She's spotted me following her, too. You're right. I don't think we'll recoup that BMW any other way." He told me he'd get back to me, and we disconnected.

I said to my spy partners, "Well, that's it. Can't do anything more."

Since the three of us would have a hard time fitting into my little subcompact, although we'd done it before, I dropped my two buddies off at the coffee shop before heading to Byron's lot to store the truck and retrieve my Fiat. When I'd completed the exchange and arrived back at my apartment, a white four-door Chevy Silverado pickup with *Sheriff - Clear Creek County* painted black-on-white, was parked in my usual place. I was about to have another Ephraim encounter.

My pulse quickened and I took a glance at myself in the visor mirror. I finger combed out my hair, sniffed the front of my tee-shirt with coffee spills from work this morning, and tried to keep an excited expression off my face. Out of breath from rushing up the stairs, I paused at the door and gulped fresh, calming air.

Ephraim sat in one of the deep loveseats, minus the sofa pillows Boss had chewed up, and Axle and Kristen faced him from the opposite couch, looking small and scrunched together. The three of them glanced over at me. Kristen had tears on her cheeks, Axle appeared stunned, and Ephraim had on his serious cop-face. The Rottweiler was the only one glad to see me. When I'd entered through the door, the Rotty had rushed over and sniffed at my hands.

Axle stabbed a finger in my direction. "Clem's dead and it's your fault."

I reared back in shock. "I just saw her this morning." My voice came out weak and my heart thumped under my coffee-stained shirt.

"You didn't tell me you saw Clem." Axle's voice sounded accusatory and full of pain.

Ephraim stood. "Delaney, let's take this outside." He held onto my elbow as we went out the door and down the stairs. Opening the passenger side of the sheriff's truck, he settled me in the seat.

After he got in the other side, I asked him, "What happened?" My voice quivered, on the edge of panic.

"She was shot. When did you see her last? Did you say, this morning?"

"I dropped off Axle after we went to Quincy's funeral. I was on Main Street. She came out of the police station with a guy." Tears spilled from my eyes and I couldn't catch a deep breath. I didn't like her and I wanted her out of Axle's life, but *dead?*

He handed me a Kleenex from a box on the console. "Back up. What were you doing at the funeral?"

"Axle and I paid our respects." I pressed the tissue against my eyes, then blew my nose and spoke from behind the tissue. "The guy I saw with Clem, he's a drug dealer."

"How do you know that?" Ephraim's tone came across ice-cold, in interrogation mode.

I explained about the drug deal that went down at Roasters and showed him the picture I'd taken. "Do you know who I'm talking about? Is he a suspect? Have you questioned him?"

He only studied the photo for a moment, then said, "I'll check with the city police and have him picked up by a sheriff."

"Tell me, was Clem wearing yellow heels with bows when she was shot?"

His eyes went wide. "Yes."

"She had on those shoes when I saw her this morning." My nose stuffed up and my voice sounded congested. Clem had been so adorable in my yellow pumps. She stole those heels from my closet. But I would've given them to her; she didn't need to ask, even if she broke Axle's heart. Cue the music, my sympathy chromosome had kicked in.

Ephraim reached across the counsel and pulled me close, but a hard knob of equipment between us blocked his attempt at an embrace: a tablet and other computer stuff I didn't recognize. He stroked my hair and I breathed in his musky jasmine smell.

I yanked back to admire his eyes, but he stared over my shoulder. Then he chuckled.

I stiffened and gave him a reproachful look. "What's so funny?"

"Your jealous boyfriend just drove by. Sorry, but you'll have some explaining to do." He didn't appear sorry. I slumped back over to the passenger side with a loud sniff, drying up my tears. Ephraim turned toward me, serious again. "Mrs. Davidsen called me after you talked to her. She told me you asked about Clem's ring." He gave me a glance that said, *you can't get away with anything.* "Mrs. Davidsen had reported a ring stolen several weeks ago. She wondered if it was the same one."

I jolted upright as if I'd been struck by lightning. "Why would Clem ask about that ring if she'd stolen it?"

"My guess is, a MacGuffin. She used it as an excuse to get you to open Quincy's car, then she tried to get a key to his apartment to get inside there, too."

"She did keep changing the description of the ring. First, it was feathers, then leaves, like she was making it up. But it was pretty stupid to ask about it if she'd stolen it. I still don't understand why she would do that." I blew my nose in the tissue one last time and crumpled it into a ball.

Ephraim stayed silent, playing the *wait-it-out* game to see what I'd say next.

I said, "Let's talk over what we've got so far."

"I can't discuss the case with you." He shook his head side to side.

"Come on, work with me here. I'm guessing Clem wanted to check Quincy's car for drugs or money, right?"

He tapped his fingers on his steering wheel. "But we'd searched the vehicle and his apartment. We didn't find drugs in either place."

"Aha!" I shoved the balled-up tissue into my pocket and faced Ephraim. "So, this *is* about drugs, then?" He kept his mouth buttoned tight. I asked, "But you didn't find any?"

"Not in Quincy Davidsen's possession."

"Could the stash have been hidden where you wouldn't find it?"

"The Gang Crime Unit brought in tracking dogs. They have the resources to do that."

I thumped the side of my head. "If I could just figure it out."

He threw his hands into the air. "That's not your problem, Delaney. Let me do my job."

"You must have a reason to suspect drugs..." I trailed off, leaning with my back against the passenger door.

He didn't give me the reason, but said with authority, "Drug dealing is dangerous. Stay out of it."

"I will, Ephraim, I promise I will. I don't want anything to do with drugs. But, what about Clem? Did she have the stuff on her? Remember, she stayed with me for a while. She could've brought something illegal into my apartment."

"That's what I'm talking about. You shouldn't open up your home like that."

"You know she moved into Lance Palmero's place. That's Demented."

"I'm not going to ask how you know that." Ephraim shook his head. "The news release is going up on our website later today, so I might as well tell you something you'll know soon enough. The killer left cash in Clem's purse at the crime scene, so robbery wasn't the motive. There were almost three hundred dollars in her purse."

"I didn't suspect robbery." I felt a strange mixture of despair and relief. Beautiful Clem gone, causing a hard ball of pain at the top of my chest, but at least there were answers. Ephraim all but admitted the case had to do with drugs. It was some consolation to have that fact, at least. "Where was Clem killed?"

"Some hikers found her body off the canyon trail, the one just outside of town. Look, there's nothing more I can tell you. From now on please keep away from the investigation." His attention seemed to be caught by something behind me as he said, "And stay away from the country bar, too, unless I'm with you. We never finished our dance."

A knock sounded on the passenger window, and I wrenched around to see who was there.

Tanner stood at the other side of the glass, his black tow truck in the space next to the sheriff's vehicle. I tried to open the door, but the lock didn't work. I attempted to roll the window down and couldn't.

"Hey, let me out."

"Oh, sorry." Ephraim hit a button and unlocked my door.

I stepped out and asked Tanner, "Did you hear the news?"

"What news?" Tanner put his arm around my shoulder, glared at Ephraim, and steered me away from his rival.

"Clem's been shot. She's dead."

Tanner's face went white. "What the...uh, hell, Laney. What are you getting mixed up in now?"

Chapter 16

I'll be honest with you, I'd wondered from the beginning if Clem killed Quincy, or more probably, was in league with the killer. But Clem was a less convincing murderer now. Of course, she could've shot Quincy, then someone else shot Clem, but my bet was on one person killing them both.

At five the next morning, I made my way down to the coffee shop. We had a few minutes to spare once Kristen started the beans roasting, so I brewed her a vanilla coconut milk latte and me a double espresso. We took a break at a table near the front. We both said several times to each other, "I can't believe it," and "Poor Clem," as we sipped our coffees and nibbled on apple crumb muffins. Neither of us had an appetite.

I mentioned, "I hope Zach stops by this morning."

"He will. And a new girl starts today. Her name is Violet. Cute name, huh?"

Perhaps one of the rich girls in town, one whose parents wanted her to have a dose of real life and thought working in a coffee shop would do it. Unlike me. I had to support myself. No reflection on Lavender or whatever her name was.

Once the doors opened and customers entered, I forced myself to chat with them all, asking about their plans for the day. Day trippers no longer stopped on the way to the slopes because mud season had arrived, the time between winter sports and summer tourists. Most of the regulars were locals on their way to work, so I sneaked in the opportunity to show them the photos of Quincy and Clem, but no one recognized them.

After the initial rush ended, Tanner walked through the door with Axle right behind him. Tanner said, "Axle called me for a ride to work and we're just stopping in for coffees before heading out." I didn't give Ax a lift today since I had to be at work early.

I made their drinks, a vanilla frappé for Tanner and a caramel latte for Axle. I glanced at my lil' cuz', but Axle didn't say a word. I gave them their drinks on the house. Axle gave me the cold shoulder.

Violet—yes, I did know her name—showed up at ten, and I trained her on the espresso machine…pull a blank shot to preheat, tamp the grounds, and time the shot. She'd previously worked at one of the big coffee chains, so she knew the routine. Blonde and perky, she was already generating tips. Zach also stopped by, but he only had eyes for Kristen and no additional information for me.

Once the morning rush ended, Kristen waved me on my way, so I tossed my sneakers into the drawer in the backroom, shoved my feet into the flat green sandals I'd worn many times—green because the green tow truck driver weighed on my thoughts—and I left to pick up my truck. Today was my turn for the towaway zones. Plus, I had another errand to run.

I steered my truck over to the much familiar Spruce Ridge Police Station and asked for the Code Enforcement Officer. He was available and came up to the window in the shiny lobby with the rows of ugly plastic chairs.

I asked him, "Am I still on the city tow rotation? Did you get any of my messages?" His face looked blank. "I see that green truck around town transporting the orange-tagged vehicles, but I never get a call." I tried not to sound whiny.

"You Del's Towing?"

"Yes."

"I did take you off the approved list. I heard you were traumatized from finding the gunshot victim in the Impreza. I didn't think you were up for doing the work." *I knew it. I knew it. I knew it.* I growled out, "I'm fine," a little louder than I meant to. I lowered my voice to say, "Please put me back on your roster."

He tapped the keys on the computer terminal in front of him. "All right. Done."

"Are there any vehicles that need to be towed now?"

He strode over to the intake desk and came back with a clipboard. "An abandoned vehicle out on I-70 near mile marker 410, a Dodge Durango, has just been tagged."

"I'm on it. Thanks." I sprinted to the door, then sped my self-loader over to I-70. I had to beat that green tow truck to the Durango. I just had to get there first. But when I glided up to the side of the road, the green truck had the tail end of the Durango, rear-wheel drive, up in the air. I was too late!

Owen Eckerd gave me a wave as he pulled onto the highway, the Durango in tow, and I used every ounce of self-control I had not to return a different hand gesture. I recited the mantra, *Keep it together, keep it together, and you're better than this.*

My cell jingled from my purse and I answered,

"Tanner?"

"I'm behind you."

I jammed the gear in park, got out and walked back to his truck. I hoisted myself up into his passenger seat, and he wrapped his arm around my shoulder. "How are you doing after yesterday? You know, after Clem…"

I forced Owen out of my mind. Time for an attitude adjustment. Tanner didn't deserve my *poo-face*. "Still in shock, you know. Did Axle say anything when you drove him to work this morning?"

"He's angry."

"What exactly did he say?"

Tanner stared out the windshield. "Umm. Well, he didn't talk much, just listened to his music."

"Okay." I sighed and looked out the windshield, too. It hurt that Axle was mad at me, but there wasn't much I could do about it. I wanted to know, "You pretty busy?"

He glanced at the time on his dash. "There's a Chamber of Commerce meeting today. Want to go with me? It would be a good idea for you to network and get your name out there."

He was right. I needed to do some actual marketing or the competition would edge me out—like the green tower. Promoting myself to the other business men and women in town might show everyone I can still do my job in spite of the trauma of finding a corpse in a car.

Note to self: put the monthly Chamber of Commerce meetings on my calendar.

"Good idea. I'd love to go."

"Great. Should we drive separately?"

"Sure." I got out and followed him in my truck to an office complex on Industrial Lane.

Tanner opened the door for me and I walked into a huge conference room with buzzing florescence lighting and folding chairs arranged in a circle. Against a far beige wall, a long table held refreshments, platters of cookies, and a humongous silver pot, the type that brews bitter coffee in massive quantities.

Hailey, in her professional business suit, perched on one of the metal chairs. I once again wore a coffee-smelling tee-shirt along with my blue jeans. At least my green sandals were in good shape and I'd painted my toenails with a fresh coat of emerald varnish to match.

Tanner greeted her with, "Hello, Hailey," and took a seat next to her. I was about to sit down, too, but a man with a long beard down to his chest, wearing an orange tee-shirt, ripped the chair out from under me and parked his well-padded backside down. I hated orange. I couldn't wear orange because of my red hair. And maybe my carrot-top nickname was another reason I loathed the color.

I stumbled a few steps back. It was Owen Eckerd. I recognized him, plus it said so on his name tag. Of course, it would be him. The poacher.

Owen tried to break in on the conversation Tanner was having with Hailey, so I cut across to the other side of the circle and lowered myself into an empty chair. Then I brooded, squinting a foul look in his direction. I really should talk to the obnoxious tower and give him a piece of my mind. But maybe I should do that in private, not in such a public place. When the man to my right urged me to get a nametag, I set my purse on my seat, wrote "Del's Towing" with a marker on a blank tag, grabbed a cookie from the refreshment table, and plopped back into my chair.

Many of the other attendees were recognizable business owners from the upscale boutiques on Main Street, and I waved at Nancy Abington when she arrived five minutes before the session was to begin. I now understood how Tanner obtained the contracts for the towaway zones.

The chairman—no one I recognized—took the podium. The meeting was more interesting than I thought it would be, with updates on new construction projects, street improvements, and economic forecasts for the city. Afterward was a chance to mingle and exchange business cards. I gave the man on my right my card and he gave me his. He owned the coffee shop on Main Street, Kristen's competitor. I'd force, I mean *invite*, Kristen to come with me to the next meeting.

I noticed Owen filling his plate with cookies while Nancy Abington chatted up the chairman, so I joined Hailey and Tanner by the door. Tanner said, "Owen Eckerd asked Hailey for repo work."

"No!" I gave her a dirty look.

Hailey held up both palms. "I didn't even take his bond application." She fastened her gaze on me, her dark eyes behind long black lashes. "Tanner told me about your friend's death, Delaney. I'm sorry to hear about it."

"Quincy? Or do you mean Clem? I knew her only slightly." Why would Tanner mention this to Hailey? Were my so-called friends talking about me behind my back? I hoped Tanner and Zach hadn't told people I was too stressed to do my job. That would sabotage my business, for sure. Or, was I being paranoid? Tanner did invite me here, after all.

Hailey made a forward motion with her hand. "See

that man talking with Owen?"

I stood on my tippy-toes and sized up the crowded room. I recognized the tall man with short dark hair wearing a golf shirt with the logo *Davidsen Designs*. Quincy's dad! "I see him."

"His son is the one who was killed. He owns a website design company, and he created the website for Friendly Finance."

"Right. Greg Davidsen."

"That's his name."

Tanner spoke up. "I developed my own website."

I said, "I don't know if I want to do my own, and I could use some help. Can you introduce me, Hailey?"

Tanner gave me a quick narrowing of his eyes before I followed Hailey to where Greg stood. I nudged Owen out of the way, and I squelched the impulse to slap Owen's grin behind the beard.

Hailey was saying, "...and Delaney wants to talk to you about designing her website."

Greg asked, "Do you have an idea what you want your site to look like?"

"I'm not sure."

"How many pages do you think you'll need? Are you planning to blog? You want a landing page?"

Blog? Landing page? "I'd like for customers to have a way to schedule a tow."

"Sure, I can design that for you. Look around at other websites, find a couple with the appearance you like, and send me the links." He handed me his business card. "Then we'll make an appointment."

"Sounds good." I shook Greg's hand and turned to leave, but bumped into Owen. I quickly glanced around to make sure we couldn't be overheard, then said,

"You'd better not steal another of my tows!"

"What do you mean? When did I do that?"

"That Charger. I got there first," I hissed. I hadn't meant to bring it up here, but *oh well*.

"I saw your truck but not you. Where were you?"

"I was, uh, right there." I didn't mention I was underneath the vehicle. It was all too humiliating. "You stay away from me or else." I accidently stumbled back on my sore ankle. "Ow!" I hopped around on one foot.

Owen asked, "You okay? Here, sit down and let's see your ankle." I fell onto the nearest chair. He pulled my leg toward him with gentle hands. "You've got a bad sprain. Wait here." He disappeared out the door, and while I was still rubbing my foot, he returned with a small backpack.

"What are you doing?"

"I'm a paramedic. You need to keep your ankle immobilized." He spun orange gauze around my ankle and secured it with clingy material that resembled plastic wrap.

"I've never seen an orange bandage before. I hate orange." I gave him a weak laugh.

"Is it orange? I'm color blind."

"Oh, hunh, well, thanks." That explained his loud green truck and his ugly orange shirt. I tugged my jeans over the dressing to hide it from view. Maybe I was all wrong about Owen Eckerd. What can I say? He was being so helpful. "Owen, I heard you were on County Road 6 and drove by the Impreza the night that man was killed."

"How'd you hear that?"

"Someone I know saw you. Did you stop at the Impreza?" I studied his expression.

"The car wasn't tagged, so I turned around." He let go of my foot. "Now, stand up and see how that ankle feels. Don't put your full weight on it," he warned.

I pushed myself off the chair and took a few steps. "Thanks, it does feel better." Could this bearded man be lying to me about the Impreza? I had no reason to suspect him, nothing to connect him to Quincy Davidsen...yet.

People proceeded toward the door, so we awkwardly said our goodbyes and I caught up with Tanner. The two of us walked together to my tow truck. He said, "It's almost time to monitor the towaway zones."

I said, "Heading over now."

He gave me a discreet hug and a light kiss on the lips, then we went our separate ways. I wanted a shower and fresh clothes that didn't reek of coffee and some time alone with Tanner. But what I got was a friendly peck, not the longed-for spit swap. No privacy and too many interruptions.

I double-backed to Byron's to pick up Axle. Concern for the angry little stinker won out over the towaway zones. When I pulled in and saw my cuz' in the office with Byron, I honked, but Axle didn't even glance up. I lunged out of the truck and stalked inside, trying to ignore my sore ankle. "Are you done for the day, Axle?"

He didn't meet my eyes. "I don't need a ride."

Byron's gaze bounced between us.

"Is someone else picking you up?" My mind went to his buddies from the shady mechanic's shop where he used to work.

"I'm moving out of your place."

My throat constricted and I had to swallow twice. "What?"

Byron said, "You move out and I'll fire ya'." A dangerous light glinted in Byron's eye.

"No, stop, Byron." I yanked on the Old Man's arm. "It's all right. If Axle wants to take a hike, he can." I blinked back a tear, hoping neither noticed.

Axle threw up his hands. "Yeah, deal with it."

Byron gave us a concerned look. "You two need ta' talk and work this out." His low, soothing voice calmed me and I took a deep breath, glancing at Ax.

Byron must have had the same settling effect on him, because the twerp said, "All right, let's go." He stomped over to the truck and thrust open the door, then banged it shut behind him.

"He's upset about Clem," I explained to Byron.

"I know, but he shouldn't take it out on you. I'll have a chat with him."

"No, I can speak to him." I might as well since we'd be riding together across town.

But when I got in the truck, Axle had his earbuds in and his arms crossed, and he glared out the window. Talk about *badittude*! I wasn't used to this kind of angry silence from *Mr. Pissy Pants*. Teasing, joking, insulting, all in a normal day, but not this rage.

I said, "I don't know why you're mad at me, it's not my fault what happened to Clem." I had no idea why I got the blame.

He acted like he didn't hear me. His music made a tinny sound from his buds, and I upped the volume on the truck radio. Two could play that game.

By the time we ascended the stairs to our apartment, my feelings were hurt, my heart ached, and my cheeks blazed. Kristen popped her door open as I unlocked ours.

She gave us her usual caring smile. "Hey, you two."

Axle said nothing, but I said, "He's moving out."

Kristen followed us inside. "Why, Axle?"

I answered for him, "He thinks I'm the reason Clem was killed."

Kristen shook his shoulder so hard he stumbled backward. "How can you think that? You can't blame Delaney. You know better than to behave like this."

He batted her hand away. "Delaney might as well have pulled the trigger. She showed Clem's picture around like Clem was a suspect or something. Delaney made Clem a target!" He gave me a death glare. "And you said the Clems of this world could take care of themselves. You were wrong."

"I had no idea this would happen!" I'm afraid my neck cords bulged and spit formed at the corners of my mouth. I turned and ran for my room and slammed the door. Axle drove me crazy. He was a pain in the rear end…driving him back and forth, washing his dishes, picking his shoes up off the floor…I'd even thrown some of his dirty laundry in the wash with mine. What a bother he was…the ungrateful bozo…but darn it, he was like family and his anger stung. Sometimes your friends hurt you worse than your enemies.

I kicked off my green sandals and pulled on a clean pair of jeans and a tee-shirt. The black ballet flats would work for tonight. Black for Axle's black mood. I was about to fling open my bedroom door—I needed to get over to the Main Street no-parking zones—when I heard a soft knock, along with a low whine from the

Rottweiler.

I hesitated, then said, "What is it?"

"It's me. I'm sorry."

I cracked the door. "Did Kristen make you apologize?"

Axle's eyes hardened and he had the air of an unrepentant teenage driver caught in a speed trap. "She threatened to tell my mom on me."

Another knock sounded from outside the door to the apartment. Axle and I gaped at each other as if we were both thinking, *What now?*

I answered the door to find Lance Palmero on the top step with another thug looming behind him. Adrenaline surged into my chest like an avalanche danger-high. "Dementor?" It took all of my efforts to hold Boss back by his collar.

"It's Demented." The lightning bolt on Lance's forehead peeped out from under the sideways ballcap. He pointed his chin toward the other scary dude. "This is Haxxed." I recognized the gangbanger from The Centerpiece Tavern, the guy with the shaved head and the thigh-wide arms and the teardrop tattoo.

Should I offer to shake hands? *No.* I couldn't let go of Boss, besides my hands trembled and my knees knocked together and my heart churned faster than a coffee grinder gone berserk.

Demented said, "Did Clem leave anything here at your place?"

"Like what?" I thought money, drugs... "A ring?"

"No. Anything else?"

I almost tipped over as Boss yanked me forward, striving to get outside. "Not that I know of."

Axle said over my shoulder, "If we do find

anything, we'll give it to the police, not you." He tried to sound tough.

"You won't do that. You'll call me." Demented rattled off his phone number. "I mean it."

I stumbled around, still tugged by Boss. "Wait, say that again."

Demented's number might come in handy, that is if I could work up the courage to call him and ask a few questions sometime when Axle wasn't around. Demented whipped a felt tip pen out of a pocket, grabbed my left hand, and wrote the number on my palm. Then he and his friend, Haxxed, bounded down the stairs and disappeared into the parking lot.

I closed the front door with a sigh of relief that could be heard two blocks away. "Axle, did Clem leave anything in your room?"

"Let's find out." He did an about-face and scurried down the hall with me and Boss on his heels. The canopy had disappeared and the bed was made up with a black comforter, not the pink, frilly one of before.

I stopped in the doorway. "Where'd all the pink go?"

"I took apart that thing on top. The pieces are in the closet. Kristen gave me the blanket." *Ha! Maybe he wasn't leaving after all.* He opened the closet door to show me the canopy propped in the corner and the pink comforter balled up on the floor. Other than that, the space was empty. The room contained nothing except Axle's backpack, an old pillow for Boss, a dirty, wet towel, and Axle's smelly shoes, triggering my gag reflex.

Note to self: get Axle a dresser, maybe some shelves. Oh wait, he's moving out. Or, is he?

I chewed on my bottom lip as I gave the room one last scan. "I wonder what Demented is looking for."

Axle shrugged a *who-knows* gesture.

"Let's take Boss for a walk, then come with me tonight, Axle. I admit I have the *heebie-jeebies*."

"Okay." Maybe Axle felt the same.

We walked the big dog around the parking lot. He took care of business and I reminded Axle to pick up after him. We fed him dinner, then I gave the Rotty a long ear rub.

I told him in my sternest voice, "Boss, be careful while we're gone," and I added in a whisper, *Watch out for Demented...*

And Haxxed...the one who hadn't said a word, but who was likely a killer. Quincy's killer?

Chapter 17

My whole body still shivered in the aftermath of the visit by Demented and Haxxed. I squared my shoulders and put on a brave face for Axle, since I was the older and wiser of the two of us. I would allow myself a much deserved breakdown moment later after the frightmare ended.

The crabapple trees on Main Street formed double rows in front of the quaint tourist stores and boutiques, the blooms having showered the sidewalk and given way to hard, little apples hanging on the branches. Red hummingbird feeders swung from ornate light poles alongside flowering baskets of purple and white petunias. I reminded myself of where I lived. In a peaceful tourist destination, safe and crime-free—other than the murder, of course. And there's the drug trade, too, I guess.

A Toyota Prius blocked the exit behind the antique store. But the Prius, front-wheel drive, had its nose against the building, so I could either grab the wheels from the side like Tanner had shown me or use the tow dollies. The dollies might be quicker. I was by no means an expert on the side-extraction method.

"I'm glad you're along for the ride tonight, Ax," I said. "Honest. Straight up truth."

He unbent a little and helped me roll the dolly wheels out from under my self-loader. Axle pumped up a dolly under the right front tire and I worked on the left. Back in the truck, with the Prius' rear-end scooped up in the air, I was just about to put my foot on the accelerator when a man ran down the alley, his arms full. He came to an abrupt stop and threw rock-hard crabapples at us!

My window gaped open and I took one in the eye. "Ow!"

Axle rolled his window down and yelled, "What's your problem, you fwack-head?"

"Axle, this is his car," I explained, as the man came around to Axle's side.

"Oh, I get it." A handful of apples hit Axle in the face and he slapped a hand on his cheek. "Shit, man, that hurt!"

I whirred both our windows up and lowered the Prius back to the ground. "We're going to have to get out to retrieve the dolly wheels." I made a face at Axle and he scrunched his face back at me. Getting caught was getting old.

I popped open the door an inch. "Quit throwing the apples and I'll let you have your car back."

"All right." The man dropped his armful and made a *get-on-with-it* impatient gesture.

Axle and I collected the dolly wheels, but I left my truck blocking the Prius. I told the man, "You need to pay me the drop-fee. Sixty dollars. I'm not moving until you do." Axle and I stood shoulder-to-shoulder facing him, two against one.

He was not at all happy about it. "What's a drop fee?"

"I'm allowed by law to charge you a fee to return your car to you. You're parked illegally here."

He balled up his fists and I squeezed my eyes shut, but Axle bumped my shoulder and I opened my eyes back up to see the man extracting money from his wallet. He only had forty-five in cash and I took it. I couldn't get out of there fast enough.

Once we'd sped off, Axle said, "Your left eye is all red."

I glanced over at him. "Your right cheek is bruised. It's turning black and blue."

He rubbed the spot. "It hurts."

"Sorry, I owe you one." I hid the truck behind a dumpster in the next block and we sat there shooting glances down the alley every few seconds, but the angry crabapple man didn't return. I handed Axle the forty-five bucks. "At least we didn't get beat up by Demented and Haxxed or anyone else from the Thunder Knuckles gang, and I got some money for the drop fee."

"What am I supposed to do with this?" He waved the bills in the air.

"I'm paying you for riding with me. You should be compensated for your time."

He gave me a disbelieving snort and stuffed the bills in the cupholder.

"Don't even start," I warned him.

He said, "You're pathetic."

"Tell me what you really think of me." This wasn't our usual teasing, this was all too real. Axle was sullen and I was a bit grim myself.

We kept out of sight most of the evening, except for prowling up and down the alleys a few more times. Axle searched for tow truck websites on his phone and forwarded some links to me. I picked out the ones I liked and sent them to Greg Davidsen. Greg texted me back right away, and we scheduled a meeting for the next afternoon. Good, maybe I'd run into Pierce or his mom and have the opportunity to ask more questions.

Axle and I captured two more unlawfully parked cars, and I collected the entire fee both times. Normally I'd be jumping up and down and screaming with joy, at least in my mind, but it was a hollow victory since my lil' cuz' and I weren't quite right.

I drove over to Byron's lot to drop off my truck. After I unlocked the Fiat, I counted out the cash for Axle's share because, yes, I was going to pay him.

I said, "I wonder what Davidsen is going to charge me for designing the website. Rent is due in a couple of weeks and I have a few other bills to pay, too. I'm still trying to catch up from taking all those days off after finding Quincy's body." And from passing up stalled vehicles and losing out on the city rotation. At least I'd earned some dough tonight.

Axle's eyes darted around and his lips turned down. "I'm not moving out. I'll give you half the rent, don't worry."

I stopped shuffling the cash in my hands. "Sorry, I was just thinking out loud. You can move out if you want, but I hope you don't." I handed Axle twenty-five percent of the take. "Here, this is for you. And the forty-five in the cupholder."

"I'm not taking your money. Look, you're giving me a break on the rent already. I don't mind riding along, so consider it part of my share of expenses." He jabbed my shoulder.

I gave him a playful shove back. "Thanks, Axle, but are you sure?" He nodded, and I stuffed the cash in my purse. "So, I don't owe you one?"

"You always owe me." He smiled slightly.

We were starting to feel normal again, like we were on the mend, and I wanted the feeling to last. I drove us home in the Fiat, and we continued our cage-match, pushing each other up the stairs to the apartment.

I hopped on my right foot, "Ouch, ow. Remember, I'm injured."

He smirked. "You goofball."

Kristen came out on the landing, hands on her hips, feet spread apart. "You two still fighting? It looks like you came to blows!"

Axle and I met each other's eyes. I said, "What are you talking about?"

Kristen pointed a finger at her cousin. "You gave Delaney a black eye?"

His mouth dropped open, a dimwitted look on his mug.

Her finger swiveled in my direction. "And you slapped Axle. I can see your handprint still on his cheek."

"Gimme a break. We're tight like this." I held out two crossed fingers. My friend obviously didn't believe me.

Axle waved his arms around. "Some guy got mad because Delaney had his car on the truck and he threw crabapples at us. Man, they stung just like rocks."

I said to Kris, "Sorry we disturbed you."

Axle said, "Yeah, sorry."

Kristen pointed to me again. "That's okay, Delaney." Then she waved her finger once more at Axle. "Nice try, Axle."

I snickered out a *tee-hee*. Yes, it seemed funnier

now. Axle chuckled, too. *OMG*. I had to admit this was hilarious. I gave out a belly laugh, a little too hard, and couldn't catch my breath, like when you're cry-laughing because you're snorting snot up your nose until it hurts. Axle was busting a gut, too, hanging onto the door frame. That's when I knew we were *honkey-dory* again. Kristen rolled her eyes, then we went into our separate apartments. Axle and I were still giggling when he headed to his room.

I texted Ephraim to let him know about Demented and Haxxed's visit earlier in the day. Ephraim said he'd have a patrol car drive by a few times during the night. I went from cracking up to wigged out in ten seconds flat.

Buck up. Snap out of it. I forced out another laugh, *HA!*, but that didn't work.

All through my sleep that night, gang members chased me with rotten apples up and down County Road 6, right up to the Impreza with a skeleton hogtied in the front seat.

****

On Friday morning I called the repo agent, Patrick Crump, about the BMW court order, but I could only leave a message. Next, I phoned Mom to get together for lunch at the Spruce Ridge shopping center. She was glad to hear from me, of course. Mom often drove to Spruce Ridge to practice consumerism at the upscale mall with her one and only daughter—me—and her adopted daughter—as she thought of Kristen. Sierra and Violet could handle Roasters on the Ridge for the hour we'd be gone, so my friend and I headed over to the soup and salad bar.

Mom took one brief glimpse of my face and said,

"Laney, I told you this tow truck business was no work for a woman." Kristen's demeanor seemed conflicted, as if she agreed with Mom this once.

My eye did appear worse this morning, but I said, "It's nothing, Mom." I tucked my sore left ankle farther under my chair and applied lip balm to my dry lips.

She insisted on hearing the full story over our fast-food lunch, but she didn't find the childish apple-throwing incident funny. She said, "After this, we're going over to the cosmetic store to get you some concealer."

"I can't stay for that," Kristen said.

Mom said, "I'll drive Laney home if you have to take off."

Kristen nudged me. "You don't need to come back to the coffee shop. Sierra and Violet have it covered, remember?" Even though I tried to give her the silent communication of *no-no-no*, she'd thrown me under the bus.

When I hiked myself onto the stool at the makeup counter, Mom told the salesclerk to give me a total makeover. And when we walked out, I had a full bag of toners and concealers. I felt ridiculous and clown-like and planned to scrub off the layers as soon as I got home.

But my cell rang with a call from the Spruce Ridge Police proving I was back in good graces with the city. Not to get too excited...it was a five-car pileup on the highway. Both state patrol and city traffic cops had responded and tow trucks were needed to clear the traffic. I asked Mom to drop me off at my truck and suggested she take a detour home to avoid I-70.

A dozen officers swarmed over the scene and a

firetruck had all the lanes blocked, but I drove up the shoulder, my tires crunching on the gravel, and pulled in behind Tanner's flatbed. I climbed out in my tall, denim wedges and approached Tanner. One car balanced on its roof and another was missing most of its front end, but the other three were in better condition. My self-loader would be able to tow either the Chevy Cruze, Hyundai Elantra, or Toyota Avalon. All front-wheel drive. Tanner's flatbed had a winch to extract the Kia Stinger, rear-wheel, which was on its roof. His flatbed would also work to remove the Subaru BRZ, rear-wheel, with the front-end damage.

I asked, "What happened?"

Mesmerized with morbid curiosity like the rest of the rubberneckers, Tanner stared at the grisly sight. He waved a hand toward the wrecks. "Those two cars got tangled up and the others couldn't stop in time either."

"How bad are the injuries?"

"Pretty severe. Highway speeds, you know." He crossed his arms and watched an ambulance nose its way between vehicles before taking off at high speed, hospital-bound, sirens blaring. Several officers stepped away from one of the busted-up cars, revealing a pool of bright crimson streaking the asphalt.

Black dots blocked my vision and I felt dizzy. The image of blood splatters on hands, hands that were tied to a steering wheel, swam on the other side of the dots. Quincy's spilled blood. Quincy's bound hands. I clutched Tanner's arm as my legs gave way beneath me.

"Delaney!" Tanner lowered me to the pavement. "Help, over here!" he shouted at one of the officers.

I tried to tell him I was all right, but only a

strangled sound came out of my throat. With my head in Tanner's lap and my feet elevated by the officer, the black dots stopped their frenzied dance, so I leveraged my feet under me and rose to a stand.

Tanner still had his arms wrapped around me, his eyes wide with alarm. "Delaney. You're so pale. Even your freckles are pale. They've disappeared!"

I pried away from his strong hold. "It's makeup, that's all."

He rubbed a thumb across my cheek to test my answer, a crease between his brows. "You never wear makeup."

"It's my mother's fault. I'll explain later." Actually, I wore a ton of mascara and blackened my pale eyebrows, but why point that out? I turned to the officer and gave him a weak smile. "I'm here to help remove the vehicles."

The Spruce Ridge officer, not one familiar to me, signaled to another patrolman, and Zach legged it over. "Delaney, are you okay?"

"Just got a little lightheaded." *Darn flashbacks.* I'd been to a few accident scenes without fainting, but none as bad as this one and not since I'd found Quincy's body.

Zach peered at me. "You look different."

"Yeesh. Okay. Okay." *Darn Mom.* I told myself, *do not blush.* But if I did, would anyone be able to tell? At least believing no one could see my black eye gave me the confidence to do what needed to be done, this one time. "So, which vehicle do you want moved first?"

Zach put an arm around my shoulder to edge me away from Tanner and the other onlookers. Still a little queasy, I tripped and went face-first into his shirt. My lipstick made perfect contact with his stiff uniform, leaving a flawless red imprint of a kiss on his collar. "Oh, sorry about that, Zach."

His hands flew up to cover the stain and his face contorted in horror. "What am I going to tell Kristen?"

"Aha! So, you two *are* dating." I gave him a triumphant smile. Finally, I have proof!

He took a deep breath like he needed to muster up a cartload of patience. "You're in no shape to tow anything. Do you want a ride home?"

"I'm fine." I tried to avert my gaze from the smudges on the road. I didn't want to lose out on the city's business again. I needed to prove I'm competent. "At least let me grab that Avalon." The Avalon rested on its wheels in the left lane and would be easiest to extract.

He gave me a once-over and took another deep breath as if his words were against his better judgment. "All right. We do need to clear the traffic lanes."

I didn't need to be told twice. I threw my shoulders back and stalked over to the disabled vehicle like everything was fine. My right foot landed flat on the ground, my sore left was more like touch-and-go, even wrapped tight in the bandage. I took a picture of the VIN, then positioned my self-loader in front of the Avalon and swooped her up. There were a lot of people nearby: emergency workers, my boyfriend, my friend's boyfriend, and who knew how many people sitting in cars waiting for the accident to clear. *Ugh*. An audience. Self-consciously, I attached the straps to the tires and the tow lights to the Avalon's tailgate, then gave myself a pep talk to smooth out my thoughts. Good to go!

Zach tapped my shoulder. "You forgot to put on your safety vest."

"Sorry." Well, I was ninety-nine percent good to go.

Tanner asked, "You sure you're okay to drive?"

"Oh, *puh-leeze*." I feigned indignation.

"All right then. I'm staying until the other cars are released. Call me?"

"Will do. But I need to get a move on." I pulled away with the Avalon, easing through the blocked traffic, and made it to clear road. I dropped the Avalon at Tanner's gated lot, and now I was running late for my appointment with Greg Davidsen.

Fortunately, I didn't need directions because I'd been there a couple of times now.

When I rang the bell, Greg answered the door. He didn't comment on the makeup—maybe he thought I wore it every day. He led me inside to a separate office above the garage, a room with smoky-black glass desks holding two gigantic computer screens, larger than some flat-screen television sets.

He motioned for me to take a seat at one of the laptops and he nabbed the other. I straightened my shirt over the top of my jeans and settled into the chair.

"Given the sample websites you sent, I've come up with a few ideas. I'm thinking of a picture of your truck on the home page and your logo on the menu bar."

"I like that."

"I recommend a professional photo of your truck. There's a photographer on the Chamber if you don't have another in mind."

"Greg, phone call!" came a shout from the bottom of the stairs.

He called down, "Take a message, Francie, I'm with a client," in a sharp tone. I sat as quiet as an electric Tesla with a silent engine, and he continued as if we hadn't been interrupted. "Think about a video, too. Maybe an interview where you talk about how you got into the business, or get someone to act like a satisfied customer—"

I butted in, "—I have real customers who are satisfied."

"Okay, but you want the recording to be professional, so you might need to stage it. Anyway, that can be added later. Consider blogging, too. You could journal about women in the towing business, or…" He glanced down at my denim wedges, back up at my logo, and chuckled. "Or write about women's shoes. That will generate traffic to your site." He opened a website on his screen. "Let me show you the one I designed for a restaurant. See the menu, there? And links where customers can place orders for delivery and pay for their food, here? You could have a similar page, but I'll need your fee schedule, what you charge for a local tow, roadside service, and the like."

"I determine the charge once I get to the scene. Sometimes I need to figure out how difficult the tow is going to be or the distance to the drop off point. So, I don't want a place where customers pay in advance. How about a button they can click to schedule a tow? How would that work?"

"Sure. I can do that. The customer will have an option to click and dial your phone or send you a text. Now about the blog page…"

I started to squirm. "There's only a limited number of customers in Spruce Ridge. We're a small community, right? Do I really need blogs and videos and all that?"

He tipped his chair back on its hind legs and scratched his dark scalp. "The idea is to reach more people. Be a regional tower. There are plenty of tourists with car trouble in the mountains and they will find you through your website."

"That's true." I scooched forward and peered at the screen. "Okay, show me what else you've got."

He thunked his chair back on all fours and leaned in. "I'll design the site to look best on phone screens. Most of your customers are going to be seeking out a towing firm from their phones."

I took a second to respond. "What you're telling me makes a lot of sense. I should sign up for some marketing classes."

He chuckled, "I wish my wife would. Maybe she'd develop the skills needed to answer the phone."

I laughed, uneasily. "Do they teach that in college?" Was this the opening I was waiting for? *Yes.* I took a deep breath. "You had a son in college, right?" *Uh-oh. Too obvious?*

His mouth tightened and he gave me an uncertain glance. "You know my kids?"

"I met Pierce at Roasters on the Ridge." Yes, that was how I was going to play this.

"Oh, that's not the son in college. It was the older one, Quincy."

I couldn't tell him I knew Quincy had dropped out. How would I explain how I knew? I reached into my own experience for a common denominator between parents. "University is so expensive. My folks felt I drained their budget when I went to school."

"Yeah, we called Quincy *the money pit*." He shook his head and tapped on the computer screen. "Let's just do four pages to start with, a *Home* page, and then *About the Company, Satisfied Customers, and Contact Us*. Write up the content you want to be included. I'll do all the pages for $400. This will cover the domain name and registrar, too."

We tossed a few more ideas back and forth and I agreed to his price, then we bade each other goodbye. As he walked me to the door I craned my neck all around, but neither Quincy's mom nor his brother was in sight.

The sun sank low on the horizon when I reversed out of the driveway. I paused to glance both ways before entering the county road and took a moment to give the house a last once over. No one peeked out the windows. No one waved from the door. The twilight gave the place an empty feeling, unlike my childhood home that was warm and welcoming. What was it like to grow up in this sterile, cold house?

Talking about the chills, Mr. Stepdad didn't seem all that broken up about Quincy's death. He seemed cold, like the house. Of course, everyone showed bereavement differently. Maybe he was just acting professionally, not revealing his emotions since I was a client and a stranger to him. Unlike his wife who'd made no attempt to cover her grief.

The Davidsens appeared to be an average family on the surface. Two parents. Two kids. A typical teen, Pierce, wrapped up in himself. A mom, understandably in the first stages of grieving. A stepdad, trying to keep it together and carry on as usual. But what if this family had other problems beside the death of a member?

Were the Davidsens hiding something sinister?

Chapter 18

I groaned inwardly at the number of people waiting at the cash register in the coffee shop on the day of the video game tournament. The only other time it had been this busy was opening day of ski season. I tightened my apron strings and stepped up to the espresso machine.

The crush finally came to an end when players took their seats in front of their laptops, their voices and occasional coughs carrying through the café. Some of the competitors had placed fantasy figures around their screens as if for good luck. The gamers comprised about twenty mostly male teens but included nine or ten older men in maybe their forties and surprisingly—to me, anyway—three or four normal-looking women in their thirties. I even recognized some of our regular customers who didn't fit the mold, the crazies who routinely stayed awake all night slaying monsters and collecting coins.

I worked my way around the crowded tables, clearing empty dishes and making sure the players had everything they needed. Figuring someone in the crowd might know Quincy or Clem, I flashed the same old pictures around, but no one recognized them. When I got to Pierce's table, I crammed my cell into my pocket. No need to ask Pierce.

A loud whistle came out of Roscoe's mouth where he'd inserted two fingers. "Listen up everyone. Thanks for coming out in person. Non-virtual. In the flesh. In human form. It's nice to meet each other, am I right?" None of the gamers answered. He shouted a second time, "Am I right? Isn't it great to get out of your caves?"

One of the older men said, "Yeah, yeah. The only reason I came is 'cause you said we had to be here to collect our prizes." All the players' heads turned toward the awards table holding packages of controllers and an expensive-looking soundbar.

Roscoe said, "That's if you win and don't get stuck in the newbie zone."

Everyone laughed and someone muttered something like how he needed the hand of protection—if I heard that right.

One of the women told the person on her left, "You look exactly like your avatar."

Her neighbor responded, "You look nothing like yours. Let me teach you the ways of the force, young Padawan."

This was a foreign language to me. Time to get behind the counter since another cluster of gamers had walked in the door. Roscoe went over the rules while Sierra took orders and Violet and I made the drinks. After I'd fastened on the lids and cardboard sleeves, I called out the names. "Mark. Donovan. Haxxed."

Haxxed?

The hair on the back of my neck stood up. I hid behind the espresso machine when the gang member with the muscular arms and shaved head and teardrop tattoo came up for his drink. I watched him between the stacks of jumbo-sized cups to see if he sat next to Pierce, but he took a chair on the other side of the room.

Kristen bent down to ask, "What are you doing?"

I hissed, "Kristen, that's one of the Thunder Knuckles gang."

"Where?" Her voice sounded alarmed. She parted the cups to see better.

"The table second from the back, see that knuckle-dragger?"

"Not funny." She scanned the tables until she spotted him, then scrunched down to join me behind the counter wall.

"What's he doing here?" I still whispered, as if he could hear me with his headphones on across the crowded room.

She said, her voice faint, "Maybe it's just a coincidence? Maybe gang members play video games like everyone else?"

I gave her a *get-real* look. "Fat chance."

"What do you think he wants?"

"Something he and Demented believe Clem left behind." I knew that much.

A man cleared his throat and we both shot up to a stand. Sierra took his order, an iced Americano, and Kristen and I escaped to the backroom. Someone had to cover dish duty, right?

Just then, Axle came through the employee entrance with a small box in his hands. He said, "The part came in for the dishwasher."

"Thank God," Kristen said, literally meaning it. Too many turns at the sink had given our hands red rashes.

Axle tore the carton open and threw the cardboard packing into the trash. He manhandled the dishwasher, wiggling it out first one way then the other until he could get behind it, then he disappeared. We both stared at the machine waiting for it to come back to life before our eyes.

"How's Tanner?" Kristen asked without looking away from the action. "I haven't seen him around in a while."

"He's handling my calls today." I dug in my pocket for my phone. A thump and an oath sounded from behind the dishwasher. "Except for the one job I have to do myself. The BMW. I should find out about that court order while I'm thinking of it."

She squeezed my arm. "Go ahead and make the call. I'm going to brew more coffee." She stole back out front.

Patrick Crump answered after a few rings.

I sat at Kristen's desk and spoke above the racket, "Hi, Patrick, just checking on the BMW."

"The attorney scheduled the Forthwith Hearing for Monday. I'll have the court order then, and I'll call the police to break the lock. I'll let you know the exact time."

"Sounds good. Thanks for being on top of it." I only towed the vehicle, I didn't have to go to the hearing. I didn't have to do the breaking-in part either. That's what the police were for, as long as Patrick had the signed order in hand. It was a huge relief to have the cops there.

He chuckled, pleased. "Of course. We're going to get this car back."

"Patrick…I'm sorry we got off on the wrong foot." The repo agent for Abington Auto Store hadn't been helpful in the past. In fact, he'd put obstacles in my way. Once Nancy had taken over the dealership, Patrick seemed more willing to cooperate with me. "I'm glad we're working together now."

He must not have known what to say, because the phone went silent for a long stretch of four or five seconds. "Yeah, me too." He hesitated again and I waited, holding my breath. Was he going to apologize for treating me like crap? *As if.* What he did say was, "So, be expecting my call."

"I'll be ready."

Patrick Crump had not only worked for Rob Abington, Nancy's husband, for a bunch of years, but he was related to my ex-boyfriend in a roundabout way, too...in the custom of small towns where everyone knows everybody else. Did he know my dad, as well?

What could it hurt to ask? "Patrick, did you know my dad, Del Morran?"

"I did. Seemed a nice guy." Patrick's tone struck me as kind, even sympathetic.

I gasped an intake of breath. Never once had I imagined Patrick to be sympathetic. "Maybe we could get together sometime for a coffee or a beer?"

"Sure."

"Okay. Talk to you soon." We both disconnected. What just happened? Would he and I become friends? At least, hold a truce?

After a stunned moment, I drifted out front to wipe tables and empty the trash can. On my way back from the dumpster, I spotted Hailey setting up a laptop near the front window. I skidded to a stop. Hailey? From Friendly Finance? Into war games?

I worked my way through the crowd. "Hailey, I'm amazed to see you here." Amazed didn't begin to describe it.

With her power cord in one hand, she felt under the table with the other, and her eyes took in my coffee-stained apron. "Delaney! I didn't know you were working here again. Did you quit the towing business?"

"No. No, no, no." My chapped hands flew about in all directions. "I'm just helping out." I tossed the attitude right back with, "And I thought you ran the loan company, but in reality, you're a gamer."

She laughed, not seeming to mind the tease. She found the outlet and plugged in her computer. "I don't play, but Haxxed talked me into coming."

My jaw hit the floor. "Haxxed?"

She twisted at the waist to scout behind her. "He's over there."

"I know who he is." Can't mistake him for anyone else! "How do you know him?"

"He put the security systems on the computers at Friendly Finance."

I collapsed onto the empty chair next to Hailey's. "I never would've guessed."

Her gaze skimmed side to side as she leaned closer to me. "He's a computer hacker, understands how the bad guys think, so he knows how to set up the best firewalls. He's cheaper than a lot of those security companies that charge an arm and a leg."

Chances are she paid him under the table. Mutually beneficial to both. I stared straight over at Haxxed, looking at him in a new light—a gang-banger, computer hacker, and entrepreneur contributing back to the economy, all in one. Six gamers crowded around Haxxed. They let out a shout, fists pumping and high-fiving each other.

"I'm a little behind. I'd better sign in." Hailey

cracked open her laptop and seemed to forget about me.

"Enjoy the tournament." I shoved out of the chair and ambled over to Pierce, wondering if he knew Haxxed, too. Pierce didn't glance up even when I stood at his elbow for a few beats. I pointed to his cup and mouthed, "Refill?

He nudged aside his headphones. "Oh, it's you."

"More coffee?"

"Sure."

"What's your drink?" He told me, so I went to make another nitro cold brew. After setting the iced drink on his table, I asked, "Do you know Haxxed? He's sitting over there." I jutted out my chin in Haxxed's direction. "He must be doing something cool since those guys are watching his action."

"Yeah, one of Quincy's friends." Pierce paused his game and turned to me. He whispered, "That's the guy who killed my brother." Despite the loud voices and *click-click-click* of keyboards, I could still hear his words. He gave me a scowl that said, *what-do-you-think-about-that*?

I splayed my hand across my chest, goosebumps rippling in every direction. "Do you have proof? Have you told the police?"

"Nah. I don't have proof. That's their job." He turned his gaze back to his screen. "Hey, I'm up. I've got to get back in." His fingers tapped the mouse in rapid fire. I hovered over his shoulder for several more seconds, but he shot me a look to kill. Gamers usually *looooove* showing off, but he wanted me out of his space, so I hustled away.

Axle came out of the backroom. "Dishwasher's fixed." The aroma of dirty dishwater, like spoiled milk and old cabbage, hung on his clothes.

I patted his back. "Great! I'll go load 'er up now! We have about seven loads that have to be done, like, yesterday."

"I'm heading over to Byron's. He's got a job for me."

"You need a lift?" Shit, if Axle wanted a ride then I couldn't fill the dishwasher. I needed some help here! I swept my eyes around the room for the other baristas.

"Nah, a buddy's picking me up."

I felt relieved, then annoyed, because that meant I actually had to fill the dishwasher. Axle grabbed a caramel latte to-go and rolled out the door.

I stacked the cups and plates in the new and improved machine, then ran back out front to make drinks. The gamers had their earphones off and were milling around the awards table. Someone by the handle of *Dragonix* won first place and was happily opening up the box with the soundbar. Two of the older guys insisted they'd both won the consolation prize for most coins lost or least monsters slain or something like that.

Finally, we handed out the last drink and shooed the sole remaining gamer out the door. Not an easy feat to empty the place of caffeinated gamers high on social interaction with their tribe. I turned the *closed* sign, appreciating the quiet after the dull roar of so many people. We got busy mopping, and before long the shop shined and smelled like pine cleaner. Kris handed Sierra and Violet each a bonus and tried to shove an envelope into my hands, too, but I said, "I told you I'd help out and I meant it."

"Then, I'm not going to take your rent for this

month."

"No way."

"Way."

We went back and forth like this until I agreed to a slight break on the rent. "I'd hug you, Kris, but I'm sweaty and gross."

"Oh my gosh, me too! Hug you tomorrow."

"Never mind." GLOMP! I dove in for the biggest coffee-stained sweaty hug ever. I guess I was delirious from a crazy, loud, busy day. I couldn't wait to clean myself up. Let my hair down. Put my feet up.

Thinking about a warm shower and comfy yoga pants, I let the coffee shop door shut behind me and started toward the stairs…when all of a sudden Haxxed appeared out of nowhere!

The deadly gangster right here in front of me. Me by myself. No one else around. *Yikes*.

I sprinted for the bottom step, but he caught the back of my shirt and my feet only cycled in place like tires spinning on ice.

Haxxed flung back his head and laughed.

I stammered, "Not f-f-funny!"

"I'm here for Clem's stuff." The man speaks! His voice was commanding like a tyrannical character right out of a scary video game.

Cold sweat ran down my spine and my pulse raced like I was on a caffeine rush. "She-she took everything over to Demented's pl-place when she moved out."

"Everything?"

"I swear." I placed my palm over my heart.

"On your mama?"

"Sure."

He stared hard at me before releasing my shirt. I

ran up the steps, feeling his eyes searing my back, and I dived inside the door.

I threw the deadbolt and stepped away, out of breath. Boss sniffed around my ankles while I pressed in Ephraim's number with shaky fingers. I shrieked into the phone, "One of the gang members was just here. He cornered me in the parking lot when I was by myself."

Ephraim's voice came back loud, too, "Is he still there?"

I checked the peephole, then scoped the lot from the window. "I don't see him. But I'm sc-scared."

"I'm on my way."

I wanted to make sure Kristen or Axle didn't show up if a gang member was hanging around, so I pounded out a text to Axle, focusing on trying to sound normal, not freaked out: —*Stay at work. Don't come home!* Whoops. That sounded too bonkers, so I deleted that and keyed in: —*Everything's fine here. No need to rush home.* I hit send, then smacked myself up the side of the head. That text still came across as psycho.

He replied: —*I'm busy on a paint job for Byron.*

Okay, then. I exchanged texts with Kris and found out she was still at the bank.

I breathed a huge sigh of relief, then considered warning Tanner, too, but if I told Tanner about Haxxed, he'd rush over. None of the gang had seen my boyfriend and I wanted to keep it that way. Ephraim was the one I needed right now, anyway, not Tanner, because Ephraim had a gun and the law on his side. I leaned my butt against the kitchen counter, Boss sitting on my foot, and I faced the door, willing Ephraim to *hurry, hurry, hurry*, expecting him any second. Yet, when his knock sounded I jumped a mile.

After I thrust open the door, he charged inside. "You all right?"

"Yes," I lied. "This is the third time either Haxxed or Demented or both have shown up here...I hate these stupid nicknames."

He held me up by the tops of my arms. "I checked around the parking lot. He's gone."

"He's after something of Clem's."

"Can I search your apartment? Informally."

"I don't care. I have nothing to hide. Let's do it. I'll help." Now that the lawman was here, my knees had quit knocking and my heart no longer jumped around like roasting espresso beans.

Boss and I watched while the sheriff searched. He examined under the couch, beneath drawer bottoms, along baseboards, in the toilet tank, and in the freezer. He took quite a while. He found nothing.

Ephraim rubbed his chin. "Did Clem give you anything to hold for her? Or maybe she gave you a gift?"

"No." I closed my eyes and pictured Clem, with her short, straight black hair and big blue eyes. I knuckled my own eyes to scrub away her sad memory.

Ephraim's features softened, and he took my face in his hands. "Do you have a black eye?"

"An irate customer. This wasn't from Haxxed."

His dark eyes went darker, his fingers tensed, and I wondered if he was about to swoop in for a kiss.

"Wait!" I almost shouted. Ephraim's eyes went wide and his hands dropped like he'd touched hot metal. "I just remembered. Clem let me borrow her leather jacket." I turned and bolted for my closet, Ephraim behind me.

Sliding the hangers first right, then left, I found the jacket and ripped it off the clothes rod, flinging the hanger against the wall. I pushed the garment toward Ephraim, and he took it and laid it out on my bed. A quick run of his hands down the lining made his eyes narrow. He pulled out the pockets, inside out. "See these stitches?"

I leaned closer for a better look.

"She opened the pockets and sewed them back together again."

"Who knew Clem could sew?" I ran for the scissors and hurried back. Ephraim sawed through the seams and poked his fingers into the lining. He withdrew his hand and extracted thin plastic gloves from one of his many pockets. After snapping on the gloves, he reached back in and pulled out wads of money and a few pieces of jewelry wrapped in a small scrap of cloth.

"Clem hid this loot." I hovered at his elbow as he felt along the rest of the lining. "And she lent me her jacket! Why would she leave it here with all that money in it?"

"She may have felt it was safe with you."

"But I wore it to two different bars!"

"Two?" Ephraim glanced up and gave me a questioning look.

"I could've easily lost this jacket or someone could've taken it from me."

"But no one did. At least until now, because I'll need to take this with me."

Bummer. It was such a bitchin' piece of clothing. I sank onto the edge of the bed. "This is what Haxxed was after. What'll I tell him?"

Ephraim folded the jacket on my down comforter, then he stuffed the jewelry inside a plastic evidence bag he brought out from his duty belt. "Don't tell him anything. Don't talk to him at all. If he shows up again, dial 9-1-1. Then call me."

The clear evidence bag held a gold ring circled with feathers, not leaves. Clem had described it both ways. "You were right, she made up the story about losing that ring."

"I want you to witness as I count the money, okay?"

I swiveled to the side so I could watch. He threw each bill down and counted out loud, stacking the cash in neat piles. All were hundred-dollar bills, five hundred of them. *OMG!* No wonder the jacket had felt heavy and warm with all this loot for insulation. And I never even noticed any lumps.

Ephraim gathered the contraband and stuffed it in the bag with the jewelry, sealing it all together. He sat next to me on the mattress and slung an arm around my back. I tried not to think about the very hot and available sheriff in my room. Sitting next to me on my bed. With his arm around me and fifty-thousand dollars in cash.

Ephraim tightened his biceps for a squeeze. "This money is most likely proceeds from drug sales. The Thunder Knuckles are not into committing robbery, although I wouldn't put it past one or two of them."

Remembering I still smelled like coffee, I inched out from under his shoulder. "Was Clem a dealer?"

"Maybe." He dropped his hands into his lap. "I can't believe you let her stay here."

"It wasn't me, it was Axle. Should I tell him about

this?"

"It'd be a good idea if you kept it to yourself until we determine where this money came from."

"It's obviously gang money. They've been looking for it. They killed Quincy over it, and Clem, too."

"That could very well be the case."

"Why didn't she just turn the money over to them?"

"Maybe they didn't give her a chance. Or maybe she forgot where she'd put it. Who knows?"

I gave him a look of disbelief. "Forgot where she hid fifty-thousand dollars?"

He held his palms up and shook his head. "You wouldn't believe the amount of cash dealers have lying around."

"Well, this solves the murders, both of them." I brushed a hand over my forehead, feeling relieved and safe. "Are you going to arrest Demented and Haxxed?"

"Delaney, probable cause is required to make an arrest. We need evidence linking this money to them."

"Maybe they left fingerprints?"

"Currency changes hands so often, it can be difficult to find viable prints on bills," Ephraim explained. "And the money might not be related to this crime. There could be another reason for the victims' deaths."

"Like what?"

"Well, we know Clem hooked up with several gang members. She didn't limit herself to Quincy. So, maybe jealousy could be a motive. Or, their deaths could be revenge or retaliation for something we've yet to learn about. You see, I need more than just a theory."

The front door banged open and Boss barked. I

froze. Ephraim leaped to a stand and assumed a wide-legged stance, his hand on his duty belt near his gun.

Were Demented and Haxxed here for the drug money?

Were we about to be whacked?

Chapter 19

Axle shouted, "Delaney, you home?"

The sheriff and I both let out a long breath. He marched down the hall with me tagging after him.

When we reached the kitchen, I asked Axle, "Did you get a ride?"

"Byron dropped me off." His gaze pinged between us, then he averted his eyes and appeared unable to speak for a moment. He found his voice and blustered, "Where's Tanner?"

My face turned scorching hot, just about as hot as milk out of the steamer. "Working."

Axle noticed Clem's jacket in Ephraim's hand, but the evidence bags were out of sight, hidden under the fold. "Is that Clem's?"

"I'm taking this into custody." Ephraim cut past Axle but stopped with his hand on the door. "Keep in touch, Delaney." His words sounded like an order.

"You, too."

He nodded and I shut the door after him. I swiveled around toward my little cousin. "Axle, it's not what it seems like. Clem left her jacket in my closet. Ephraim went with me to the bedroom to get it."

A smile twitched at a corner of his mouth. "Too bad that's all that happened."

"Shuddup!" I punched his shoulder.

He smacked my arm. "No, *you* shuddup!"

I rubbed the spot. "We need to take Boss for a walk. And, I have some good news. Kristen is giving us a discount on the rent this month."

He gave me a limp high-five, but it was better than nothing.

****

I longed for a quiet Sunday and wanted to avoid thinking about killer gangsters. So, after my first cup of coffee, I scrubbed the kitchen and bathroom and forced Axle to give me the sheets off his bed. Laundry going, I sat at my computer and composed a couple of paragraphs for my website, explaining how the heck a girl like me had gotten into the tow truck business. Not my best work since the crime still distracted me, but I emailed the script to Greg to see what he thought.

Axle appeared listless and I was antsy, too. Tanner had taken his brother to a soccer game and I had no idea what Kristen was doing. The apartment felt like it was closing in on us and we needed to get out.

I nudged Axle's foot with the toe of my plum-colored cowboy boots. "Quit being a sofa spud. Come with me. I'm going to cruise around to look for abandoned vehicles."

He clicked off the remote. "All right. Let's jet."

After picking up my tow truck, we turned west onto the highway and started up the pass. The broad reach of the sun illuminated the long, winding canyon in a golden glow. The air smelled dry with dusty pine needles. I was sailing along over the speed limit, enjoying the ride, when we came over a rise to see a police car in the median with its light bar rotating.

I hit the brakes to slow the truck and said to Axle, "An accident?" then said to myself, *Don't faint. This could be an opportunity.*

He didn't hear me, so I gave his earbuds a tweak. "Look ahead."

He clutched the dashboard. "Should we stop?"

"Maybe. Let's take a look." As my self-loader climbed the hill, a vehicle came into view on the other side of the squad car. The green tow truck. What if the state patrol was issuing Owen a speeding ticket? *Heh-heh.* I gave the bearded driver a smug over-the-shoulder look as we cruised on by. We got off at the next exit and returned to the highway going the other direction so we could have another good laugh.

"You're gloating." Axle shook his head.

"No way." But after I took the exit again and made the circle once more, I admitted, "Maybe I am gloating."

"Real mature."

We listened to the police scanner under my dash while driving around some more. We didn't hear of any accidents or spot any abandoned, orange-tagged vehicles, but witnessing Owen's ticket made the effort worth it.

****

"This is your last shift." Kristen wiped her hands on a dishcloth. "I'm good to go after today since Violet's working out so well. I really, really appreciate all your help." She gave me a kissy-face.

"No problem. I've enjoyed myself." I wrapped the apron around my hips and got to work.

Monday was bean roasting day. Some of Kristen's employees said they couldn't smell the beans anymore after working a few weeks, but that hadn't happened to me. The rich scent of java never faded or got old. All of

Kristen's usual customers came in and once the rush ended, I tossed my apron in the laundry bin and hitched my bag over my shoulder, getting ready to leave for the final time as a volunteer worker.

I poked my head in the office to say, "so long," to Kristen, then turned to the front. A man with big blue eyes and straight black hair walked in the door. The drug dealer! He'd been with Clem the last time I'd seen him. And, I hadn't forgotten he'd sold drugs right here on these very premises. The nerve of him coming back.

I pointed my finger at him. "What are you doing here?"

"I'm trying to find Guy. He works at this place." His gaze took in the whole coffee shop.

"Not anymore." I put a little sarcasm in my voice. "You here to do some dealing?"

He shuffled his feet. "I'm here for a coffee."

Should I call Ephraim and turn him in? But Ephraim had said he was going to bring this dealer in for questioning—along with the gang bangers, I hoped. Had the dealer been taken in and released so soon?

"What'll you have?" I zig-zagged my way behind the register and gave Sierra a jerk of my head as if to say *I've got this*. She frowned but got out of the way.

"Chai latte."

What a sissy drink. I gave myself an internal eye roll. "You want vanilla in it?"

"Nah. I like it spicy, not sweet."

Maybe not so sissy after all…or else he used this as a pickup line. No way this girl was charmed. *Not just no, but hell no.*

I took the chai tea out of the refrigerator. Kristen made her own chai with cardamom, cloves, peppercorns, and black tea. I heated and frothed the milk and added the hot milk to the cup. After snapping on the lid, I said, "It's on the house. Let's talk outside."

He took hold of the drink and observed me as I came around the counter. I made an arm sweeping gesture and he went out the door in front of me.

I pulled out a chair from the patio table and dropped my purse on the ground. "Tell me what you were doing downtown with Clem Vargas the day she was killed." I sounded like the DA on a television drama.

His blue eyes did a shifty thing as he sat. "Is that what you want to talk to me about?"

"Uh, yeah." I tugged on my long red braid, wondering whether he was dangerous. Was I safe? What if he had a gun in his pocket? Would a chai drinker have a concealed carry? Traffic at the corner of Pine Street and Eagle Avenue was always busy and he couldn't shoot me in front of all these witnesses, right?

"Why should I talk to you? You called the cops on me last time I was here."

I reared my head back, tucking my chin down. "I did what?"

"You called the cops."

Oh yeah. I'd forgotten that little white lie. "Ha, ha. I didn't really call the police. So, what were you doing with Clem?"

He raised his hands in the universal sign of surrender. "Look, Clem was my sister."

I gasped out loud. "Your sister?"

"Clementine Vargas. I'm Leonardo Vargas. Everyone calls me Leo."

I sucked in my cheeks. I'd showed his picture to

246

Clem. I'd asked her about her own brother! "She told me she didn't know you."

"I'm not surprised." Leo lowered his gaze and turned his face away. He did have Clem's same big blue eyes and straight black hair, even the razor cut in a similar haphazard style. I hadn't seen the family resemblance before, but here was the matching male anime character.

"I'm so sorry about your sister…" I trailed off, my throat tight. Words were always inadequate.

He fiddled with his to-go cup, seeming a lot less sure of himself than when the drug deal took place. "Yeah, she was on a downward spiral. I couldn't help her. Goddamn did I try."

"What do you mean?"

His eyebrows drew together. "You're asking an awful lot of questions. Why should I tell you anything, even if the coffee's on the house?"

Okay, different approach. "You're right. You don't owe me an explanation, but I hoped you might want to talk about Clem. I have a feeling you have the answers." That was my best attempt at flattery. I had no idea where else to go. Seriously. "So, did Clem ask for your help?"

He gave up a sigh. "Yeah. She told me Quincy had locked her out of the apartment and she needed me to talk to him. So, I called him, but he was driving and had to pull over. He stopped and phoned me right back."

"What happened then?"

"Quincy didn't say what the argument was about, but he promised to speak to her. I don't know if he did. That was the night he died."

"That's it?"

"Look, that's all I know about it. There's nothing more I can tell you."

"Can we talk about Clem? What was she really like? I hardly knew her, but she did mention a few things, that she'd been in foster care growing up."

"Yeah, all right. We were raised in separate homes. Actually, she was tossed around to a few different ones. She had a lot of anger issues and hated her life. She was even mad at me, and that's probably why she didn't tell you we were related."

My social worker training kicked in. I knew sometimes Family Services had to split siblings up and not all situations were equal. The muscles bunched in my throat as I said the words, "Every kid deserves a good home."

He snickered. "Get real."

Could I blame him for his doubts? "What about your parents?"

Leo shrugged. "Mom abandoned us. We didn't know our dad. Clem tried to find him but never could. I didn't bother."

My eyes watered, and I blinked a few times. "I never saw my dad when I was growing up, either." I had to ask, "Who do you think killed your sister?"

He rested his blue eyes on me. "I don't know. I wish I did."

"What are you going to do?"

"Nothing. I've learned life's just a big bag of trash and there's nothing you can do about it."

"No, that's not true. There is something you can do."

Leo placed his tongue against his teeth, like he was about to make a *tsking* sound. "Yeah? And what would that be?"

"Make good choices," I said. Clem's life sucked and life wasn't fair, but she had some control over her own path. And what did she decide to do? Get into gangs and drugs. Was Leo any better, selling narcotics in Kristen's coffee shop?

A chocolate gray Kia Sportage, LX, which was an all-wheel drive, pulled into the parking spot on the other side of our outdoor table. The gangsters in their low-slung jeans, Demented and Haxxed, climbed out. My heart sped up to the beat of the rap music thudding out of their car.

Leo's eyes went wide. "Shit. They're following me."

I shrank back in my chair. "I think they're after me." We gave each other terrified looks. I rooted around in my purse, my hand feeling here and there for my phone.

Demented crossed his arms and planted his feet wide. "We want Clem's stuff."

"I told you before, Clem took all her things with her. I have no idea what you're after," I bluffed, my voice breathy, my fingers reaching for my cell, but only finding my wallet.

"No, she didn't, not to my place." Demented asked, "You still have my number?"

Leonardo and I said in unison, "Yes."

Haxxed told us both, "Call Demented when you find it. If you don't, you better live in fear. You better watch your back."

The two Thunder Knuckles returned to their car and the Kia hurtled down Pine Street. Leo and I stared at each other.

He stood. "I'm outta here," and dashed to a white sedan in the parking lot. I was so rattled, the make or model didn't even register with me.

No way was I sticking around. I fled, too, and sprang inside my Fiat, hit the door locks, then dialed Ephraim and got his voice mail. I left a message, describing the Kia and the direction the gangsters took. After I hung up, my phone rang with a call from Patrick Crump.

He said, "The BMW is in the garage, I saw her pull in. And I got the court order."

I'd forgotten all about the hearing today. With so much going on it had blown right out of my mind.

"I'm on my way." My voice came out shaky, but I had to get over it. I had a job to do. *Don't think about gang members and drug dealers. Put them out of your head. Get back to work.*

Before disconnecting, I asked Patrick, "Do you need me to contact an officer? I know who to ask."

"I was just going to phone the police next, but if you have someone who'd show up on short notice, then by all means call them."

"Will do." I hung up and called Zach, asking him to meet us at the owner's garage, then I put the Fiat in gear.

Ten minutes later, I arrived at Bianca White's house in my tow truck, and Zach's squad car pulled in next to me. I cast glances left and right over my shoulders—no Demented, no Haxxed. We both got out of our vehicles and Zach followed me over to the locked garage where Patrick Crump leaned against the frame. He was about my age, five-foot-eight and slightly built, in jeans and an untucked dress shirt and tie.

I said, "Hey, Patrick. Glad to see you, Zach." The officer gave me a curt nod, having no idea I'd come from a gangland encounter, but just standing next to him gave me my confidence back.

Crump handed Zach the paperwork and Zach said, "Wait here a moment."

He walked up to the front door and rang the bell, while Patrick went back to his car and I waited in the tow truck. Zach stood on the porch for a few minutes, but no one answered.

If the owner was home, an officer could hand off the court order to open the garage. The owner could have done so, and there would've been no need to break in. But most people in collection kept out of sight in fear of being served some kind of summons. They think if they hide, the police can't do anything. They don't know law enforcement can smash the lock.

And that's what Zach did. He extracted a crowbar out of the back of his squad car, snapped it between the handle and the door, and *voila!* With a loud, splintering crack, the door rolled up.

I reversed the back end of my truck a little closer to the garage and pushed the magic button on the yellow remote hanging out from under the dashboard. My self-loader gave an almost imperceptible sway and another of its moans and tings. On the other side of the truck's back window, the rear of the BMW rose into the air.

I gave a thumbs up to Patrick and he returned a broad smile. I stepped on the gas and my truck moved forward, tugging the black BMW behind. Zach would close the garage door and we could all leave.

Okay, then. This was a successful repo. *Look at*

me! I did it! This made me feel like an honest to God, bona fide repo agent, instead of a pretender. Some folks wouldn't be proud of it, but it took guts to do this job. *Jussayin.* You have no idea how scoring the vehicle and satisfying the client lifted my mood. The fear of the Thunder Knuckles gang was replaced with...the feeling of *dang awesomeness.* I felt giddy.

I buzzed over to Abington Auto Store and hung a left past the showroom to where the service department was located. I disconnected the BMW, walked around to make sure all was well, and hiked myself back up into my truck cab.

Would Dad have been proud of me?

Patrick was. He texted me: —*Well done! Let's meet for coffee tomorrow.*

I called Tanner. "I got the repo! The BMW."

"Hey, good job. I know how hard that one was. You can tell me all about it later."

"Sure thing." I'd catch him up on the bad stuff, too, eventually. Now was the time to celebrate. Business was good. At least the repo work and towaway zones were.

Now, if only I could make sure the city was really going to use me instead of that Owen Eckerd...but did I need the city contract? I had done so well with everything else.

Forget the city. Forget Owen. Forget Demented and Haxxed, too. Surely I would be given more repo assignments now.

Plus I was going to be a regional tower, I reminded myself.

Chapter 20

The next morning, I showed up a few minutes early at Greg Davidsen's house. I followed him up the steps to his office above the garage and sat next to him in front of the two ginormous computer screens.

He clicked his mouse and opened up my new website. "What do you think?"

The red Fulcan Xtruder, with Del's Towing logo of the stiletto outlining my phone number, made a pretty picture even if I took the shot myself. The photo filled up a banner stretching across the top of the page. Underneath was the menu: *Home, About the Company, Satisfied Customers, and Contact Us*. He clicked on the *About the Company* page and the words I'd written appeared.

I felt my face flush with pleasure. "It's so polished. I love it."

"I still think we should add a video, one of you towing a car, wearing your high heels, shaking the hand of a satisfied customer, something like that. You should have the footage done by a professional, along with another photo of your truck. You like this now? You'll like it even better with some first-class photos and video clips."

"All right. You've convinced me. I'll talk to the photographer. The next Chamber meeting is another month away?"

"Yes, but I've got her business card here." Greg handed me a card from a stack on his desk.

I had on a broad smile. "If I give you some of my cards, will you promote me, too?"

"Sure. You need to add your website address to your business cards." Greg pressed a couple of keys on the keyboard. "Here's the button for people to click for a tow. They'll have the option of sending a message or, if they're accessing your site from their phones, they can dial your number directly. You ready?"

I nodded.

He tapped a key with one finger. "Your site is now live."

I felt a great leap of excitement as I handed him a check. I couldn't wait to get my first call from the site. I practically skipped out of his office, my sore, bandaged ankle all but forgotten.

But, on the way down the stairs, we ran into his wife. She stood with one hand on a hip and her mouth open, her eyebrows elevated in a question. She said, "Delaney, what are you doing here?"

Greg stepped closer, giving me a look of *what the...*

Whoops. Trapped! The narrow hallway felt close and claustrophobic now.

Francie said to her husband, "She's the one who found Quincy."

I fixed my eyes on Greg, giving him a steady look. "Yes, you see, I towed the Impreza. This is a small community, as you know, and it was a coincidence I ran into you at the last Chamber of Commerce meeting. Remember Hailey at Friendly Finance introduced us?"

He took a second to respond, "I remember that, but

you could've mentioned before now that you discovered my son's body." His voice had a hard edge.

I flinched. "I...I...guess, but I couldn't think how to bring it up." My gaze ricocheted between the two of them.

Francie's face crumpled. "Greg, I'm sure Delaney didn't want to be the one to find him. None of this is her fault." Tears sprang to her eyes and her hands shook.

"Francie, you should go lie down." Her husband reached out to her, but she took a step back.

Her eyes seemed to look through the wall behind me, and then she clenched her eyes closed. "I feel so bad." She clutched the collar of her blouse, twisting it into a knot. "Quincy needed me. I let him down. How could I do that?"

"Why don't you go up to your room, hon, get some rest?"

"But I failed our son." She swayed, unsteady, then reached out to support herself.

"Francie, Francie, you didn't. In fact, just the opposite. You did too much." Greg's voice was laced with worry. "Go lie down," he pleaded. "You need to take control of yourself."

"I'm sorry, Greg. I can't help it. Will you ever forgive me?"

He took her elbow. "There's nothing to forgive. Just let it go."

"I didn't realize the money was all gone until it was too late, Greg. I'm so sorry." She blinked rapidly, her chest heaving.

"I know, I know, but we don't have to talk about it right now." His eyes darted to me, unease coloring his face. Part of me wanted to disappear, but another part wanted to stick it out.

She sagged away from him, against the wall. "I guess I couldn't help Quincy anymore."

Greg said, "That's not helping. That's enabling. We've talked about this before. We don't need to go over it. Quincy understood you did everything you could."

She looked up, hope etched on her face. "Did he? Did you talk to him? Did he say that?" Her voice came out faint and wistful.

"No. I didn't get a chance to talk to him, but I meant to."

She picked at Greg's sleeve. "You tried, though, right? You tried?"

"I stopped at his place, but he wasn't there. Clem answered the door, so I talked to her."

The two looked into each other's eyes in silent communication like married couples do. Greg put one arm around her shoulder, "Come on then, how about a cup of hot tea? If you won't go rest, have something warm to drink."

Francie slid out from under his arm, seemingly gathering herself together. "I'm sorry, Delaney. We're being rude. Come back to the kitchen, I'll make coffee."

I rarely refused coffee. But could I actually intrude on them like this? Yes, I could. "I'd love a cup."

Greg and I trailed after her to the back of the house. The wall of windows framed the snowcapped mountain peaks and the pine valley floor. A calming scene, but tension had followed us into the room.

Francie hit the start button on the coffee machine.

She and Greg remained ominously quiet while the dark brew dripped into the carafe. Their eyes shot my way, and I hoped they'd be able to work out their problems, but the death of a child, and financial troubles on top of that, would be difficult to overcome.

Greg didn't look at me fully when he said, "Delaney, I'm embarrassed you heard that. We should've kept our business to ourselves."

"But I understand. Everything is so raw and you're still processing your son's death." I turned to Francie. "Are you getting any help?" I'd taken only a few grief counseling classes in college, and those did not equip me for this mother's deep anguish.

Her shoulders spread back. "Yes. You helped me understand I need closure, Delaney. That's why I started therapy." She gave me a tight smile. "Thank you for that. How about you? Are you still having nightmares?"

Greg's eyes scoured my face. "What?"

I explained, "I'm having some bad dreams. I'm upset, too, not that I can even begin to feel your loss."

Greg brushed a hand down his face. "It's been hard on Francie."

Francie nodded and the three of us went quiet for a moment. I asked, "Is there any news?"

Greg answered, "The sheriff called to let us know he found money in something that belonged to Quincy's girlfriend. He told us to keep quiet about it, though."

Francie said, "And my ring. He found it, but I don't even want it back."

I chewed on my bottom lip, then said, "I can't help wondering what Clem's ruse with the ring was all about."

Francie frowned. "Clem was a liar and a thief. Who knows what she was after."

Greg stared at me. "You knew Clem, too?" I nodded. The coffee machine dinged, signaling the brew was done. Greg said to his wife, "I'll get it, hon. Why don't you sit down?" He brought three mugs out from the cupboard and poured us each a cup.

Francie took a chair at the table. "I wanted Quincy to break it off with Clem. This was all her fault." Her voice sounded bitter, and I couldn't really blame her.

"Quincy did ask Clem to move out." I set my coffee mug on the counter. "At least that's what Clem's brother told me."

Greg asked, "You know her brother as well?" His voice had lowered an octave.

"I only just met him, Leo. He told me Quincy locked Clem out of the apartment." I paused for a couple of beats, then asked, "Did the detective mention how much cash they found?"

The parents both stared at me wide-eyed.

"Did you know it was fifty-thousand dollars?"

Greg whooshed out a big breath of air. "That much? We had no idea."

"It wasn't yours, right? I mean, did you give it to Quincy and he gave it to Clem?" Considering what Greg had said about *the money pit* bleeding them dry, it wasn't out of the range of possibility.

Francie shook her head. "I never gave him that much."

I held up a finger. "I think Clem stole that money from the gang and Quincy kicked her out. Maybe he was trying to distance himself from Clem or maybe he was trying to get her to give the money back. Something like that."

Francie's hands trembled as she clasped her mug, her knuckles white. "What gang?"

"It could be gang money, probably from drugs."

"That Clem! This is all her fault." Francie's wild eyes landed on Greg, but he had on a closed, angry face.

He said, "You know Quincy embraced the whole gangster persona, getting those tattoos, wearing the clothes. That's when he dropped out of school."

So his parents did know about that.

Francie started rocking, still clutching her cup with both hands. "I don't believe it. My little boy wouldn't join a gang. My child was better than that. My Quince."

I tried to think of a positive spin, but all I could come up with was, "The police said your son's death many have nothing to do with the money. It's all guesswork right now."

Francie stopped swaying. "My therapist told me not to expect total resolution. I hoped someone would call on the hotline with helpful information, but no one did. The counselor said my son's memory does not live on by knowing who killed him. His memory lives on in here." She tapped a finger over her heart.

"She's right." I glanced at Greg and gave him an encouraging nod, too, but her husband kept a tight-lipped silence.

Francie continued, "I'm having lots of flashbacks of when he was a little boy, but I found out it's part of the process. Let me show you his picture." She disappeared down the hall and quickly returned with an eight-by-ten frame in her hand. "This is Quince with

Pierce. Aren't they adorable?"

The boys seemed to be in their pre-teens, maybe thirteen and eleven. They had their backs to one another with their arms crossed, as if in contention. I had a similar photo of me and Axle, giving each other the same belligerent looks. I smiled. "You can tell they're brothers."

Greg said, "Stepbrothers."

"Yes." She set the frame on the counter.

I placed my empty mug in the sink. "Francie, there are support groups for mothers of murder victims. You could join one of them."

A bit stronger now, Francie took a bracing sip of her coffee. "I'll think about it. I don't know if I can deal with all that drama at the moment. It might make it all worse. I'll just stick with the therapist."

I had my purse on my shoulder and my keys in my hand. "Thanks again, Greg, for all the work on my website. And, take care, Francie." I headed down the hall.

The front door shut behind me, and Pierce loomed up from the porch swing. "What are you doing here?"

After a moment of astonished silence, I said, "Your dad designed a website for me."

A look of relief passed over his face, then his features hardened. "That better be all there is to it. I want you to leave my mother alone. Quit nosing around or you may end up like Clem."

I flew down the steps and made a beeline for my car. I gripped the wheel and tried to keep my foot steady on the pedals as I pulled onto the county road. Unwinding my window, I took in deep breaths. The woodsy fragrance of pine sap gave way to the scent of approaching rain. A thunderstorm threatened behind the peaks and heat lightning sliced the sky, so I careened down the canyon hugged on all sides by the steep mountains, driving to beat the storm.

Chapter 21

When I zoomed into Byron's parking lot, Byron bustled out of an open bay like he always did, glad to see me. Large raindrops began to splatter the cement.

He gaped at me through my half-closed window. "What happened to you?"

I ran a hand down the length of my braid, then flicked the visor for a glance in the mirror. My eyes were wild and my cheeks flushed. I drew a deep, solid breath. "I'm here for Axle."

"Axle!" Byron shouted over his shoulder.

The teen sauntered out of the shop, waved goodbye to the Old Man, and wedged himself into my Fiat. "You're not taking the truck?" It was my turn to monitor the impound lots, but it was early yet.

"I just want to get home. But I need to stop for groceries first." Real life had demands that included food, especially since Axle inhaled everything in the pantry. Even though Ephraim warned me not to, during the short drive to the grocery store I brought Axle up to speed about the Davidsens and the contents of Clem's leather jacket and Clem's brother and the latest visit by the two gang members. It all came tumbling out. A lot had happened since we'd had a chance to talk.

He said, "This is a friggin' nightmare," and I agreed.

"The refrigerator's bare," I said as we scurried

through the rain into the supermarket. "So, get what you need." I had something in mind for dinner, so I snared a cart and began to fill it. I asked Axle to pick up some things from the pet department for Boss, too, like a new sleep pillow and some dog dishes and food. We met up at check out, and while waiting in line, I called Tanner to invite him over for a slapped-together meal. I texted Kristen to be there as well.

Once we lugged in the groceries, I set Axle to browning hamburger with chili powder, garlic, cumin, and red pepper flakes, while I diced up tomatoes, onion, avocado, and black olives and tore lettuce into pieces. Axle did a good job. There was hope for him yet. I dumped everything into individual bowls, including shredded cheese, and set taco shells on a baking sheet to warm in the oven. Axle poured some dry food into the new dish for Boss.

Axle was in the shower when Tanner arrived. My boyfriend pulled me into an embrace and gave me a deep kiss. "I've missed you."

"You, too." I snuggled in his arms, my first moment to relax.

Kristen burst through the door. "Hey, you lovey-doveys. Aren't you a precious couple?"

We broke apart. I said, "Hope you're hungry."

Kristen eyed the bowls on the counter. "Tacos? Yum." She swept onto a stool and nabbed a tortilla chip out of the bag.

Axle padded down the hall in bare feet. "You better save some for me." His wet locks stuck up all over and water dripped down his neck like he'd undertaken nothing more than a towel-dry.

I teased, "Love what you've done to your hair.

That's a good look on you." Then I said, "Dig in, guys," and we all scooped our taco fixings into the hard corn shells. While we ate, I told them about the fifty-thousand dollars in Clem's jacket that'd been hanging in my closet all this time and about everything else, too. Axle had heard it on the drive home, but listened again anyway.

Kristen peeked out the window where the sun broke through the clouds. "Are we safe here?" Tanner and Axle exchanged arm-flexing glances like they'd made a silent pact to protect the women-folk.

"Ephraim's keeping an eye on the place," I said. Tanner shot me a sharp look. I continued, "So, this is what I think happened, Clem stole drug proceeds from the Thunder Knuckles and they came after Quincy for it. Quincy and Clem got into an argument over the money and he kicked her out of his apartment. Quincy fled, thinking he'd hide out at his parent's house, and the gang caught up with him and killed him. They searched the Impreza for the cash. Papers and stuff from the glove compartment were thrown all over the front seat. Those knuckleheads shot Clem, too, and they're still hunting for the loot."

"No!" Axle's voice came out loud. "Quincy stole that money and hid it in Clem's jacket. She didn't even know it was there."

"Hey, cuz', Don't go nuclear on me." I bit into my taco, and lettuce and tomato squirted out.

"Just telling the truth, man." Axle raised his eyes to the ceiling and stuffed a chip in his mouth.

I gave them all a warning look. "Ephraim didn't want me to tell anyone about the cash, so nobody say anything." I was amazed at myself for keeping it from my friends for this long. But Quincy's parents knew. So, the word was out, as far as I was concerned.

Tanner asked, "Why did Clem want inside Quincy's car? What was that about?"

I said, "I have no idea. And she wanted in his apartment, too."

Kristen set her taco on her plate. "Why haven't those gang members been arrested yet?"

Axle said, "Because you're all wrong. They didn't do it. They don't kill one of their own. They're like brothers."

"How do you know that?" I pinched Axle's ear.

"Ow." He swatted my hand away. "Byron told me. He said the Thunder Knuckles claimed to have nothing to do with Quincy's death."

I explained to the others, "Byron did a little digging around at a gang-hangout. The gang denied killing Quincy, but of course, they wouldn't admit it. They probably did kill him."

Tanner blinked, then shook his head. "Byron did what?"

I trod carefully, trying to make it sound like nothing. "He just talked to a couple of guys he ran into."

Kristen said, "Well, Delaney's right, it's clear the gang killed them both."

"Clem didn't know anything about that money. Quincy was the one who hid it." Axle's eyes entreated me not to let go of his theory. "That's why she left the jacket behind at the apartment. She didn't know the money was inside. Quincy put it in the jacket. There's no other explanation."

Since I had my mouth full, I lifted my hand in a

wait-for-it gesture and swallowed. "Why did someone kill her if she had nothing to do with it?"

Kristen asked, "And would Quincy be handy with a needle and thread?"

I nodded. "For that matter, would Clem?"

Tanner put in, "Sure. It can't be that hard." Okay, Kristen and I gaped at him for a few moments, like *have you tried it, lunkhead?*

I said, "Does it make any difference who stole the money? Bottom line, one or both of them hid the stash in the jacket, and the gang killed the two of them."

Tanner gripped his hands into fists. "And now they're after you, Delaney."

"Yay, me!" I bounced my hands off my chest.

Kristen said, "If Haxxed or Demented show up again, you should tell them the police have the money."

I made a quick decision. "You're right. They'll leave me alone then. I should've told them already, but Ephraim warned me not to talk to them again."

"What if they shoot you out of pure malice?" Tanner's face puckered with worry. "I agree with Ephraim, don't speak to them."

Kristen said, "Ask Ephraim to have the sheriff's department issue a press release that the money's been found and the police have it in their possession."

I said, "That's a good idea." Everyone's heads bobbed in agreement and Tanner appeared placated.

I started to feel better about the whole thing myself. "I'll avoid those two. I'm not working at Roasters anymore, so I won't run into them there, and I won't answer the door unless it's one of you guys." I scanned my friends' faces. "Kristen, if you see anyone suspicious in the coffee shop, call Zach right away."

She brushed her hands together in brisk motions, like dislodging crumbs. "Of course, I will."

I pressed my fingers to my temples. "But what if it's not the gang?" Axle was the only one who nodded. "I think it *is* them, but what if we're coming at this from the wrong direction?"

All three stared at me, tacos forgotten. Boss whined from under the table, hoping for scraps.

I broke the silent moment. "The family has financial problems."

Kristen said, "How did you find this out?"

"After I met with Greg about my website design, I ran into Quincy's mom, Francie. She admitted Quincy drained their bank accounts. Greg called Quincy a 'money pit.' There was a lot of resentment." I warmed to this idea. "What about Pierce? There was a rivalry between the brothers. They were stepbrothers, not brothers, and maybe it was toxic between them. Rory went to school with the Davidsen boys and he told me they didn't get along. Rory Rearden, you know, from the coffee shop."

"He's one of my regulars," Kristen explained to the others.

Tanner said, "But the dad adopted Quincy, right? That shows closeness. Family ties can be pretty tight."

"I guess so." I sneaked a crumble of beef to Boss under the table. "But there's something seriously wrong with Pierce. He has anger issues."

Kristen weighed in. "What about her brother? You said his name's Leo, right? Clem's brother would want to protect his sister. He shot Quincy because he'd gotten Clem mixed up with the gang."

Axle's lips flattened. "Even if Leo killed Quincy,

who killed Clem? Not her own brother."

"They weren't close. Not raised together. And Leo may have been the last person to see Clem alive. He was with her the morning before she died." I slapped the countertop and everyone turned my way. "I'm about to give up. I don't think we can solve this." I lifted my shoulders and let them fall.

Kristen agreed, "This crime might never be solved."

True, that. And Francie had said something similar. There were too many loose ends. The mystery of the dead man in the Impreza, the mystery of the dead girlfriend, and the mystery of the fifty-thousand dollars in the jacket.

****

I pulled into Abington Auto Store the next morning to collect my fee for the BMW recovery. Two hundred George Washingtons. Nancy seemed glad to hand over the money and thanked me for the capture. I wanted to jump up and down in my heels and scream into my hand, but I refrained.

Patrick Crump came out of his office. "You ready to go for a coffee?"

"Sure. Meet me at Roasters on the Ridge."

I made certain no recognizable gang members were in the coffee shop before I went inside. Violet brewed our drinks and Kristen refused to take our money. Once settled at a table, me with a double espresso and Patrick with a two-pump mocha, I asked him, "Are you working on any more repos?"

He screeched his chair closer and said in an excited voice, "We have two, but I'm negotiating with one to voluntarily surrender the car." He loosened his tie. "I can't find the other vehicle, but I'll keep you in the loop when I do."

"I appreciate that." I twiddled with my coffee cup. "There's something I've wanted to ask you about. You said you knew my dad? Del Morran."

"I only met him once."

"When was that?"

"He came into the dealership to talk to Rob Abington." Patrick didn't need to explain to me about Mr. Abington. The whole town knew what had happened to him. He was serving time in prison, and Nancy, his ex-wife, was only too happy to have taken over his business. She'd rebuilt almost all of the goodwill that had been lost when the scandal came to light.

"Do you know why they met?" I asked.

Patrick shook his head. "No. I walked in on them and Rob introduced us. Del seemed like an even-tempered kind of guy, polite, soft-spoken, even though Rob was obviously ticked off."

"Why?"

"It wasn't unusual for Rob to be upset about one thing or another." Patrick rubbed his chin.

"Did it seem like they were doing business together?"

"I couldn't tell."

"Did my dad say anything about his towing business? His truck?"

"No."

Darn. No clue as to why Dad gave me the truck. No hint as to the cause of his hit and run. The owner of a car dealership would be acquainted with a man who ran an autobody shop, so I suppose it wasn't surprising

Mr. Abington and Dad had conversations.

Since I knew Patrick's sister, we chatted about how she was doing before Patrick said he needed to get back to work. I decided to do the same. So, after depositing the cash Nancy had paid me, I drove to Byron's lot and picked up my self-loader.

I was ready.

Tow truck in gear, stiletto to the pedal.

I was feelin' groovy. I had a website now. A Chamber networking event to attend once a month. That nice paycheck from Nancy Abington. Yeah, I'm running with the big boys.

I'm done with the coffee shop shifts. Done with the murder investigation. With all my heart, I was finished. *I mean, come on*, what could I do if the deaths were gang related?

I'd stopped at a light when my phone rang with Ephraim's ring tone. "Just a heads up, we're releasing the Impreza from police-hold. We've gathered all the available evidence, and we're finished with the vehicle."

I gripped my cell tighter. "Does this mean you've arrested somebody?"

"No. Sorry."

"Can you tell me if you're close to an arrest?"

"No can do."

"Humpf. So, you think Quincy's folks will come and get the car?" I didn't care to run into the Davidsens again so soon.

"I'm calling them next and I assume one of them will. The car can be cleaned up and sold, or however they want to dispose of it." His voice turned soft. "You'll be glad to be out from under that responsibility."

I said, "I suppose so." But I was thinking, *darn right*. "Can I take the police tape down?"

"Yes. No longer your concern."

"Got it. Glad to be free of the whole thing."

Now, I am. That's what I told myself.

Chapter 22

The yellow crime-scene ribbon around the Impreza fluttered in the afternoon breeze coming in on dark clouds from the west. I tried to avert my eyes from the car windows while I snatched up the flapping tape, looping it around and stuffing it into a trash bag, but my gaze kept returning to the interior.

Was this my last chance to face my fears? I stooped to look through the window.

The blood had turned a dirty rust color, staining the seats and floor. Tuffs of batting showed through sizeable tears in the upholstery. Had the bullets sliced all the way through Quincy and pelted the back of the seat? I stood up fast, a little lightheaded. Leaning against the fender, I took deep breaths.

Haxxed rumbled down the street in the chocolate gray Kia Sportage, LX, all-wheel drive. His bald head turned in my direction, and I did a double-take as we stared at each other. His Kia rolled down the block out of sight while my heart rate quadrupled and lightning bolts of fear shot up my spine.

Haxxed must be after the Impreza now, even though the police had been through it.

I was about to phone Ephraim in a panic, but my cell rang with Greg Davidsen calling to let me know he was on the way. I told myself it was over and tried to get my heart rate back to normal. Haxxed would be

Greg's problem now, and I'd be sure to warn him to be careful.

After tying shut the garbage bag full of yellow tape, I tossed it in the dumpster, then hid on shaky legs behind the Impreza to wait. It took a while, but Greg finally showed up in his Lexus LS Hybrid, rear-wheel drive. By this time I was calm and composed. I punched the knob to open the electric gate, he walked through, and the barrier automatically shut behind us.

Greg removed his Bronco ballcap, then slid the cap back on. "Delaney, I didn't realize you had possession of Quincy's car. I know you said you towed it, but the police told us the vehicle was stored at a lot owned by Tanner Utley."

"I work with Tanner."

"I see. Well, I hope you didn't have to wait too long. I had to stop at the sheriff's office for the key."

"I'm just glad you're here now." I was happy to be getting this over with. "Look, you need to be careful. There's still a killer on the loose and there are gang members around town."

"Yeah, I suppose you're right."

"The car's pretty gruesome. You're going to hire a restoration company, right? Francie won't see it, I hope."

"I hadn't thought of that." He leaned over to peek in the driver's window. Greg couldn't keep from looking, either.

I said, "The sheriff has the names of a couple of biohazard outfits equipped for this kind of thing."

"I'll call them." He straightened to a stand. "Can I leave the car here while they do the cleanup?"

This meant I had to keep the Impreza for a little

while longer. *Darn it*. My shoulders fell. "Sure."

"Can you meet them and let them into the car?"

"I can do that. And I'll mail the invoice for the storage fee to you, too."

"Quincy's still costing me money." Greg shook his head and handed me the key. "The zip ties are gone."

I ducked my head down to stare through the window one more time, and Greg did the same, our heads together, our eyes taking in the steering wheel, the dashboard, and the ruined upholstery. It hit me this sight would be Greg's last memory of Quincy. My eyes moistened at the thought he would never see his son again.

The seat, right there, *that* driver's seat, was where Quincy's life ended, his hands on the wheel, zip ties around his wrists, the bullet wound…the scene that triggered my nightmares.

I pulled myself to a stand. "How did you know about the zip-ties?"

"From the newspaper."

The words hung in the air for a long minute. "Wrong. There was nothing in the news about the ties."

"Yes, there was. That's where I found out about it." His eyes gleamed as if daring me to contradict him.

A dizzy rush hit my head along with a crazy idea. I'd never told anyone. I hadn't even given Axle that particular detail. Only the police and I knew about the zip ties. And the killer. I blurted out, "You shot your own son."

Greg sucked in a breath and crossed his arms. "How could you suggest such a thing? You're nuts. Why would I kill Quincy?"

Why would he? That was a good question. My

brain went into high gear and I stared off into space, imagining the scenario. "You and your stepson never really bonded, so instead of asking you for financial help he kept going to his mom. She was weak, always giving in to him and you wanted to stop the money drain."

Greg's eyes darted around the lot, leading me to believe I was right, although he said, "That's not what happened."

"Yes, it is." I squeezed the back of my neck. "Somehow you arranged to meet Quincy at the turnout. You shot him, went home, then pretended you didn't know why he hadn't shown up."

"You're wrong." A trickle of sweat rolled down his face. "Not a bad theory, but you couldn't be more wrong."

I thought it was a pretty good theory, but it didn't explain why Clem had to die, so maybe I was wrong like he said.

I stared at the Bronco ballcap on Greg's head, triggering a memory. When I first met Clem, right here at this very spot, she got into a Lexus LS with a man who wore a similar hat. Greg drove a Lexus. Greg wore a Bronco hat. And, remember her selfie picture with Greg?

I said, "You had a thing for Clem. You got rid of Quincy so you could have her. An added benefit was that your stepson wouldn't be able to ask your wife for any more money. But Clem had moved on to somebody new, so you killed her, too."

Okay, that seemed farfetched even for me, something out of a soap opera. But Greg drew himself up, squared his shoulders, and loomed over me with his fists clenched and his eyes dilated. Had I guessed the truth after all? Had I gotten it right this time?

I turned on my heels and raced as fast as I could for the gate, my stilettos barely skimming the ground. My weak left ankle came down funny in spite of the tight ankle wrap. *Right foot flat, left toe touch-and-go...ouch...right foot flat, left toe touch-and-go...ouch.* I reached for the button to open the barrier. Just a few more steps. My fingertips hit the knob, but as the fencing started to move with a sluggish rumble, Greg whacked my hand away, and the gate motored back to a close. The gate moved too slow and the killer too fast.

"Gimme your hand." His voice came out as a growl. I squirmed, pushing and shoving, but he'd pinned me with his body against the fence and caught my left wrist in a vice grip. He shoved his free hand in his pocket and yanked out a zip-tie. He fastened my wrist to the fence, then pulled out a second fastener. "Give me your other hand." I weaved my right arm around as he tried to grasp it. "Come on, give me your hand." We struggled, my loose arm flying in every direction, and he yelled, "Stand still!"

I shouted, "Help! Help!" but no one was around. No cars. No one watching out of the apartment windows across the street. No green tow truck driver *for once*. Where was Haxxed? Why didn't he appear? I could use his muscles about now. I stretched my free hand out for the button to open the gate.

Greg caught hold of my wrist, small in his big hand, but this time I was ready. "Get off me!" I yelled as I kneed him in the crotch.

He let go of my hand and clutched at himself while I rotated my bound wrist around every which way, trying to release the zip tie at the same time I reached for the gate lock. He recovered after a short moment and lunged at me again, so I smacked him away.

"Jeez, you hit like a girl."

I batted at his hand some more, causing that second zip-tie to fly out of his grasp and land on the ground out of his reach.

Note to self: Take some self-defense classes for the love of God!

I screamed again, and he yelled, "Shut up!" and slapped me across the face. My head bounced against the chain and I saw stars. He said through clenched teeth, "I don't want to hear another sound out of you."

Since my heart rate pounded at stroke level, I took a moment to breathe. "Don't hit me. I'll be quiet."

His gaze went from my face to his Lexus. What did he want with his car? To escape? *Fine by me*. Or…to get a gun to make sure *I* didn't escape? *Not so fine*. He took a few steps toward the zip-tie on the ground, and I screamed once more. I screamed my head off. *So, I lied.*

He rushed back, clapped a hand over my mouth, and gave me a vicious shake. "You'd better not do that again. Don't yell. Don't move."

I nodded, and he let go of me, but remained rooted to the spot, staring at his Lexus, back at the zip-tie lying in the dirt, and over to my left wrist zipped firmly to the fence. My right hand was free and I might be able to get hold of the button to release the gate. I knew he wanted to secure my right hand so I wouldn't be able to, but I was afraid to try it now. He snagged his hair in both hands, as if grappling with a decision. His eyes had a frantic look.

I couldn't let him go for the second zip-tie, or a

gun if that's what he planned to do. In my mind's eye, I could see that's what had happened to Quincy. Both hands tied up, shot, left for someone else to find. Who would find me? Tanner. Dear God…what if one of his siblings came with him? A tear ran down my cheek and I felt barfy.

Sooner or later someone would come by or a car would turn down the street, so I tried to delay him by asking, my voice steady this time, "How did you get Quincy to sit still in the car while you zip-tied his hands to the steering wheel? You must have caught him by surprise."

His gaze went inward. "He thought I had money for him in my pocket, but I brought out a gun and put it to his forehead and said, don't move. He didn't even take his hands off the wheel when I slapped on the zip-ties. He was easier than dealing with you."

It had to be a relief for him to tell me after all the questions he'd been dodging and the lies he'd been telling his wife.

"Why didn't you just shoot him?"

"I wanted to talk first. If I hadn't tied him up, he could've driven away or gotten out of the car and flagged someone down. I would've had to pull the trigger before I got a chance to tell him just how much I hated him." Greg's lips curled back. "He was glad to see me at first because he thought I'd brought him the money he asked for. He agreed to meet me at the turnout. He didn't even question it."

"That was clever to search the Impreza and scatter the stuff from the glove box, make it appear like a robbery or something."

"I didn't think of it until later, but that did work

out."

My ears strained to hear traffic noise, but all was quiet. I squished my fingers together to make my left hand small, but couldn't get the locked zip-tie past my thumb. "You were searching for something? What?"

"His burner phone. He called home on his regular cell, but he kept a burner in the car. We exchanged a few texts on the burner and he'd dropped a pin on his location so I'd know right where to find him. I didn't want the police to discover those texts."

His eyes focused on the other side of the fence where he'd parked the Lexus.

There was something more, something he'd left unsaid. The loose end. Clem. "Did you tell Quincy you loved Clem?"

He stared unseeing with glassy eyes. "I told him she was too good for a loser like him."

I pressed, wanting the whole truth. "Did you tell Clem you killed Quincy?"

"She was searching for the burner phone, too. She had texted Quincy on the burner about the cash she'd taken from their apartment, the drug money. Quincy couriered for the gang, but you probably figured that out. She wanted him to run away with her, but he refused. He told her to bring the money back, and in the meantime he was hoping for a loan from his mom. His usual go-to when he was in trouble." He gave me a *what are you gonna do* look. "When Clem found out Quincy had been shot, she assumed, at first, that it was a gang slaying and she was afraid they'd come after her. That's why she hid out at your place."

I tugged my left wrist hard against the plastic fastener. I was an easy target strapped to the fence.

Greg could punch me, knock me out, and bind up my other hand so he could go for his gun. He was a killer, fully capable. I said, "Clem didn't want to tip off anyone about the phone, so she made that up about the ring."

"Yeah, she wanted that burner bad. She tried to get inside his car and his apartment to get her hands on that phone. She didn't want someone to find her texts, the same as me. But she called me and admitted she was looking for it. She thought out of everyone I was the one who would help her."

"That was stupid. The police would have confiscated that phone if it was in his car or apartment." I twisted my left hand around, holding my right arm behind me, hearing my heart thump like mad against my eardrums.

"She quit looking after I told her I'd found the burner in the glove compartment and trashed it. Unfortunately, that's when she figured out I'd shot Quincy. I told her to forget about him, that I would take care of her now. But she said she was with someone else, living with him even." His voice cracked. "She was sure a fast worker."

Ya' think? He got that right.

I said, "The guy she moved in with was one of the gang who was after the money. Where was her brain?"

"She believed somehow he'd protect her from the rest of the gang. She played with fire, but then she could always get any man to do what she wanted."

"What about your wife, Greg? I thought you cared about Francie."

He shook his head, his hair flapping under his ballcap. "I do, I do! Oh, I can't believe this happened. I wish I could take it all back. I must have been insane."

Another thing he got right.

Where was Demented now? Why didn't Haxxed drive by again? Or Tanner—alone, of course. Owen, even. But no one was going to come along and rescue me. I needed to figure this out myself. *I can do this! I will do this!*

How? How could I get away? By sacrificing one of my black stilettos, that's how. I lifted my right foot, with all my weight on my left. A sharp pain went up my ankle into my calf, but I reached down with my free hand and ripped my shoe off before Greg even realized what I was doing. I smacked him on the side of the head with the pointed heel and blood spurted everywhere.

He screamed out, but I struck him again and he went down to the ground, out cold.

As for me? I didn't faint or nothin'.

It pays to hit like a girl, a girl with high heels.

I let go of my shoe and dug the Impreza key out of my pocket. I sawed away, back and forth with the key's serrated edge, until the plastic split open and fell free. I ran over and grabbed the zip-tie he'd dropped and bound Greg's wrists together.

Ha! Foiled with his own evil device.

Then I phoned Ephraim. "I'm in Tanner's lot. Come get your killer."

Chapter 23

When I entered our apartment, Axle and Boss faced me like a welcoming committee. I was grateful to be home, pleased to see the two of them.

"Delaney! Are you okay?" Axle knew about Greg's arrest because I'd called him during the down time between rounds of police questions.

"I'm okay, but I'm worried about you."

"No, *you* the one."

"No, *you*." I led Axle over to the couch and sat him down. I needed to sit, too. It'd been a very long afternoon and my left ankle still throbbed.

"I'm fine." Axle raised his eyebrows. "Where are your shoes?"

I'd folded my bare feet under me. "The sheriff kept them since I fought Greg off with one of the heels." We stared at each other, both of us sad. I said, "You weren't wrong in falling for Clem. You can't help who you love." I waggled his hand. "I know you'll miss her, but time heals all wounds."

Axle gazed at the ceiling with a look of *oh-no-not-that*. I wasn't as good as Kristen when it came to giving comfort.

"Why don't you ask Shannon out? Get back on the horse and all that?" Another cliché, the best I could do.

Axle looked down. "She's the boss's niece. She's like a daughter to him. He feels about her the same way he does about you. Just drop it, Delaney." He tickled the bottom of my bare foot.

"Got it. Nuff said." But, I could tell he was doing better and on the rebound. "Kris and some of the others are waiting for us at the coffee shop. Come on down with me."

He gathered his phone and earbuds, and I went to change into a clean top, new jeans, and flat, spotless and crime-free flip-flops. Axle clambered down the stairs behind me and we came in through the employee entrance.

Ephraim and Zach sat together in deep conversation at a table near the window, while a couple of gray-haired men played chess at a booth in the corner. Otherwise, the coffee shop had emptied of customers.

Kristen and Violet made drinks behind the counter, so I teamed up with them while Axle joined the guys. Violet pulled shots with a loud whirr of the espresso machine. Kristen told me over the noise that she and Zach were not staying long unless I needed her, having planned to visit Guy in the hospital before he was to be released later today. We carried a trayful of drinks over: non-fat cappuccino for Zach, a cold brew for Ephraim, a caramel macchiato for Axle. Kristen and I had our coffees in hand, too—iced vanilla coconut milk latte for her and double shot for me.

Zach's salt and pepper mustache appeared freshly trimmed and he smelled strongly of aftershave, like he had a date. And Kristen wore makeup!

Note to self: Find out what's up with them.

Ephraim was in the middle of his story, so I said, "Wait, hold on, start at the beginning. I want to hear the whole thing."

The sheriff sat up straighter. "I was just telling Zach that we didn't know about the burner phone."

Zach added, "Quincy's regular cell phone had no records of calls around his time of death except for one he made to call home and the one from Leonardo Vargas." He must know this because he was a part of the initial investigation before the sheriff's detectives took over.

"Right, we identified Leo fairly quickly." Ephraim pressed himself back in his chair. "But Leo was nowhere near Spruce Ridge when Quincy was killed. Several witnesses placed him in Denver, as well as his phone's GPS, so we didn't have cause to arrest him."

I asked, "Did you ever find the gun?"

"Not until after we took Greg into custody. He had the weapon in his car when he confronted you, Delaney. He should've gotten rid of it when he disposed of the burner phone. Lucky for us he didn't."

I swallowed a lump in my throat. If Greg had made a run for his car after he tied me to the fence, he would've come back with that gun and shot me for sure. "Why didn't you find the gun sooner?"

"We searched the house, but he had hidden it in the woods at the time. He later retrieved the gun and stowed it in his car."

Axle said, "So Greg killed both Clem and Quincy, and it wasn't about the fifty thousand." His voice sounded soft, fragile-like. "The gang had nothing to do with their deaths." He gave me a squinty-eyed *I-told-you-so* look. But he was wrong about Clem. She had taken the money and hidden it in her jacket.

Ephraim said, "That's right. Greg confessed all. He

told us Pierce answered the phone at their house when Quincy called that night. Greg called Quincy back on the burner and they arranged to meet. You know the rest of the story."

I surveyed everyone nursing their coffee drinks. "Honestly, I would've guessed the brother as the killer before I'd have guessed the stepdad. I thought there was something up with Pierce, I just didn't know what. Do you think he knew his dad killed Quincy?"

"It's possible, but he's not saying. He's protective of his parents."

"I could tell Pierce was smitten with Clem. Then I found out Greg was, too. Was *everyone* in love with her?" I asked. No one had an answer. Axle just gave a helpless shrug.

"I found out you told your friends about the money in Clem's jacket." Ephraim nailed me with a glare.

"I can't get away with anything, can I? Jeez, you win again, Lopez." Then I blushed warm because Axle had on a knowing smirk, the little twerp. I returned his snarky look before glancing back at Ephraim. "I never told anyone about the zip-ties. When Greg mentioned the ties, that's when I knew he was the murderer."

Ephraim said, "You could've been killed. You should never have confronted him on your own. Why didn't you just walk away? You should've called me and let me handle it."

"You're right." My cheeks burned hotter. "But I'd only figured it out while talking to him. The more he talked, the more danger I realized I was in and then it was too late. I hope I didn't hurt Greg too bad when I hit him with my shoe."

"He needed seven stitches." Ephraim winced and

rubbed the back of his own head. He added, "Greg could get a life sentence."

"Good. I can picture him in a prison uniform."

Kristen said, "It's so sad that, in a way, Quincy's mom lost her son and her husband. One dead, the other going to jail." We all took a moment to reflect on that over our steaming espressos.

A man burst through the door and everyone glanced up. The man with a lightning bolt tattooed on his forehead, a silver lightning bolt earring pierced through one earlobe, and a metal barbell stuck through the thin skin of his neck.

Demented gazed straight into my eyes—I shivered in my seat—and he gave me a salute.

None of us said a word as he strode up to the counter and Violet took his order, a skinny, sugar-free vanilla latte, what baristas called a *why bother*. When the espresso machine began its whirring sound, we turned back to the table.

"Are we done?" Axle asked, popping his earbuds in, his thumbs flying over his phone screen.

"Yes, I have some paperwork to complete." Ephraim gave me a smile before shouldering through the door on his way out.

As I watched the sheriff leave, Tanner's truck came into view. He parked, then strode through the door, wearing his long black jeans and a tee-shirt…with short sleeves. Exposing the new tattoo. The one spelling out, *Annie*.

I stood. "Hey, Tanner. Grab a chair and I'll get your usual."

Tanner eased into the seat vacated by Ephraim as I made my way behind the espresso machine to create his vanilla frappé.

By the time I returned, everyone else had taken off except for Axle and Tanner. Just as I was about to sit, Axle, too, shoved off his stool. He said, "I'll see you guys later," his keys making a jangling sound in his hand. He'd just received his driver's license back and Byron had provided him with a loaner car, a ten-year-old Subaru. All-wheel drive is pretty much standard on every Subaru.

"Hey, cuz', we need to celebrate you getting your license. Milkshakes and chili dogs later?"

He laughed. "Kristen promised me a steak."

"Can't beat that." I told him goodbye, then turned my attention to my boyfriend. "Sorry you missed all the details. Ephraim just left."

"Axle gave me the short version while you made my drink." Tanner raised his iced coffee to his lips. "I'm so glad you're all right."

"I am." But I was sick of talking about it. I poked Tanner's arm. "Let me see the new artwork. Does it hurt? When will the redness go down?"

He held his arm out straight and rubbed lightly over the tat. "In a couple of days. Do you like it?"

I said, "Sure, sure, very nice," then I blurted out, "So, who's Annie?"

"There are two names." Tanner adjusted his elbow around to show off a second tattoo, Tate.

I asked, "Tate? Oh, wait a minute. Isn't your brother named Tate?"

"Yeah. I got these for my brother and sister."

I was confused. "But your sister's name is Treanna."

"She always hated her name, I don't know why. I

think Treanna is pretty, but she wants to go by Annie." He swallowed down a huge gulp of coffee. "I still call her Treanna but she told me I'd better not put that name on my tattoo."

I whooshed out a breath so loud it could be heard over the bean roaster. "When do I get to meet them, Tanner? We could do something casual, like go to the zoo, or a movie, something they'd like to do." I gave him a wide grin, but he didn't crack a smile.

"Okay. I'll think about it."

I secretly scolded myself. Maybe it was still too soon in our relationship. Time for a different tactic. "Good thing you don't have any more brothers and sisters, or you'd have names tattooed all up and down your arm." I trailed a finger along the inside of his forearm, and this time he did smile, his eyes going wide.

He brushed my palm. "How do I know *you* didn't get a tattoo? Maybe you got one, too, somewhere I can't see?"

A shiver went across my shoulders and the hairs rose on my arms. "I don't have a tattoo." My voice broke on the last word.

"Are you just teasing me? Come on, let's see." He tugged my shirt so it bloused out over my jeans, but stopped short of coming untucked.

Not to be outdone, I said, "How about you? You got any more hidden ink?" I snagged his tee-shirt and it flew up, exposing the top band of his underwear. *Oops.*

Tanner leaned forward, his face earnest. "Wouldn't you like to know?" He stood and extended a hand, pulling me out of my chair. "Axle's gone, who knows where. We'll be alone. I can show you how grateful I am that you didn't get hurt." He gave me a slow wink.

I tilted my head, studied the ceiling, then closed my eyes, thinking, *why not?*

Alone time. With Tanner. I did want to find out if he had more tattoos.

He must have read my mind because he placed his hand on my back and whisked me out the door. He said, as we thundered up the stairs, "Maybe we won't be interrupted for once."

A red-hot flush went over my face, and I raised my chin trying to cover up my nerves. "What about our phones?"

"I'll shut mine off if you will."

We came to a halt on the top step. I dragged my cell phone from my pocket and punched a button to turn the ringer down. Tanner made a show of doing the same. I put my hands on my hips. "Let Owen take the calls for a change. He wants to be the big tow man around town."

I had my hand on the doorknob when Kristen's door opened and her head popped out. "Hey, you love birds, come in and have dinner with Zach and me. We're having spaghetti and meatballs."

"Whaaa?" I stared at her, open-mouthed. My friend was on a date? Not only a date but *the dinner date*, the one where the girl cooks for the boy? This happens around the same time the boy wins a giant stuffed animal at the fair for the girl. I asked, "Zach is in there? I thought you were going to see Guy."

"We already made a quick stop at the hospital and now we're back. Guy's fine, by the way." Kristen gave me a wide smile. "And Zach and I have something to tell you."

289

"You do?" I gave my friend a look like *what have you done?* She matched my gaze with her own look of *wouldn't you like to know?*

My fingers gripped Tanner's and I gave him a *please, please, pretty please* pout, noticing his posture slump.

Kristen said, "Yes, we have news."

I turned to Tanner. "Kris has news."

She added, "And spaghetti and meatballs."

I repeated to my boyfriend in case he didn't get it, "Spaghetti. Meatballs."

Tanner plastered a wooden smile on his face. "Garlic bread, too?"

"Of course." Kristen held the door open.

She gestured to the empty chairs across from where Zach sat at the square table covered with a linen tablecloth. A tapered candle emitted a flame, sparking high, then low. A tureen of spaghetti smothered in marinara sauce gave off a meaty aroma. They'd uncorked a bottle of red and left it to breathe.

Tanner wriggled into the seat opposite me, and Kristen set out two more plates faster than she poured a cold brew. I helped myself to a chair, and Kristen handed a basket of garlic bread sticks to Tanner.

"What's this about?" I asked, my shoe tapping the table leg.

Kristen reached across to hold Zach's hand. "We're courting now."

I goggled at her. *What did that mean? Had Zach popped the question? Was my best friend getting married?* My heart beat fast and I held my breath. "Courting?"

Kristen answered, "We're dating."

Zach's eyes twinkled. "Courting is more serious than dating." My gaze bounced between the two. What does *more serious* mean? Whatever, it didn't mean *engaged* because Kristen did not have on a ring. I'd ask her to explain later.

She beamed. "We should go on double dates."

I perked up. "Oooh, sounds great." We both stared at the men expectantly.

Tanner turned to Zach. "I guess we'll be seeing a lot of each other."

Zach asked him, "You like to golf?"

Tanner's lips pulled down. "No. You like football?"

"No. I don't even follow the Broncos." *Hoo boy*, them's fighting words. Zach swallowed hard and his eyes darted to Kristen as if to say *help!*

Tanner gnawed on a breadstick. "How about the Rockies?"

Zach blew out a sigh. "Yes, I like them."

Both men appeared relieved.

Zach tipped a measure of wine into each glass. We held them up and touched rims in the middle of the table. Tanner started to tell Zach some crazy repo stories—I'll tell you the stories another time. Right now I couldn't do them justice.

Kristen and I looked like two moms with kids on a play date, happy they were making friends.

****

After that night, time passed slowly, since Kristen was often out with Zach. Did I say *often*? I meant, *all the time*. I, on the other hand, was hardly ever on a date because Tanner and I have opposite towing schedules. I'm sure you remember that, I've complained about it enough times.

One night I had another dream.

I was back in my childhood days, a little girl in a short blue dress standing in the doorway of the two-story, red brick house where we lived in Spruce Ridge. Dad pulled in the driveway with his brand new, front-loader tow truck. It appeared shiny and big and had Dad's name written on the door. My mom blocked the entryway, but I dashed past her. She said, *Delaney, get back here*, but I kept running right into Dad's arms. He scooped me up and threw me in the air and caught me like I'd seen other dads do with their kids. I squealed. Then he set me down and I ran my hand over the cold, hard metal down the length of the door to the bumper almost as tall as me. I was short even then. I said, *I want a truck just like this one Daddy. I want to be just like you.* Then it was Thanksgiving, just like that, then Christmas, then birthdays and the Easter bunny and Halloween costumes, and then I was all grown up. Dad handed me the keys to his self-loader and said, *These are for all the days I missed.*

The dream brought me closer to Dad in a way I couldn't explain.

At least the lightning nightmares had stopped once the murder had been solved. This dream about Dad was different…sad, but comforting somehow.

****

One Monday afternoon in early June, when the azure sky was clear, not a cloud in sight, and the temperature in the nineties, I was tooling down County Road 6. I'd been tailing the green tow truck, just to give Owen a hard time. When I spied a VW Touareg, rear wheel drive, on the shoulder, Owen kept going, but I slowed down. The car did not have an orange tow tag, but I turned in anyway.

Surprise. The driver still sat inside.

I rolled down my window and asked the teenaged girl, "Do you need help?"

"I ran outta gas, and worse yet, my cell's not working. No bars. No service." She held up her phone as if to show me.

"No problem. I've got gas."

"Boy, am I glad you stopped."

I climbed down from my truck, a full-on grin across my face, my high-heels hitting the pavement. "I'm glad I stopped, too."

A word about the author...

Karen C. Whalen is the author of two cozy mystery series, the Dinner Club Murder Mysteries and the Tow Truck Murder Mysteries. The first in the dinner club series, Everything Bundt the Truth, tied for First Place in the Suspense Novel category of the 2017 IDA Contest. Whalen loves to host dinner parties, camp, hike, and read.